THE MACNEIL LEGACY - BOOK ONE

DIVERSIONBOOKS

Also by Jane Bonander

Heat of a Savage Moon
Wild Heart
A Taste of Honey
Fires of Innocence
Secrets of a Midnight Moon
Warrior Heart
Dancing on Snowflakes
Forbidden Moon
Winter Heart
The Dragon Tamer

Diversion Books
A Division of Diversion Publishing Corp.
443 Park Avenue South, Suite 1008
New York, New York 10016
www.DiversionBooks.com

For more information, email info@diversionbooks.com

First Diversion Books edition August 2015.
Print ISBN: 978-1-68230-289-7
eBook ISBN: 978-1-68230-288-0

Especially for Richard.

A big thank you to Nancy Pirri and Jill Barnett.

Prologue

When the night was dark and the moon hovered over the flat Texas horizon like a giant white ball, Shamus MacNeil told his son of his homeland, where ancient ghosts still roamed the castles, where wee people hid inside bluebells or under stones, and where a great "beastie" lived in a loch of immense depth.

Young Fletcher had hung onto every fanciful word. He heard high tales of his two uncles who lived back in Castle Sheiling on the Isle of Hedabarr. Stories of their prowess with the bow and rifle made Fletcher practice his bow until he could do it with his eyes closed. Tales of their bountiful fishing made him cast his line for hours. All that Shamus MacNeil had done as a lad, he passed on to his son. To die and leave behind no remnant of Scotland would mean the MacNeils had no past.

Only when his father spoke of lineage and inheritance did Fletcher's mind wander to subjects more interesting, like tracking a bear or watching an eagle soar overhead. At the tender age of nine, Fletcher's world was Shamus. There was only the two of them.

Then his father remarried, and everything changed.

Fletcher, Maker of Arrows, pressed one knee into the grass beside his father's grave and rested his forearm on the other. He had thought he would weep; he could not. His sorrow went deeper than tears.

Under this pile of loosely packed earth was Shamus MacNeil, the man he loved more than anyone else in his life. He had guarded that love possessively, even jealously.

Soft footsteps sounded behind him over the coarse, dry grass, stopping close by.

"He forgave you long ago." The old man slowly lowered himself to the ground beside him.

Fletcher could hear the creaking of his grandfather's ancient bones. "And now I will never forgive myself."

The old man gazed up into the clouds. Fletcher studied his profile—hawk nose, sharp cheekbones, both of which Fletcher had been granted. He resembled his mother's people more than the other siblings.

Grandfather spoke. "I was not happy when my daughter married a white man. It took me time to discover what Gentle Dove saw in him from the very beginning. Shamus MacNeil was a kind man, a gentle man who knew that although we were different from him, we were equal. He lived as we did, embracing our ways, but he never forgot where he came from." Grandfather continued, his voice holding humorous warmth, "And he spoke unlike any white man I had ever known, his words sliding and gliding across my mind long after he had stopped talking."

Fletcher remembered his father's Scottish burr, the gentle humor he found in life, the kindness in his heart. All of the things Fletcher had abandoned when his own small, petty pride made him leave home so many years before.

"When your mother died, I was saddened. No father should outlive his children," Grandfather was saying. "But when your father followed tradition and married my other daughter, I knew that he was a man who believed in the strength of family."

Fletcher had received the news of his father's and stepmother's deaths only days before. Running Deer had been washing clothes at the river. Fletcher's grandfather and Shamus went to check on her and had found her floating face down in the water. His father swam out to get her and after pulling her body ashore, his chest seized and he fell over dead.

"I was always unkind to Running Deer," Fletcher admitted. He had been jealous when his brother and sister, Duncan and Kerry, were born and he had to share his father. But when Shamus rescued and adopted Gavin after a raid on his family's ranch, Fletcher had felt completely abandoned. "I didn't want to help care for them; I wanted to hunt and fish with my friends." He had been so young and so selfish. "I wouldn't do my chores; instead, I did what I pleased. When I returned, he would ignore me. That hurt more than anything, to be ignored by him." Fletcher had overheard Running Deer defending his antics, explaining to his father that it was only his age that made him distant, surly, and unruly. Emotion made him disinterested in the stories his father now told his brothers and sister.

"You were young, and hurting."

"That was no excuse for my behavior, Grandfather."

"No, but it is the truth."

Not long after his fifteenth birthday, Fletcher turned his back on his family and left. Until today, he had not returned. Foolish pride had prohibited it.

"What will you do now?" Grandfather asked, using Fletcher's knee for support while he attempted to get to his feet.

Fletcher helped him up. He'd come to a decision, albeit grudgingly. "I will stay."

Grandfather's rheumy eyes were shrewd. "Is that what you want?"

Fletcher's gaze slid away. "Of course it is."

"You feel guilty, but that shouldn't be your reason for staying. We will be fine. You have your job with the army. Go, my son."

Fletcher's relief could not dissuade his guilt, but he would have to live with that. He glanced at the house one more time. It looked solid, like it wasn't in need of any repair, but it wasn't home anymore. His brothers and sister played nearby. They hadn't recognized him when he returned. At least they would remember him now and his job with the army would guarantee they would have food and shelter. They didn't need him to stay, either.

"I will send you my army pay." Fletcher pulled out his buckskin money sack and handed it to his grandfather. "This should help you for a while. I'll send more."

Early the next morning, Fletcher waved goodbye to his family and rode away.

Chapter One

Fort Wiley, Texas—1857

The rough muslin bed sheets lay in a tangle around them, the air still musk-scented. Fletcher glanced at his partner, whose breathing was as ragged as his own, and whose face was bathed in sweat. It had been a month since he'd bedded a woman. He stretched, flexed the muscles in his legs, and put his hands behind his head. He'd sure as hell made up for it tonight, he thought, feeling satisfied and just a little bit smug.

Hours earlier, she had opened the door wearing only a flower in her hair. Her luscious breasts with their big, brown nipples had jutted straight out, as if reaching for him, begging him to put his mouth around them—which eventually he had. The thatch of dark hair between her thighs had looked inviting; he went down on his knees to have a taste. From her scent, he'd thought he was going to burst the seams of his buckskins; his erection ached. She had tasted sweet and tart, and she was very, very wet, her labia swollen and her clit as round and hard as a pea.

Before she came, she had pulled him to his feet, reached down, and unbuttoned his pants. She pulled out his erection and then hopped into his arms, wrapping her legs around his waist, pressing her wet, naked center against him.

He'd barely made it to the bedroom. They collapsed on the bed, already hot, sweaty, and eager. She'd almost torn his shirt off of him; had there been buttons, they would have flown all over the room. The first time was short, hot, and intense. She screamed when she came; he'd had to close his mouth over hers to muffle the sound. Then she dragged him into the kitchen, swung her arm across the table, sending the cloth and a basket of wildflowers flying, and perched on the edge. Spreading her legs wide, she invited him into her pink wetness with, "Come inside."

He liked it that way, standing so he could watch himself move in and out of her, watch the moisture glisten on his erection as she became wetter and wetter, so hot and ready for him that her ankles were shaking as she balanced them on his shoulders.

Now, four hours after he had arrived on her doorstep, she reached over and moved her hand to his groin. "Are you ready for me, half-breed?"

He was already hard.

She squeezed him; he got harder.

"I can make it stand up again and salute that flag." Her voice was heavy with seduction and the promise of sexual delights as she nodded toward the window, where the flag from the fort flapped in the dry wind.

He watched her closely, saying nothing. But as she continued to stroke him, he knew he wanted her again. In spite of his reluctance to stay, he couldn't resist the urge to reach for her breast. Her nipple pebbled at his touch. He licked it, then the other. He raised his head. "When does your husband come home?"

"There's time…" She purred and moved closer, nuzzling him like a big, warm cat. She threw one leg across his thigh and rubbed her calf over his groin. "He won't be home until morning. I told you that." She made more catlike sounds in her throat. "You sure feel ready, honey." Then she pushed even closer and caught his thigh between her legs, pressing herself against his skin.

He slid his hand up to the furry patch between her thighs. "Some nice, proper white girl you are; you stay so damned wet."

She gave him a lazy chuckle and spread her legs wide. "It's you that makes me wet, half-breed."

She had never used his name, although he was sure she knew what it was. Hers was Lindsay Bannerman. Her husband was a captain, an arrogant son of a bitch. She wasn't exactly pretty, but she radiated sex like it was perfume. She had an ample ass—something that usually didn't excite him, but once they had fallen into bed, it was there for him to grab as he battered into her while she begged him to do it harder and harder.

If he had any respect for her at all, he wouldn't be lying here, exploring her wet and swollen folds. But like other white women of her kind, all she wanted was an Indian in her bed. He was half Indian; that was enough. He had no respect for a woman who cuckolded her husband.

He could bed them; he just didn't respect them.

Early in his youth he had learned that his looks and silence drew women like this one, eager for what was between his legs and for the native wildness they thought came from his Comanche blood. The first time had been nearly ten years ago, when he was eighteen. He had screwed on horseback, with his partner facing him, her legs wrapped around his back and him deep inside her.

"C'mon, honey," the captain's wife murmured against his ear, nipping at the lobe, her hand touching him in long soft strokes. "I want you inside me, now."

He heard a sound across the room and flipped her on her back, his hand over her mouth.

She fought him, clawing at his fingers.

"Shhh!" He listened for the sound again.

She pried free and tried to hit him. "You son of a bitch!"

All at once he faced a gun barrel. And the room exploded in light.

SOLICITOR'S OFFICE, VILLAGE OF SHEILING, ISLAND OF HEDABARR, SCOTLAND

Geddes Gordon had feared this moment, had dreaded it. The old laird was dead and in no time at all, the laird's grandnephew, Fergus MacBean, came sniffing around, waiting to be handed the estate. The prig sat before him now, buffed and polished, smug and arrogant.

"I don't see the problem, Mr. Gordon." MacBean flicked an

imaginary piece of lint from his fawn-colored pantaloons. "The old man is dead and I'm a legal heir."

"Aye," Geddes answered, "but there is still the question of Shamus."

MacBean expelled a derisive snort. "No one has heard from him in decades. He could be dead for all we know."

"But we don't know that for certain, do we?" Geddes countered.

MacBean stroked a bushy sideburn with a stubby finger. On an impatient sigh, he said, "My wife and I are traveling the Continent soon; we leave within the week. We're spending a lengthy time in Paris, then we're off to Vienna. She has relatives in Switzerland who are anxious for us to visit, then we'll leave for Barcelona. Trust me, Mr. Gordon, I will return in one year to collect my inheritance. Make no mistake about it." With that, he stood, picked up his greatcoat and his top hat, and, without so much as a nod, went to the door. Before he left, he added, "By the way, I'll be requiring a new staff and will hire my own solicitor. Your services will no longer be necessary." Then he was gone.

Geddes rubbed his hands over his face. If this entire estate was going to be saved from that spendthrift braggart, something had to be done. And Geddes feared he knew what it was. The idea did not appeal to him at all.

• • •

Six weeks later, Geddes Gordon looked out the stagecoach window, trying not to compare the hot, dusty, dry, monotonous landscape to the fresh, clean hills on the isles of Scotland. He failed miserably. This was where the old man's heir lived? He closed his eyes against the harsh scenery. It was unfathomable that anyone with Scots blood in his veins could tolerate the hellish heat and constant dust. By the holy, it was winter and still hot as the very devil!

He tried to relax and gave himself up to the rocking of the coach, his thoughts returning to his last conversation with his sister, Rosalyn. It irked him to think she found him so weak. Yet he knew she was right—he detested traveling even as far as Edinburgh, but as the late Duke of Kintyre's solicitor it was his duty to see the complicated terms of the will fulfilled. To do that, he had to find the new duke, the youngest son, Shamus MacNeil.

If he were unsuccessful, the fortune would go to Fergus MacBean and his profligate family, and then he and Rosalyn, who were living at the castle and caring for the estate, would be forced to find other lodgings. Not that they couldn't, but they both loved the castle and its grounds. It would be a shame to see it all pissed away by MacBean.

"Do you remember much about Fergus MacBean?" she had asked him that same night.

He had related to her his last meeting with MacBean but did not go into detail or tell her of the prig's plan to replace them. Rosalyn had looked worried, then asked him about Shamus. He told her what he knew: that Shamus was a good, God-fearing young man, whom many had thought might enter the church, until he suddenly left Scotland, almost overnight. Perhaps he knew that as the third son he had no reason to stay, perhaps wanderlust called to him. Soon after, Jamie died suddenly, but there was still Munro. Who'd have thought he would die, too? The MacNeil believed he would never die, and Geddes wondered if he had believed that, too. No one ever tried to locate Shamus and no word came back from America.

He remembered looking at his sister and again being amazed at how lovely she was. Rosalyn had perfect skin, a pert little nose, and thick hair the color of wheat shimmering in the sunshine. It was so fortunate that she was the pretty one, with her smaller features instead of his big ears and pointed beak of a nose. When he said as much to her, she scolded him.

"You are a handsome man, tall, broad-shouldered, and charming when you wish to be. And you have always been the cleverest and kindest man I know, Geddes, although you are a bit stubborn." She had looked up from her sewing. "What will happen if Shamus is dead?"

"I can only hope that he has a bairn, Rosalyn, and let's pray he's a wise, upstanding young man, just as Shamus was, one who will continue to need our services."

She had laughed then, a truly amused sound that had annoyed the very devil out of him. Rosalyn had this uncanny ability to laugh at the situations he found most distressing. She had told him he was too serious. He supposed he was. Yet her greatest liability was that she was too stubborn by half. When they were children, they had gotten into their mother's garden and eaten berries until their faces were stained and their bellies so full they were ill. Their mother, not usually a violent woman, whipped them with a switch. Had she told them she was going to bake a pie for a very special visitor, they might not have partaken, Geddes had whimpered as each of the blows came. But Rosalyn had not. She stood straight and tall, unwilling to even flinch. Even her breathing did not change. Rosalyn did not show the world her pain.

"And what if this heir is a rakehell and a rogue, like his brothers and his grandfather?"

"Then God help us all," he said aloud inside the coach. He had no idea who he might find at the end of his voyage. At the last stage stop there had been a message waiting for him. Shamus MacNeil had died a number of years before, but at the fort outside Cedarville, he would find Shamus's son, the MacNeil heir, the next Duke of Kintyre. It gave him some hope that the heir would be an army man; the MacNeils had always been excellent soldiers in the service of their kings.

The stagecoach rocked as the whip master shouted, "Cedarville!" then stopped next to a dreary building.

Geddes got out, brushed off his gray wool trousers, buttoned his black cloth frock coat, and stared at the stark platform.

His grimy valise raised a cloud of dust as it landed at his feet.

Geddes coughed and waved away the parched soil that rose from the dirt-packed street, brought out his handkerchief, and coughed again. Sweat popped out on his forehead and quickly trickled through his eyebrows into his eyes. His body, laden with wool, seemed to scream for air. He squinted up at the sky. The sun beat down relentlessly.

Merciful God, how did people live in this oven? No lochs to be seen, no glens, no snow-covered hills. Nothing was green. Everything around was coated with a dry, dull film of dust that probably never went away. The only shade came from the slant of an overhang on the adobe station building. There wasn't a tree in sight, just scrubby brush and gray bramble without roots that seemed to have the good sense to tumble away from this hellhole.

A cluster of enormous, dark, ugly birds circled in the distance. Buzzards, the whip master had called them, carrion crows that fed on the flesh of the dead. Geddes brought his handkerchief to his nose once again.

A gangly youth in a dusty, dark blue uniform ran out from the side of the station, his limbs loose and his sleeves so short his bony wrists protruded like bleached and dried animal bones. His trousers stopped at his boots, both grimy with dirt. His grin exposed big, horsy teeth. His shaggy dark hair stuck out in all directions. "You that Scottish fella who wired ahead? The lawyer?"

Geddes gave him a little bow. "Geddes Gordon, solicitor tae the MacNeil."

The lad chuckled, as if Geddes had said something more amusing than merely his name and station. "I'm here to take ya to the fort."

"Well, dinna keep me waitin', 'tis anxious I am to meet the new MacNeil."

The lad gawked at him. "Say, what?"

Geddes sighed. "Take me to the fort, laddie."

• • •

Fletcher, Maker of Arrows, dropped to the dirty floor and did fifteen rapid push-ups, focusing on one of the many tiny holes in the adobe where thin rays of light shone through. Barely winded, he stood, avoiding the window and the sight of the scaffold barely twenty feet away. It was less than forty-eight hours until his death.

For the hundredth time he thought about his two younger brothers and his sister. Although his grandfather was looking after them, Duncan, Gavin, and Kerry had been Fletcher's responsibility for three years now, ever since the deaths of his father and stepmother. At fifteen, fourteen, and twelve, they were still too young to fend for themselves. The letters he received were usually from Kerry and occasionally from Gavin. Duncan, it seemed, was not interested in writing his older brother. But the other two assured Fletcher that everything was well, that he should not worry about them.

Fletcher couldn't stop blaming himself for the mess he had made of things. What he feared was that there had been trouble. Perhaps Grandfather had died; he had been an old man when Fletcher was young. But why, then, hadn't one of them written? It wasn't like Kerry, especially, to ignore him. The possibilities of what could be wrong gave him nightmares.

He placed his hands on the jail wall and stared down at the floor. He was a selfish ass, and felt a rush of self-loathing. Once he was hanged, they would be abandoned. What would happen to them when the money quit coming was anyone's guess. He had made a promise to always care for them, and now he felt a deep sense of shame. He had lived his life with too many bad decisions. The trial was over. He was a convicted murderer and rapist. No one believed a half-breed over an army captain.

As he stared at the floor he asked himself if his life could have been any different. Could he ever have found a woman and settled down to raise a family as his father had? He didn't know; he had never tried, nor had he ever met a woman with whom he desired to spend his earthly eternity. Hell, he was anxious to be rid of most of them after just one night.

A shout made Fletcher look outside. His gaze swept over the garrison, stopping briefly at the stables. He loved everything about horses—their power, their beauty, their lusty aroma, especially after a long, hard ride. He didn't even mind the manure. From his cell he could smell them. He inhaled deeply, bringing the scent into his lungs and holding it there as long as he could.

He wondered if there were horses in hell. Probably not; they didn't deserve to be there.

He caught the familiar stout figure of Captain John Bannerman exiting the infirmary with his arm in a sling from a knife wound. Anger and hatred welled up in Fletcher's throat when he looked at the man. *Wife killer.*

Fletcher was guilty of stabbing him, in self-defense, but Lindsay Bannerman had died from a gunshot meant for him. He had bedded her, but Bannerman had murdered her, and then blamed him. There was one brief moment when he'd held the dying Lindsay in his arms, blood spreading in an ever-widening circle from the hole in her chest, and he had wondered what demon had brought him to this point in his life, when his selfish actions had been the reason this woman died.

He slumped onto the hard wooden slab with the dirty blanket that served as a bed. He heard voices, and then the heavy door between the jail and the cells creaked open. The sound of keys jangled from a chain. The sergeant in charge appeared. An oily man with bad teeth and a nasty, swaggering manner, he wore a look of mean superiority. "Breed!"

Fletcher looked up.

"You got a visitor."

A big man wearing a dark coat and woolen trousers stepped up to the cell. He carried a leather case in one hand and a black top hat in the other. His thick, pale blond hair, heavy with sweat, lay flat against his scalp. Moisture glinted off his forehead like beads of water sizzling on a hot skillet. The man smelled of perspiration and damp wool.

With one mocking eyebrow raised, he studied Fletcher from his head to his boots, his expression less than pleased. He wore small wire-rimmed glasses that did nothing to hide the disapproval in his light blue eyes. He considered Fletcher, as if wondering how to proceed, then glanced at the sergeant and spoke. "Open the cell door and be gone."

Fletcher hadn't heard that lilting burr since he'd broken his father's heart and ridden away. He never saw his father alive again. Another twinge of shame—if his father were alive, he would be so disappointed in him.

The sergeant muttered an oath under his breath, opened the cell door, and locked the man inside, giving them a scurrilous look as he left.

The Scotsman stared after him briefly, and then once again looked at Fletcher over the rims of his glasses, his expression drenched with disapproval.

"Who in the hell are you?" Fletcher asked.

"I'm Geddes Gordon, solicitor—"

"A lawyer? You're a goddamned lawyer? Wasn't one of you enough? They've already tried me. Look outside at those gallows." He nodded toward the window, where the scaffold stood waiting. "How many lawyers does it take to hang a man?"

"You didna let me finish. I am representing the MacNeil, your late grandfather. I'm not here to hang you, Your Grace; I'm here to set you free."

"'Your Grace'?" Fletcher snorted with derision. "You've got the wrong man."

"I don't think so. You are the Duke of Kintyre."

"Sure," Fletcher said with a sarcastic smirk. "And some days I'm Napoleon Bonaparte, and yesterday I was President Buchanan, and, why, just last week I was your bonnie Prince Albert, but not today. Today, I'm just a half-breed who's going to hang by a rope for a murder I didn't commit."

"I understand your confusion, Your Grace, but I don't appreciate your sarcasm."

"You don't understand a damned thing if you think I'm going to get out of this hellhole."

"I'm hoping that to be the case, Your Grace."

The words began to sink in. "Who are you?" he asked again.

The lawyer fished into his pocket, brought out a card, and handed it to him.

Fletcher stared at it.

"Can you read?"

Fletcher gave him a scathing look and then read the card aloud. "Geddes Gordon, Solicitor to the Duke of Kintyre, Erskine MacNeil. Of the Clan MacNeil, Isle of Hedabarr, Scotland." Once again he looked at the man before him.

"Your late grandfather."

It had been many years since Fletcher had given any thought to his father's name and what it stood for. When Fletcher had fled his home at fifteen, he had claimed his Indian name, Fletcher, Maker of Arrows, leaving the MacNeil surname far behind. "Explain why you're here."

"Your grandfather, the MacNeil Himself, died. You are his heir, since your da, Shamus, is dead."

"But my father wasn't the heir. He told me so years ago. His brother Jamie was, then Munro. He joked about how his father had an heir and a spare, so he knew where he stood."

"Aye, until Jamie was struck with influenza and died, then about six months ago Munro broke his neck racing his horse. Shortly thereafter, the MacNeil, God rest his soul, passed on. Shamus MacNeil, your father, became the next Duke of Kintyre."

"And my father is dead."

"Aye, so that leads me to you." The lawyer looked around him, once again lifting one mocking eyebrow. "Here in prison."

Fletcher just stared at him.

"I was hoping that you'd be an honorable army man. I didna think you'd be a bloody redskin…or a murderer."

"I didn't kill her."

The lawyer offered him a wry smile as his gaze swept the cell. "Aye, right. You're just sitting in here for the pleasure of it. I can see how you might enjoy the place—the splendid accommodations and all."

"I didn't kill her," Fletcher repeated.

"No? Then why are you here?"

"Because this," he said, his voice heavy with disdain, "is United States Army justice."

"In a bit of a pickle, then, aren't you?" The lawyer gave him a wry look.

Fletcher barked another short, wicked laugh. "To put it mildly, yes, I'm in a bit of a pickle," he answered, mimicking the burr of his visitor.

They studied one another for a long, quiet moment, and then Fletcher asked, "So, now that you've found me, what are you going to do? Use your clever lawyer double-talk to get me out of here?"

"You're the heir," Geddes answered simply. "You have money and title and a castle."

"And I'm sitting in this stinkhole of a jail, sentenced to hang."

"Yet you say you're innocent."

"I am," Fletcher shot back.

The lawyer took a step back. "Well now, don't go apoplectic on me, Your Grace. Open your mind to other possibilities."

I'm here to set you free. Fletcher wanted everything the Scotsman said to be true; God, how he wanted that. He began to pace. Bits and pieces of memory filtered back to him, like the stories his father had told of Scotland, the castle, the land. But could any of it be real?

The Scotsman seemed to read his mind. "You're a rich man now."

"Here, even a *rich* half-breed can't buy justice."

"It wasn't justice I was thinking of buying."

Fletcher crossed his arms over his chest and digested this. Money. A title. Land. "If this is some kind of cruel, monumental joke you're pulling just two days before I'm to die, then I'm sorry if I don't find it one damned bit funny."

"'Tis no joke, Your Grace."

Fletcher sobered. It sounded very, very appealing, like some kind of tale right out of a child's book, one where no one died in the end. Resisting the urge to fully believe something that was clearly a miracle, he snorted a humorless laugh. "How do you propose to get me out of here?"

The lawyer gave him a sly look. "Don't you worry, I have the means and I have a plan. Soon you will be out of here and on your way to Scotland, Your Grace."

Your Grace. It beat the hell out of *breed.* Fletcher's brain buzzed as he continued to think. "There is something you must do for me. I have two younger brothers and a sister." He gave the solicitor their names and then added, "I want you to find them and arrange for them to come and live with me."

"Three more bairns of the MacNeil?" The lawyer frowned, scrubbed his chin, then nodded. "Aye, that can be done." He gave Fletcher a skeptical glance. "Find them, you said. You don't know where they are?"

"I did. They've been living with their grandfather. I've been mailing money to a bank in Abilene for their care, but I haven't heard from any of them in two months. No letters, nothing. I can't find them from this cell. I'm worried that something has happened."

The lawyer's visage was grim. "And armed with this meager bit of information, I'm to find them?"

"You found me, didn't you? I can tell you where they were last living. If you won't give me your word, I won't go with you." Perhaps a hollow threat—if he didn't get out of this cell, he was a dead man. Not quite the scenario he'd pictured for the remainder of his life. "And didn't you say you work for me? Consider it your first job."

"Getting you out of here is my first job. But…" The solicitor sat on the bed and opened his satchel. He leafed through the contents and apparently found what he was looking for. He handed Fletcher another card, this one with the name of a detective agency out of Galveston emblazoned on the front. "'Tis how I found you. I'll wire them immediately. Give me all the information you have."

Fletcher gave him the material he needed, then said, "You have two days before I'm out there swinging from a rope." He wondered if he could really believe any of this, and every time he looked at the scaffold, he was afraid to let himself hope.

* * *

It was almost dawn when the night guard woke Fletcher.

"Come here," the guard whispered.

Cautious, Fletcher rose and went to the bars. The stink of liquor was heavy in the air.

The man glanced toward the door and then quickly unlocked the cell. "I've unlocked both doors. Don't go nowhere 'til you get the message," he said under his reeking breath. "I'm turning my back and leaving town with the wad of money that Scotsman paid me. Run, breed, run like me." With that, the guard stumbled away.

Moments later a rock came in through the barred window and landed on the floor. Fletcher picked it up and opened the note attached. It read:

Detective agency on board; the search has begun. A horse is tied behind the jail house. Meet me in Galveston, my lord, onboard The Bonnie Lass.

It crossed Fletcher's mind that this could be a trap, but he was going to die tomorrow, so what did it matter if they shot him tonight? He crammed the note into a pocket inside his shirt, walked over to the cell, and pulled open the door. He glanced around him and listened, hearing nothing but the strong drumming of his heart as it slammed his ribs. He stepped into the dark walkway and moved quietly toward the heavy wooden door that led from the cells, grateful there were no other prisoners locked up.

So this was how Fletcher, Maker of Arrows, MacNeil, with the help of a wily Scotsman, escaped his death sentence and disappeared into the mist on *The Bonnie Lass*, which ferried him to his new home—and freedom.

Chapter Two

Sheiling Castle, Isle of Hedabarr, Scotland, January 1858

Rosalyn tugged the shawl close around her and paced the cobbled drive. Sima, the pregnant wolfhound, followed close behind.

"Aye, Sima lass," Rosalyn crooned, reaching down to stroke the hound's furry ears. "Walking might jar those pups loose." The dog's belly was huge; Rosalyn didn't envy the delivery.

A burst of biting wind whipped around the castle, gusting through the trees and riffling the grass. Rosalyn shivered.

Geddes had sent a messenger from the ferry with the news that he and the new duke would arrive within the hour.

Rosalyn felt skittish, rather like a new colt. Why she was nervous she couldn't explain; she and the maids had scoured and swept and cleaned until their hands and knees were raw. She herself had scrubbed the larder and replaced the gauze over the windows. Why, even the Turkish carpet in the foyer had been cleaned with damp tea leaves to absorb the sand and dirt from outside while the others were taken outdoors and beaten upon by the stable boy. The whole place was scrupulous. She glanced down at her reddened hands, inhaling a sigh at the dreadful sight of them. She just wanted everything to be in order when the new duke arrived. She had been in the old laird's employ since the disaster that took away her lovely daughter two years before. As the old laird's new solicitor, Geddes had been in charge of finding a housekeeper to replace the one who had recently left to nurse an ailing sister. He had immediately thought of Rosalyn, and she was very grateful.

Now her curiosity was piqued because the old laird had been

a bawdy and stingy old sot. Heaven only knew what type of man Geddes had found in Texas. Geddes had wired her that Shamus was dead but that his son was alive and well. So, it would be a younger man who would arrive with her brother. Perhaps that was why she was nervous—a younger man might want sweeping changes of the estate, changes that didn't include her.

The house was ready, the rooms cleaned and sparkling. She vowed to make herself indispensable. As solicitor, Geddes was already a crucial part of the duke's staff. Although Rosalyn knew she had done an excellent job with the household help, she also realized that the new duke might want a housekeeper of his own choosing.

Sima's bark heralded the carriage as it clattered over the cobblestones, sending Rosalyn's heart into her throat. He was here. She hurried inside and checked her reflection in the mirror. With shaky fingers she smoothed back the hair that had been blown loose from her carefully tucked chignon.

The door opened, banging against the wall, the noise startling her. Her brother entered, looking frazzled.

Rosalyn's stomach dropped. "Geddes? What's amiss?"

"The duke is ill." Geddes motioned to the footmen behind him. "Take him up to the old laird's room. Come, Rosalyn. You have to help."

Alarmed, Rosalyn followed as four footmen carried the blanket-covered form up the wide, winding staircase, Sima close behind.

• • •

Once the footmen had placed the patient on the bed, Rosalyn peeled back the blanket and gaped at the new laird, her mouth hanging open and her heart drumming in her ears. Sima pressed against her leg as she sniffed the man, her nose occasionally poking the man's body.

Rosalyn was stunned. No, she was dumfounded. This was a savage! An American Indian complete with long black braids that nearly reached his waist, dark skin, and fringed clothing. She finally found her voice. "Geddes Gordon, your brain must have gone soft and turned to porridge somewhere over the Atlantic. I don't believe what I'm seeing." Rosalyn stared down at the unconscious man, tossed a doubtful glance at her brother, then returned her gaze to the bed. "Are you sure 'tis the right man?"

"Aye," Geddes said. "He's a half-breed Indian."

She snorted a dry laugh. "You say that so matter-of-factly. He's a savage, Geddes, a bloody savage. Look at him. How can you be certain he's Shamus's son?"

"Oh, he's Shamus's son. And whatever you think of him, sister, he is the duke."

She couldn't stop gawking at him. "When you wired that you had found him, you said nothing about this."

"I thought 'twas best to let you see him for yourself."

Aye, she would not have believed it if he'd simply told her in a letter. "What kind of duke wears braids that hang to his waist?" She reached out to touch one, then thought better of it. She caught a whiff of something unpleasant and wrinkled her nose. "And what in the world is he wearing? They smell like they've been dipped in goat grease. Och." She waved away the air, as if to dispel the odor. "They stink, Geddes, they stink to high heaven."

"I need you to nurse him. Doctor Russell is away from the island for a week."

She sincerely loathed the island physician, who was drunk more often than sober. "You'd think he'd make himself available for the new bloody Duke of Kintyre," she murmured as she continued to stare at the unconscious form on the bed.

"I'm sure when he returns he'll come posthaste. And by the way, dear sister, your language has become quite unacceptable."

"Hang my language. If Fen wasn't abed with the grippe, I'd have her take a look at the savage," she mumbled.

"I'm certain Fenella Begley is the reason your language is improper. The woman spent far too much time with soldiers, doing God knows what."

"You know very well that she saved men's lives in the Crimea and helped more people than you could ever know, Geddes. We've been over this before."

"Stop!" Geddes raised his hand. "I don't want to hear how saintly the woman was. She is a nuisance and a *besom*."

She may be an irritating woman in Geddes's eyes, but she is my only friend, Rosalyn thought. But she knew Geddes turned a deaf ear when she talked about Fenella. Each time they were in the same room the tension between them was so thick one could cut through it. Inviting Fen for dinner always ended up in a debate over something, like the rights of women against putting women in their proper place. Often, Fen had called Geddes *bodach* behind his back, which amused Rosalyn because Geddes was anything but an old man, although at times he sounded like one.

"It just occurred to me that perhaps you enjoy sparring with her. It's probably the solicitor in you."

"I don't like arguing with anyone, Rosalyn. I'm a pacifist by nature. And don't presume I have anything but distaste for that woman."

Rosalyn raised an eyebrow, wondering if perhaps he protested too much, then glanced back at the bed and caught a glint of something gold. The big, savage man even wore an earring. She was flabbergasted by the idea of such a man as the new duke. Astonished, stunned, and…she couldn't think of enough words to describe how she felt. "Where did you find him?" Her words came out in a rush.

Geddes coughed and cleared his throat. "He was at an army fort."

Rosalyn examined him closely. "He's not dressed like a soldier."

"I, ah, believe he said he was a scout, or some such thing."

"Scout," she repeated. "What in the world is a scout?"

"He worked for the army in some capacity, Rosalyn; I'm hardly in a position to know everything."

"Well, surely you learned something about him. You were together on the ship."

"For God's sake, what does it matter?" he said sharply.

He wasn't telling her everything. When her brother became impatient with her he was usually trying to hide something. "What's his name?"

"His name is Fletcher."

"Maker of arrows," she mused. "Fletcher MacNeil. Very Scottish sounding, wouldn't you say?" To look at him, however, sent another message. She shivered.

She turned back to the bed. Sima continued to sniff the man, as if wanting to remember his scent. "Well, in his current state he appears harmless enough."

"Of course he's harmless. He is the son of Shamus MacNeil. He is educated, not a savage, although he does look like one. When he was awake, we got on famously."

"No doubt you sat up until the wee hours of the morning playing lively games of chess," she said dryly.

"Aye, we did. He won every game."

Rosalyn changed the subject. "When did he get this fever?"

Geddes stood beside her. "It started a few days ago. It's been getting worse; he drifts in and out of consciousness. And his cough has become more pronounced. The fever rises at night. The ship's surgeon seemed to think it would pass."

She put her hand on his head. He was warm but not burning up. "He needs cleaning up," she said, gingerly touching the new duke's clothing, "Here, we'll have to get this animal hide off him."

Sima let out a short yelp, and when Rosalyn looked back Geddes was almost at the door. Thank the lord Sima was there to alert her to Geddes's attempt to escape.

"Just where do you think you're going?"

"I'll get Barnaby to help."

"Oh, don't be a fool, Geddes. The man's ancient. That poor old sod can barely climb the stairs."

"He is the valet."

"Barnaby Phigg *was* the valet. I know he's been in the MacNeil's service since he was a lad, but he cannot help. Lifting this…lug could kill him. Just look at the man. He's huge and unconscious. He's dead weight."

Geddes returned to the bed, muttering.

Together they shifted the new duke and stripped off his

buckskins, leaving him naked as a new bairn—which, Rosalyn thought as she studied his scarred and well-developed body, he was not. Never had she seen such a man. She tossed his clothing onto the rug and something clattered to the floor. It was a knife, one wicked enough to flense a whale. "The bloody savage carries about a knife?" She pinned her brother with another withering look.

"'Tis no different than someone toting a hunting rifle."

"A rifle is a more civilized weapon. Huns and savages wield knives," she answered.

Geddes sighed. "I'd like to know where you learn some of your facts, dear sister."

Ignoring him, she carefully picked up the weapon by the leather handle and laid it on the table beside the bed, scrubbing her palm against her skirt when she'd finished. "They use knives to scalp women in America, after they've raped them."

"Europeans brought scalping to America, Rosalyn. He's really quite civilized."

Still skeptical, she eyed her brother. "If he can truly beat you at chess, I'll eat one of my roses."

He gave her a rather smug grin. "Then cook it up, dear sister, cook it up and prepare to dine."

She shook her head at his nonsense, then kicked at the skins that lay on the rug. "Take those filthy things out of here. They smell like dead cattle and cow dung. And send up Marvella with bath water. Not Annie." Rosalyn gave an indelicate snort. "That's all we need, one gossipy maid to tell the entire island that the new Duke of Kintyre is a half-breed savage. We'd have all the nosy, superstitious villagers camped out on our doorstep waiting to get a look at him."

"They'll find out sooner or later."

"Aye, that's what I'm afraid of," Rosalyn said, turning back to the duke. He lay there, all brawn, carved in granite, but his skin began to glisten with sweat and was flushed all over. "Run along with you now. Get the water. It looks as if his fever is rising. The bath should help him."

Geddes left the room in a hurry.

Rosalyn continued to study the unconscious duke. *You are hiding something from me, brother. I will find out what it is.*

Next to the bed, the stinky buckskins were heaped on the floor. Sima had become interested in them, poking through them as if searching for a tidbit. Knowing her dog, she wouldn't be surprised if Sima attempted to eat the hide.

"Nay," Rosalyn scolded. "You'd probably get a bellyache and be too sick to nurse those pups when they come." She picked up the clothes, holding them away from her, walked to the fireplace, and tossed them into the fire. They sputtered and burned and smelled worse than a hot day in the stables before they were mucked out.

If the villagers thought Fenella was an oddity because she had served as a nurse in the Crimea, what in God's name would they think of their new duke? This was the man who was supposed to rescue the MacNeil legacy and fortune. A true-to-life American Indian. A redskin, complete with braids and a knife, and the body of a warrior. Aye, she'd read about them. Had what she'd read been real or exaggerated? Could he possibly gain the respect of the islanders? Certainly they would fear him.

His chest was wide and smooth, muscles defined sharply beneath the dark skin. She wondered what it would feel like against her palm. Lower, his genitals rested impressively in a nest of thick black hair. Interesting, she thought, that he would have so much hair there and on his head, and so little everywhere else. She forced aside the pleasurable pang that cramped her lower belly and quickly covered him with the blankets.

For so many years she had been as celibate as a nun. She'd felt no passion looking at a man, so she was surprised she could feel anything at all in this case. Perhaps it was fear, but she didn't think so. Yet even covered he was dangerous. His face was darkly intriguing, his cheekbones sharp and his full lower lip sensual. "Well, my savage duke," she murmured, "just what is to become of us now that you're here?"

Chapter Three

A noise woke him. He listened for other sounds, but heard nothing familiar. The smell was different, too—no stale, salty air. No dampness. At least he was on solid ground; his stomach had stopped rolling and tossing with the ship.

He struggled to open his eyes. His gaze met a huge, wooly head with a long dark snout. Enormous eyes peeked out from beneath thick furry brows. "What the hell?" He jumped to a sitting position, but he had moved too quickly and felt faint. Expelling a vile curse, he fell back against the pillows, coughing as though he'd bring up a lung. He slowly opened his eyes again. The animal was still there. Its giant tongue came out and slathered his cheek with animal spittle.

Another figure appeared at the bedside. He peered up. It was a woman. She whispered something that Fletcher didn't understand and the great gray behemoth left the bedside.

Fletcher swore soundly again; he ached all over. Every muscle in his body screamed in pain. With effort, he surveyed his surroundings, noting the high, intricately stuccoed ceiling and the wide shaft of light that came in through a long window across the room. "Where am I?" he asked, and then swore once again, as even the sound of his own voice made his head ache.

The woman blinked and continued to stare but said nothing.

Fletcher rolled his tongue over his teeth. His mouth was dry and he coughed again. "Who are you? Ah, hell, never mind. The inside of my mouth tastes like buffalo shit. Get me some whisky."

She didn't say a word, just stared at him, her expression one of shock and bewilderment.

He cursed loudly once again. How could he communicate if she couldn't understand him? "You do speak English, don't you?"

Her expression quickly changed from confusion to impatience. "Aye, but from the sound of it, not as colorfully as you do."

Oh, God, he thought, *a sharp-tongued woman*. They were the worst kind. "I asked for whisky," he repeated. "Please." He felt like hell and needed a drink.

"To wash away the taste of buffalo dung, I imagine," she answered, her voice sharp and sarcastic.

Fletcher frowned. "Whisky."

"You're ill." She paused, then added, "Your Grace."

The first few weeks of the voyage he'd spent with his head over the side of the ship, relieving himself of anything he tried to eat. And then the fever and cough had hit him, making him as weak as a kitten. He was glad the trip was over, but he still felt like hell. He studied her, noting her starchy demeanor. "Do you work for me?"

She opened her mouth and then closed it and finally said, "Aye, I'm in your employ."

"Then get me some goddamned whisky! Now!" Christ. Suddenly he felt as though he were rocking with the waves again, and he fought back the nausea that climbed his throat.

She backed away from the bed but did not appear afraid. Her gaze grew hard and she didn't look away.

He looked down at himself. "Where are my clothes?"

"In the fireplace."

"You burned my clothes? You *burned* my clothes?"

She looked completely unapologetic. "They stank like cow dung, or, if you prefer, buffalo dung, and were not fit to be saved. And my dog found them irresistible, and I was afraid if she tried to eat them, she'd get ill. So, aye, I burned them."

Ah, so the behemoth was a dog. It was almost as big as a horse. "That wasn't your decision to make," he groused. "There is a way to clean them."

"'Tis done, and there's no retrieving them."

Hell. He saw his knife resting on the bedside table. "At least you didn't burn this." He picked it up. "Are you ever going to get me that whisky?"

Her gaze was focused on the knife. "Are you threatening me with that barbaric weapon?"

"If that's what it takes to get me a drink," he countered.

She tossed her head; he noticed the fine, porcelain line of her neck and thought he detected a pulse at her throat. "As you wish."

Her tone was like ice. Everything about her was icy. Cold. Wintery. Just like the damned weather in this place. The last time he'd been awake they had been skirting the Scottish shore. The seas were wicked, the air was damp and bone-chilling, and the sky shrouded in misty clouds. He missed the Texas heat.

She returned with a glass and a bottle.

Ignoring the glass, he took the bottle from her and drank deeply, the liquor burning a path to his stomach. He lay back and felt himself relax, although there was still a chill in the room. He swore he could see his breath. "It's cold as a witch's tit in here." He pulled the blanket higher, cradling the bottle close.

"I'll have someone add peat to the fire. Surprisingly, your clothes didn't generate as much heat as I thought they might, considering all the raw animal fuel they contained."

She was pretty damned rude for a servant. "Who in the hell are you?"

"I'm Rosalyn Marshall. Your Grace," she added, as if it were an effort to address him so.

"Geddes's sister."

She gave him an imperious nod.

The widow. The veritable paragon of womanhood, according to her brother. She was pretty, but she looked like the kind of woman who would never dream of shedding her clothes and sliding naked into bed next to a man and pressing her breasts against him. The kind of woman who wouldn't dream of grabbing him between the legs and giving him a good, hard squeeze. The kind of woman who could freeze a man's balls off by just looking at them. *Brrr.*

In other words, she looked like the kind of woman he had avoided all of his life.

"Is there someone else besides you working here?"

Her head inched up a notch. "You're not happy with me?"

He scrubbed his face with his hand. "I would say, ma'am, that you're not happy with me. I get the impression that you feel you have better things to do."

"I think it's best if I deal with you. I'm not afraid and your bellowing won't send me running from the castle." She crossed her arms over her generous bosom. "If you must know, Your Grace," she said, once again appearing hesitant to use the term, "you are not what we were expecting."

"Just what were you expecting?"

She blushed but did not break her gaze. "Geddes wired me that he'd located you, but he neglected to inform me of your unusual lineage."

Fletcher puffed himself up and scowled. "He didn't tell you I was a goddamned red-skinned savage? Well, then, off with his head!"

She looked at the floor and appeared to stop a smile. "You may tease if you like, Your Grace, but you have no idea how people will react when they first see you and realize that you truly are the new duke."

"Believe me, ma'am, sometimes even in Texas we breeds attract more attention than we wish to."

"Nevertheless, I am here to take care of you. You have a fever and your cough is troublesome. I am a suitable nurse." She had haughtiness about her, a cool superiority that made him want to give her trouble. God, women like her really brought out the worst in him.

He kicked off the blanket, leaving himself bare. "I want a bath, and some clothes. And I've got to get up; my ass is getting numb from lying here. And where's the piss pot?"

A pink stain crept up her neck, into her cheeks. "The chamber pot is under the bed."

He swung his legs over the side of the bed and stood, testing his strength—and her resolve. He felt dizzy. "Whoa.... Will you get it for me?"

"What?"

"Get me the piss—ah, chamber pot. Please."

With obvious reluctance, she got to her knees, reached under the bed, and brought out the pot. From his position he could see the swell of her breasts. They were creamy and soft looking. She removed the lid and dropped it on the floor; it clattered noisily. She started to walk away.

"Where are you going?"

She leveled him with a gaze that, though carefully controlled, could not hide her anger. "To give you some privacy."

"I may need your shoulder to lean on. I feel weak."

"Then I suggest you use the bedpost."

Good one, he thought. "As my nurse, aren't you supposed to help me?"

She nudged the pot with her toe and moved it toward the end of the bed. "There. Use the bedpost." Then she disappeared behind a folding curtain.

When he finished, he took the blanket and wrapped it around himself, and then sat down on the bed again. "I'm done."

The door opened and a dour-looking middle-aged woman with sad eyes entered, carrying two steaming pails of water. Geddes strode in behind her, carrying two more. "We have your hot water, Your Grace." They disappeared behind the folding partition and he heard water splashing into a tub. The woman left, carrying the empty buckets, and Geddes stoked up the fire. "How are you feeling?"

Out of the corner of his eye, Fletcher saw the sister stop what she was doing and watch the exchange. "I feel like a herd of buffalo has trampled me."

"Yes, well, my sister Rosalyn will see that you feel better."

Fletcher raised an eyebrow in her direction. "She burned my clothes."

Geddes gave the woman a pointed look. "You did?"

"They stank." Her voice was matter-of-fact.

"Unless you want me to walk around stark naked, I suggest you get me some clothes," Fletcher said.

"We will find something," Geddes promised, then added, "My sister will be your nurse. She insisted that she alone will tend to you, my lord. Isn't that right, Rosalyn?"

Rosalyn shot daggers at her brother.

He crossed to the door. "I'll leave you in Rosalyn's very capable hands."

When he left, the room was quiet, except for the ticking of the clock on a long table below an enormous painting of some young dandy in a long wavy wig and ruffled shirt.

"You alone? How flattering," Fletcher commented with a smug smile. "How very flattering, indeed."

"I offered to nurse you, that is all. Barnaby is the valet. I will send him up to you while you bathe, but…he's really quite decrepit, and the less he is required to climb the stairs, the better for his rheumatism."

"Hmm, he sounds useless," Fletcher said around a purposefully careless yawn. "Why is he still here?"

"He has been in the employ of the MacNeils since he was a lad." She became fiercely protective. "Your grandfather has stipulated that Barnaby be allowed to stay on here until the day he dies."

Fletcher knew this; Geddes had gone into detail about everyone in the household. But if the widow could treat him with contempt, he could give her a hard time. "We'll see about that."

Her clenched jaw and narrowed eyelids spoke volumes.

He grasped the bedpost to steady himself. He really did feel weaker than he'd imagined. He shook his head and felt the floor come up.

She was immediately at his side. "Maybe you should lie down." Her voice was kinder, less icy.

"I'm not getting into that bed again until I have a bath."

"Fine," she said sharply, but placed his arm around her shoulders and helped him to the tub. He could smell a flowery scent in her hair, as if she had rinsed it with roses. It was the color of Texas wheat, and looked soft and abundant. He glanced down at her chest again, outlined by her fitted dress. She had a bosom most women would envy. Odd, he found himself wondering what she would be like in bed, curious to know what secrets lay between her thighs.

Alone, he sat in the water for a long time, his mind fuzzy, yet not entirely asleep. He did need a woman; it was simply that he hadn't had one in so long, even this one tempted him.

• • •

Too impatient to call for her gig, Rosalyn threw on her cape and gloves and took the short cut through the coarse marram grasses and rocky sand that led to Fen's cottage, barely noticing the slicing wind that came up off the sea. Sima lumbered along at her heels. Rosalyn needed the time to walk off some of her frustration since her cowardly brother had rushed to an appointment as soon as he had seen that the duke was all right. Once the savage had fallen asleep, she'd left him in Barnaby's care.

The new duke bore absolutely no resemblance to any of the MacNeils. Strutting around naked, taunting her with his knife. And he wouldn't dare get rid of Barnaby, who was a sweet old man with absolutely no place to go if the new duke booted him out.

Once over her initial shock, she'd vowed to give him the benefit of the doubt, promising herself she would not be unfair, just because he was...well, what he was. It was absurd. He had no sense of breeding. He was rude, crude, and abominably ill-mannered.

At one point she got the sense that he was toying with her, but even if he was, he did not appear to know the first thing about being a gentleman. Doing his bidding was not going to be an easy task. Thank God for Geddes's management expertise, for without him, she wondered what would become of the estate. Surely this savage duke was not educated in any way to handle it. She approached Fen's cottage and as always was struck by its sturdy appearance. Unlike other cottages on the island, it had a roof made of slate stone that Fen had brought in from England. Most other roofs were constructed with thatching material, which, according to Fen, was a breeding ground for vermin and should be outlawed.

Reggie Gunn was hoeing the garden. Rosalyn waved. Reggie was Fenella's bodyguard. She had found him near death on the battlefield during the Crimean War, his tongue cut from his mouth. She nursed him back to health and he became her devoted servant from then on.

Fen came to the island as a stranger and was not trusted by the villagers. She made enemies quickly when she assisted women who were not satisfied with the care they received from the island physician. She was disliked by the men, who thought her a witch, with her remedies and strange ways of healing. And it was Reggie who had protected her twice from an angry mob.

Rosalyn approached the front door and knocked briefly, then stepped inside. Sima curled up on the stoop. "Fen?"

"In here."

Rosalyn hung her cloak on the coatrack and went into the small parlor, where Fen was lying on the divan with a blanket tucked around her.

"How are you this morning?"

Fen coughed, but Rosalyn noted that the sound was loose, which meant her chest congestion was loosening up. "Better, I think."

"I'll fix us some tea." Rosalyn went into the small kitchen and poured hot water into the teapot from the boiler. She added tea leaves to the pot and let them steep while she rummaged around for some biscuits.

From the other room, Fen chatted with her, then said, "So today is the day the new duke arrived. You must tell me everything."

Rosalyn brought the tea tray into the parlor and put it on the table in front of Fen. "I hardly know where to begin." She poured tea for each of them, adding a generous dose of whisky to Fen's. "He was unconscious when he got here; it took four footmen to get him upstairs."

"He's ill?"

"He has a fever and a terrible cough. Despite his condition, he was able to bellow like a bear."

"So he's already acting like lord of the manor, is he?"

Rosalyn shook her head. "You have no idea."

"What was the physician's diagnosis?"

"He wasn't there. A fat lot of good he is, always off somewhere else when he's needed here, and when he is here, he's more often drunk than sober."

With a frown, Fen said, "I wish I could help you."

"No. You need your rest. Anyway," she added cryptically, "I don't think medical care is all that the man requires."

Fen scooted herself up, interested. "What do you mean? Oh, come now, Roz. I won't tittle-tattle, if that's what you're afraid of."

Rosalyn leaned forward. "Och! I must tell someone or else I'll explode. He's not quite…white," Rosalyn finished lamely.

Frowning, Fen asked, "What do you mean? 'Tis Shamus, isn't it?"

"Nay. Shamus died; the new duke is his son."

Fen nodded slowly. "But what do you mean, he isn't white?"

"He's brown. No, actually, red."

Fen's expression changed. "He has red hair? Well, that's a bit of bad luck."

"No, no. Red skin, as in savage Indian." When Fen didn't respond, Rosalyn added, "He's a half-breed, Fen. His mother was a full-blooded Indian."

Fen flopped back against the divan, her mouth open. "Well, by the saints." Suddenly her eyes widened. "Does he dress like they do in books? You know, feathers and…" she paused to think, then finished, "a tomahawk?"

"No feathers, but he does have a knife, and his hair is very black and in long braids that come nearly to his waist." Rosalyn nearly stumbled over her words to get them out.

"Oh, bloody hell! What fun," Fen crowed, collapsing in a fit of coughing.

"It wasn't fun. He was wearing buckskins that smelled awful.

And when I told him I had burned them he got so angry I was afraid he was going to scalp me."

"Does he speak like a savage? You know, 'ugh' and all that?"

"He speaks like any other American, I suppose, his sentences crude and spiked with curse words."

"How is Geddes taking all of this?" Fen asked.

"He acts as if the new duke is no different from Prince Albert himself, as if every day a savage Indian becomes a peer." She thought of him as she'd helped him to the tub. Big and muscular he was, and his body grand, his touch not repulsive, in spite of everything else. "It's hard to believe he's actually the duke."

"I'd have loved to have seen Geddes's face when he first saw him." Fen chuckled and sipped her tea.

"Aye, that's another thing. I think...I think there's something more to the story than Geddes has told me."

"What do you mean?"

"When I asked him where he'd found the duke, he said at an army fort. And when I asked more about it, he became snappish." Rosalyn drummed her fingers on the arm of the chair. "Whenever he gets impatient with me he's usually hiding something."

"Considering everything you've told me, the possibilities are endless."

"Aye," Rosalyn agreed, although for the life of her she couldn't imagine how things could get any worse. "You know, I still cannot imagine Geddes traveling all the way to the American frontier. Lord, he has enough trouble journeying to Edinburgh and London. Although maybe I'm overreacting. I can only imagine what kind of trip it was for my brother. What does an unadventurous soul like Geddes talk about with such a person?"

Fen laughed again. "I suppose chess was out of the question."

"According to Geddes, the duke won every game."

"This gets more and more interesting, doesn't it?" Fen looked sharply intrigued.

Rosalyn sipped her tea. "I suppose I shouldn't gossip about him—he is the duke, no matter what else he is."

"Well, if you'd brought him here, I'd have been hard-pressed not to ask him to do a war dance."

"Fen!" Rosalyn had to laugh. "You can't say anything to anyone yet. I honestly don't know how people will react when they find out."

"Well, Lord knows that twit Annie will be spilling the news everywhere she can."

"Annie hasn't seen him. I'm tending to the duke myself."

"You are? Interesting. Who is watching him while you're here?"

"Barnaby is with him now, for all the good it will do. Poor old addled thing. The other day I found him wandering about in only his cotton breeks. When I brought it to his attention, he looked surprised that I had even noticed, and then said, 'The air feels good on me bum, madam.'" Rosalyn rolled her eyes and Fen laughed.

Rosalyn could confide in Fen, who knew her deepest, darkest secrets, and was the only one who knew the truth about Leod, Rosalyn's late husband. He was a monster, who had lied to her and hid a secret life until after she'd married him, and then it was too late. Rosalyn could not think of her dead husband without feeling so dirty she wanted to soak in a tub of hot, soapy water for a week.

"So, tell me more about the duke. What's he really like?"

"So far we've only sparred with one another. I got the distinct impression he was testing me."

"Testing you?"

Rosalyn nodded. "Yes, testing me. At least I hope that he was, else he is quite possibly the most boorish barbarian who has set foot in Scotland since the Vikings pillaged and plundered."

"He has got your blood up," Fen noticed.

"Why would you say that?"

"You're here, aren't you? I don't think I've seen you this fired up since the day we learned Leod had taken little Fiona, and you vowed to roast him alive."

All of those ugly memories flooded her. "Leod deserved to die; the new duke merely deserves to be ignored, and for the life of me I can't seem to let his taunting simply roll off my back. I find myself answering his barbs with a few of my own."

"I can't wait to meet him," Fen said with glee.

"Well, it shan't be too long, I wouldn't imagine. He seems like the kind of man who would want to explore his domain and meet his people, even if it's to see what kind of reaction he gets out of them." She chuckled. "And what kind of chaos will ensue after they meet him? That should be something to see."

They were quiet a moment, and then Fen said, "So Shamus MacNeil bedded an Indian squaw. Tongues will wag when people hear about his background, but he's the new duke of the isle. If he's even halfway civilized some desperate mamas will be throwing their virginal daughters at him, despite his braids and his knife. He's worth a bloody fortune," Fen said dryly.

Once again, Rosalyn thought about how the duke's future might affect her own. If he should marry, and indeed he would, she would no longer be needed. Surely any young bride would want to hire her own help. And although Rosalyn rarely thought of herself as merely the help—for she and Geddes came from fine stock and good breeding—she was, indeed, employed by the estate.

"I'd better get back," Rosalyn said as she stood. "Do you need anything before I go?"

With a quick smile, Fen shook her head. "Just return soon with more gossip about this savage duke who soon will have the entire island buzzing like flies over a dead rabbit."

Aye, Rosalyn thought, the islanders would buzz about him, and there was no way to stop it. As she made her way back home, she wondered exactly how the man's appearance in her life would change it, for indeed it would. With each step she took, her anxiety worsened.

Chapter Four

Just as Rosalyn came in the front door, Geddes rounded the corner from the library and gave her a look of displeasure. "Where have you been?"

"I could ask the same of you. Hustling out of the duke's bedroom and leaving me to deal with him." She hung up her cloak. "I went to check on Fen."

"How many times…" He raked his fingers through his hair and gave her a troubled sigh. "She doesn't even dress like a woman, strutting around in those ridiculous trousers and all. Even when she attends a formal affair, as she did when she attended the old laird's funeral, she wore those damned trousers. It's as if she has no sense of decorum at all. "

Rosalyn rounded on him. "Would that make her a more presentable friend? If she wore a gown, like most of the rest of us? Och, there are times I envy the way she dresses."

He rubbed his hands over his face. "She irritates me. Do you know that I met her in the village the other day, and she was standing nose to nose with the schoolmaster, telling him he couldn't beat his students with a switch because it was barbaric?"

"But don't *you* think it's rather barbaric, Geddes? Remember how you felt when our tutor took a switch to your backside?"

Her brother lifted his chin in defiance. "It made me a better man."

"Hogwash," Rosalyn said under her breath, then, louder, "Fenella could do so much good, if only that sot Doctor Russell would quit trying to undermine her. She knows that wounds must be kept clean and privies must be far enough away from the wells, otherwise the sewage will seep into the water. She—"

"She's sticking her nose into other people's business, that's what she's doing. And Callum Russell has been to medical school, Rosalyn. Surely he knows what's best for us all."

"He's a drunk. And he believes that washing a man's head in dog urine will cure baldness. Our very own footman tried that, and dare I say that his pate is still shiny as a new coin. What a foolish remedy," she scoffed. "And that was thanks to Callum Russell, the educated physician."

Geddes rubbed the back of his neck. "Now that the new duke is here, I expect you to spend more time at the castle."

She put her hands on her hips. "And why would you say that? You know I never leave here unless all of my duties are done."

"Well, right now, we have a little crisis in the village."

Alarmed, Rosalyn asked, "What's happened?"

"There's some argument over a dog or something," he answered.

"That's a crisis?"

"It is here, Rosalyn. God knows we're lucky if that's all that's stirring things up right now."

That was certainly true.

"And, even though the duke is ill, I think it would be a good time for him to present himself to his public. This incident is minor, but at least the people will realize that he's here to intercede when needed."

Rosalyn was incredulous. "You're going to haul him off to the village in his condition?"

"Nay," he answered. "You are."

"Why me?"

He tugged at his collar. "I have a prior appointment."

Rosalyn shook her head and sighed, realizing that when he tugged at his collar, his "prior appointment" could well be teatime.

Though Rosalyn had argued, the savage insisted he could make the trip. They found a pair of trousers and a shirt in Geddes's wardrobe, and now he was wrapped in a huge fur greatcoat that had belonged to the old laird. His dark eyes were focused straight ahead and Rosalyn glanced at his hawkish profile. To her, he looked like a mythical Viking who'd just stepped from his ship onto Scottish soil. She could only imagine how the villagers would react. He said nothing as they continued their short journey, coughing occasionally and using a handkerchief to dab at his nose.

Before entering the village, Rosalyn spoke. "There will be a small crowd surrounding the men in question in the village square."

"What in the hell am I supposed to do with them?"

"These people have simple needs," she explained, ignoring his ill temper. "They are proud and oftentimes scurrilous with one another. Old wounds come back to the surface and some old wrong that was never righted becomes a scab both parties are eager to pick at. You are their laird; they'll want you to listen to their problem and give them a solution they can both live with. Even if they could have come to the same conclusion themselves."

His Grace squirmed beside her. "How am I supposed to know what to do?"

"Use your common sense," she answered, stopping herself from adding, *if you have any*. "I'll be right beside you."

He took a deep breath, then exhaled. "Let's get at it, then."

They entered the village, met with a cacophony of noisy, raised voices. The moment one of them noticed Rosalyn and her carriage partner, he let out a loud whistle and everyone stopped talking at once. They all turned toward the carriage and stared. The quiet was deafening. Eyes popped. Mouths gaped open. Children hid behind their mams' skirts.

Rosalyn gathered her wits, stood, and announced, "This is your new laird. His name is Fletcher, Maker of Arrows, MacNeil. He comes to us from America, where the youngest son of your late laird lived and, unfortunately, died, in a place called Texas. Your new laird is the late laird's grandson." She paused and waited.

Heads turned, buzzing commenced. One of the men stepped forward, removed his beat-up watch cap, and raised his gaze to his new laird. The man was small, wiry, and had very bright red hair that at the moment appeared to have been used as a bird's nest.

"Donnie the Digger," he announced, giving His Grace a slight bow.

Fletcher turned toward Rosalyn, a question in his eyes. She leaned into him and said softly, "Digging ditches and graves is what Donnie does for extra coin."

Fletcher acknowledged the man with a nod and then asked, "What is your complaint, Mister…Digger?" He winced at the sound ofit.

"Donnie will do, Yer Grace." He motioned behind him with his thumb. "Fergie the Burn stole me prize collie, Sarge."

Fergie the Burn burst in front of Donnie, doffed his cap at Fletcher, and explained. "The dog came ta me land with no proddin', Yer Grace." Unlike Donnie, Fergie was tall, rangy, and had the forearms of a wrestler. His bald head was so shiny the sun glinted off it.

"He'd 'a never gone if ye hadn't coaxed him, ya flagpole."

"I didna have to coax the brute, ya skinny rooster; I got me a bitch in heat and I wasna plannin' to have yer mangy collie as stud."

Donnie cursed. "Ye'd be damn lucky to have me dog screw yer bitch. He be a champion sheep herder, ya beanpole wi' balls."

"At least I got balls, ya—"

"Gentlemen," Fletcher interrupted, standing with Rosalyn's help. As if on cue, everyone's gaze moved slowly upward, taking in their very tall, very dark, very menacing-looking laird.

"I can understand both of you are upset." He coughed, a deep sound that rumbled in his chest. "But I have an idea that you might consider."

Rosalyn held her breath. This first meeting of the duke and his people was so important. It would form the pattern for the future.

"Aye, and what might that be?" Donnie asked, trying to curb his belligerence.

"Mister…ah, Fergie. Did your bitch get impregnated by Donnie's collie, Sarge?"

Fergie nodded, "I'm thinkin' she did, Yer Grace."

"Is your bitch a collie, sir?"

"Aye, and a fine one, I might add," Fergie answered, his chest swelling with pride.

Fletcher turned to Donnie. "And you, sir, have you loaned your collie out to stud others?"

Donnie, too, raised himself taller. "Aye, and I've had no complaints. He's a grand stud, he is."

Fletcher ran his hand over his face, coughed, and took a rattled breath. "I suggest that when Fergie's bitch whelps, he allow Donnie here to have the pick of the litter."

Both men studied one another, bushy eyebrows pushed into a frown, mouths turned down, eyes wary.

Donnie shrugged. "'Twouldn't be a bad exchange."

Fergie's frown deepened, and for a moment Rosalyn stopped breathing.

"I can live wi' that," Fergie finally answered.

Rosalyn blinked and exhaled, grateful this first encounter had gone well.

"In the meantime, perhaps Donnie's stud could be returned to him. If the dog got the bitch pregnant, that means she'll no longer be in heat, therefore no longer a threat to Donnie, his collie, or his sheep."

Fletcher released a sigh of relief. He had no idea what he had gotten himself into. What had he expected, that he would laze around every day, hunt, fish when he felt like it and live a life of luxury? But this one was easy. He wondered what other duties he would find as time went on.

He watched the crowd disperse, odd little people, some with colorful clothing, others in what he would refer to as rags. It was a sea of white faces with big, frightened eyes that had stared up at him. Before this he hadn't thought of how he might appear to them. He actually hadn't thought of them at all, to be truthful.

The crowd dispersed and Rosalyn bit back a grin. "You did very well, Your Grace. And as you can tell, they probably could have come to terms without your intervention, but having you as go-between makes everything nice and tidy. And it's what they expect from their laird."

He turned to her, his feverish eyes burning into hers. "Fergie the Burn?"

Rosalyn glanced away. "Fergie lives by a small stream; in Scotland, we call it a burn."

Fletcher gave her a deep, rusty sigh. "Of course you do. Now take me back so I can go to bed. I'm dying here."

Later, after she'd explained the entire scene to Geddes, he studied her for a long while, then shifted his gaze to something behind her.

"I think you should get to know him better."

Suspicious, she asked, "Why?"

He was silent for a long moment and then said, "Follow me into the library."

They entered the library and Rosalyn stood for a moment, enraptured by its beauty, as she always was. On the floor was the largest and most beautiful Turkish carpet she had ever seen. The oak furniture was sturdy and regal, and the bust of Rabbie Burns gazed down at her from atop one of the bookcases. Even though it was always a dark room, for it faced the north and east to keep the sun from fading the carpet and the window coverings as well as the spines of the hundreds of books, to Rosalyn it was a welcoming room.

"I've never informed you of the particulars of the will, have I?"

"Nay. But I don't see why I would need to know."

He cleared his throat and pulled at his collar—something unpleasant was looming for her. She could read her brother's body language like the poetry of Burns, which she could recite by heart.

He studied her over the rims of his spectacles, his expression grim. "The heir must produce an heir of his own within a year of assuming the title, or the money goes to MacBean."

Rosalyn was stunned. "That nincompoop? But the castle and title are entailed; they go to the rightful heir."

"Aye, that's true. But the fortune doesn't. And although we've found the rightful heir, it will mean nothing if we can't fulfill the contents of the will."

Once again, Rosalyn felt her sense of security slipping away. "So, the savage duke must reproduce."

"Damn, Rosalyn, don't call him that. What if he should hear you?"

She ignored him, her thoughts again on her predicament. She loved it here. Edinburgh was teeming with noise and people and filth; she had left it all behind along with her painful memories. Hedabarr was clean and quiet and isolated. She went to the window and pulled aside the heavy corded drapery. The rocks outside stood as a barrier between the castle and the sea. In the distance, she watched the cold green whitecaps slap against the shore. She caught the edge of her garden, where explosions of color bobbed gaily in the wind.

"I've grown to love this place, Geddes."

"As have I."

"I thought you said that if you found him, we could stay. Isn't that why you went to America?"

Rosalyn turned her gaze to the window once more, drinking in the sight.

"There is only one way we can stay."

She glanced back and saw him tug at his collar again. "And what is that?"

"You can marry him."

She smiled, truly amused. "You are jesting, of course."

"No. I am telling you the only undisputed way we can stay here. You could marry the duke and produce the required heir."

She studied him and found no hint of humor in his eyes or on his face. "You're not jesting."

"I'm quite serious," he said.

Her answer came swift and certain. "Nay." She stepped closer to the desk. "Whatever gave you the slightest inkling that I would consider such a thing?"

"It would secure your future, Rosalyn." His gaze was calm. "Wouldn't you like another child to replace Fiona?"

She stepped back as if he had slapped her. "How can you suggest such a thing? One child cannot replace another." Her stomach churned and she felt the seeds of a headache take root behind her eyes. "No child on earth can replace Fiona." She turned away, afraid she would be ill. "I will never marry again, never. One monumental mistake was enough."

Geddes was silent.

Rosalyn moved toward the door. "Don't ask me again, Geddes, and don't ever again imply that Fiona, my dear sweet child, is replaceable." She walked out, before he could see her tears.

• • •

She all but ran to her roses, planted on the south side of the castle, next to the vegetable garden. She usually found the flowery fragrance and the earthy loam soothing. A garden was a lovesome thing. This time, however, as she bent over her flowers, she was afraid it would take more than that to calm her.

A shadow fell over her. She looked up and found old Barnaby hovering nearby, an uncharacteristically coherent look in his eyes.

"She is a bonnie garden, mum."

In spite of her angst, Rosalyn was forced to smile. The Gaelic tongue labeled everything as either masculine or feminine, and the islanders brought this idiosyncrasy over into their colorful English. She was happy to learn that her garden was considered female. "Thank you, Barnaby, she certainly is."

He continued to stand there, so she said, "Is there something wrong?"

"'Tis the duke, mum."

A bite of alarm niggled at her. Of course it would be the duke. Hadn't he been a source of her displeasure since he arrived? "Yes?"

"He's demanding…" Barnaby's face went suddenly blank.

A frisson of irritation washed over her. "What is he demanding, Barnaby?" She stood and brushed dirt off her skirt.

The old valet frowned, his wizened face compressing like

a dried-up apple. He glanced at her skirt and then brightened. "I remember. Clothes, mum. He's demanding clothes."

Rosalyn felt a wave of relief. That demand was simple enough to satisfy. He obviously couldn't continue to wear Geddes's clothing, for although Geddes was no small man, the duke was taller and quite a bit more muscular. "Go to the attic, Barnaby. There are trunks of clothing against the east wall that belonged to the old duke and his sons. Surely there will be something in them he can wear until the tailor arrives to fit him"

Barnaby appeared to mentally process this, and then tottered away. He stopped and turned back. "We destroyed Himself's undergarments."

"Himself," the old duke, had ordered his underclothing burned—God only knew why. But she remembered the rich silk stockinette drawers that Annie had washed after the old man's death. The foolish girl had thrown them in with a red blanket, but otherwise they were good as new. "I'll take care of the undergarments," she told Barnaby, and followed him inside. She found the drawers and went to the duke's bedchamber, closing the door quietly behind her.

She stopped short, surprised to see Sima lying beside the bed. With one eyebrow raised, she whispered, "Traitor." Sima's tail thumped against the floor.

No doubt exhausted from his little trek into the village, the duke was asleep, so she laid the drawers at the end of the bed, and then touched his forehead. It was still too warm, but she couldn't pull her hand away. Her skin was so pale against his, his coloring so different, like one who spent each day in the sunshine and absorbed every bit of its warmth.

She studied him freely now, this man Geddes had suggested she marry, and had to close her eyes against what she was feeling—a dark, spiraling sensation settled deep inside her whenever she looked at him. His black and wavy hair fascinated her. She'd helped him wash it, surprised to find it wasn't coarse, but silkier than her own.

Goosebumps rose on her arms when she thought about his size. He was too tall for the bed; his feet stuck out at the end. He sported a number of scars, as if he had spent much of his time fighting, as did many foolish Scots. What little she knew about half-breeds, well, she suspected there was a reason they were called savages. She felt suddenly hot, because in her mind's eye she was seeing him naked, staring down at her, his body moving above hers.

His big, brown hand clamped onto her arm, jarring her back to reality, and she let out a guilty yelp as he pulled her down on top of him. "Your Grace…" She stared into his dark, menacing eyes. Could he read what she was thinking?

"For the last time," he said gruffly, "if I don't see some clothes in this room pretty damned fast, I swear to God I'll strut around this goddamned castle naked." He released her.

She scurried away from the bed, her heart in her throat. Sima appeared undisturbed. At any other time, had someone frightened her like that, the dog would have been up with teeth bared, ready to attack. "We have called for a tailor to fit you for some clothing, Your Grace. In the meantime, these are your grandfather's drawers." She tossed them to him.

He looked at the underwear and then up at her, his expression one of disbelief. "Are they pink?"

"They are fine silk stockinette; they'll feel quite grand, I can assure you."

"But, damn it, woman. Pink?"

"Annie, the maid, washed them with a red blanket," Rosalyn explained.

"Goddamn underwear," he muttered, tossing it onto the floor. "I'd rather walk around naked than wear that."

"So you've said."

He flung back the coverlet and stood, tall and proud.

She hadn't thought it was a challenge. "It is one thing to flaunt your nakedness in front of me," she said calmly. "Anything you have I have seen before. But should anyone else catch sight of you without a stitch on, they'll be hard-pressed not to believe you're as daft as your late grandfather was." Although her heart was drumming her ribs, she nonchalantly began to straighten the covers.

"So tell me about my dear, daft old granddad. Did he run around naked, or just in pink underwear?"

"I don't believe nudity was one of his proclivities, although it wouldn't have surprised me if it was."

"Comanche warriors wear few clothes. I could walk around here like this very comfortably. I'd even ride horseback nude if my sizeable bag of tricks weren't always getting in the way." Cocky as a bull, he strutted around in front of her.

She glanced at him, noting the tightness of his buttocks as he turned, and felt the flush creep up her neck into her cheeks.

She looked him straight in the eye, and no lower. "Go prancing about the castle without a stitch on, Your Grace, if that's your pleasure. Perhaps you'll catch the grippe and die, and then we can carry your naked hide out of here on a slab and bury you next to your debauched grandfather."

He threw back his head and roared with laughter, surprising her so that she simply stood and stared at him. All of him, from his long, inky hair that hung nearly to his waist, to the thick, dark thatch at his groin that cradled his sizeable trick bag, to the beautifully chiseled muscles of his thighs. Never in her life had she seen anything quite so perfect as this savage's body.

He continued to chuckle as he crawled back into bed. "I never thought I'd enjoy a prickly tongue on a woman, ma'am, but I'm beginning to enjoy yours."

"I'm so happy I amuse you," she said, her voice tight.

"You do."

Anxious to leave him, she said, "I've sent Barnaby to find you something to wear."

"Nothing pink."

Glaring at Sima, who didn't appear interested in joining her, she closed the door quietly behind her and briefly leaned against it. She thought of his hard, smooth body with the thick, black hair in only the most important places. She thought of his successful attempts to embarrass her, of his laughing black eyes and his bawdy sense of humor. She thought of bedding such a man, and her knees shook.

She was beginning to feel something she hadn't felt in years: intense, all-consuming desire. And she was not one bit happy about it.

She shoved herself away from the door and met Barnaby on the stairs carrying a pile of garish, out-of-date clothing. "Barnaby, where did you find those things?"

He squinted at her, appearing puzzled by the question. "Why, in the attic, mum, like you said. I'm taking them to the duke."

Rosalyn bit down on her lip to keep from smiling. Piled high in the old valet's arms was a red silk coat, purple silk breeches, and a white neckcloth with a lace jabot. On top of it all was a white wig, tied at the back with a big black bow. And the duke thought the pink drawers were a problem.

"Oh, thank you, Barnaby. I'm sure the duke will be so pleased that he finally has something to wear." Rosalyn hurried away before she burst out laughing.

* * *

For many nights sleep escaped Rosalyn, both her body and her mind ever in turmoil. Sometimes she fell hard into a dream. One of the most disturbing was the one where she was drifting along in a boat and she wasn't afraid. Odd. She had been afraid of the water ever since Fiona drowned. But here she was, floating in a small boat, the wind in her hair. She was cuddling a child close to her bosom. Was it Fiona? The child smiled up at her, eyes so dark they appeared bottomless. *Mama*, it mouthed; it appeared to have no voice.

She drew the blanket away from the babe's head and saw that it had an abundance of thick, black hair. A tiny round earring glinted from one delicate earlobe.

Mama, it mouthed again, yet still no voice sounded, but the smile widened and a dimple appeared in one cheek. The bairn extended one small, pudgy hand, and suddenly she saw Fiona's hand, clutching her favorite doll, the one she'd called Little Fifi.

Mama!

I'm here! I'm here. But she couldn't reach the baby, for suddenly it was floating away from her, away.

Mama!

This time the sound reached Rosalyn's ears.

"I'm here!" she shouted.

The dream came so often she just knew it meant something. Each time she woke, she would sit bolt upright in bed. She would pant, her heart drumming her ribs, the words *I'm here* still echoing in the dark room. Many mornings she woke crying.

Chapter Five

As January melted into February, the savage duke recuperated slowly. He still taunted her, but she was becoming accustomed to it. She often found him sitting outside, still wearing some of Geddes's clothing and wrapped in his grandfather's old fur greatcoat. Occasionally someone from the village spotted him sitting outside in a comfortable chair and stopped, always asking permission to do so. Rosalyn noticed that the duke was welcoming and never rebuffed his visitors. She commented on that one afternoon after a local crofter had left, and he said, "How else am I supposed to get to know these people? When I'm strong enough, I'll spend as much time in the village and around the island as I can. I don't want them to be afraid of me."

He took infrequent walks around the grounds, but that appeared to tire him out. He ate what was offered, never demanding anything special. Each day he seemed stronger, and when the doctor finally came to call the duke told him he didn't need his services, for he was well taken care of. Rosalyn was actually relieved.

Rosalyn was haunted by Geddes's suggestion that she marry the duke. Each day the ultimatum hung over her head, briefly dipping down to engulf her senses. The dreams were not making any possible decision easier. Fen was the only one who knew the whole story of her horrific marriage, the whole story about Fiona. But only now did Rosalyn feel she could leave the castle for any period of time. Not only had the duke monopolized her time, she'd had to hire and teach new help how to handle the chores required of them. On top of that, Fen had gone to the mainland for a spell and only returned last week.

She spotted Evan, the stable boy, in the distance and waved him over. Evan, who had come to the castle after losing his family at sea, or so the story went, was a young lad of perhaps thirteen or fourteen—no one knew for sure, although to Rosalyn's knowledge no one had ever asked him. He was a handsome laddie, though, with curly black hair and startling blue eyes. He stopped in front of her, slightly out of breath. "The bitch is close to whelping, ma'am." His eyes shone with excitement.

"She is?" Rosalyn paused. "Poor thing has been carrying around her load far too long." Sima, the beautiful wolfhound, had been bred with a crofter's stud, whose owner only wanted a male pup in return.

"I was going to ask for my gig, but if Sima is ready…"

Evan assured her, "I know what to do. 'Tis anxious I am to see those pups."

"I haven't forgotten I promised you the pick of the litter," Rosalyn said. "We'd better hope there's more than one male in the bunch."

"Aye, but I'll take a female if I have to." He grinned, showing even white teeth. He disappeared into the stable and returned with the gig. Like a young gentleman, he aided Rosalyn into the seat.

"I'll be back as soon as I can, Evan. I know I can trust you'll take care of everything."

With a happy nod, he jogged back to the stables.

As she rode toward Fen's she recalled the old laird's insistence that the boy sleep in the castle—perhaps not upstairs in one of the wings, but somewhere warm and away from the weather. Since that time, Evan had been calling the room behind the kitchen, the one with a wall that was on the other side of the fireplace, his own.

It took only a few minutes to get to the snug cottage at the end of a lane near the outskirts of the northern village. Fen was at the door before Rosalyn even secured the reins. Once inside, Rosalyn removed her cape and gloves and then followed Fen, whose loose cough was muffled by a handkerchief, into her sunny little parlor.

"Do you feel better now that you're home? I know you dislike traveling, like Geddes." Fen curled up on her Persian divan. "I'm fine, but you'll never believe who showed up here earlier."

"Who?" Rosalyn sat on the faded velvet settee.

"Angus MacNab, the nasty drunk."

Angus MacNab and his wife, Nessa, owned a pub in the village. Fen had helped Nessa when Angus had hurt her and Angus had not forgiven Fen for interfering. When Fen first settled on the island and MacNab discovered she was a nurse, he caused her as much trouble as he could, inciting the village men to fits of frenzy by plying them with ale and claiming she was a witch. Although often easily riled, most island men knew better than to listen to Angus MacNab.

Alarmed, Rosalyn asked, "Where was Reggie?"

"I'd sent him for a few supplies. Obviously that bastard MacNab saw him in the village and decided it was a good time to tell me what's on his whisky-soaked mind."

"What happened?"

"Reggie showed up and threatened Angus with an ax. Angus was still cursing at me as he ran away, claiming I was going straight to hell for interfering in his life."

"Undoubtedly he knows hell well. Ungrateful sot," Rosalyn mumbled.

"So tell me," Fenella began, "how are things at the castle?"

Rosalyn rested her head against the back of the settee and briefly closed her eyes.

"That bad?"

Rosalyn looked at her friend. "Geddes wants me to marry the duke." It was the first time in nearly a month that she'd said the words out loud. They still sounded ridiculous.

"What?" Fen's laughter was loud and hard. When she'd composed herself, she said, "That's priceless. The trip from America must have addled him."

"Aye, I've told him more than once that his brain has turned to pudding." Rosalyn rose, poured herself a cup of tea, placed a scone on a small plate, and sat down again. "The will states the heir must produce an heir of his own within a year of assuming the title, or the money goes to the nasty great-nephew."

"Fergus? Good God…" Fen made a face.

"My thoughts exactly. But I can't do it, Fen."

Fen studied her, and then said, "What else did he say?"

"He had the gall, the absolute gall, to suggest I have a child to replace Fiona." Even now it made Rosalyn's blood heat up.

Fen didn't say anything.

"No one can replace Fiona," Rosalyn said fiercely. "No one."

"It's been three years. You were a good mother. You should have more children."

"Fen!"

"Not to replace Fiona, of course, but for the joy of it, Roz. Think of the joy. Maybe he just thought you might like to have another baby. You remember what it was like to love a child."

Aye, she remembered the love, the all-consuming love she'd had for her precious Fiona. How does one not love a life so wee, so helpless, and so perfect? Even now she could almost feel that precious bundle in her arms, nursing at her breast, pressing that small fist against her skin. Even now it made her weak to think of her loss.

But a baby with the savage duke? "I've had a recurring dream that I had a bairn. I would hold it briefly, and then it would float away and I couldn't get to it. It kept calling to me and I would answer, but…" She pressed her fingers against her eyes. "You know, so many times I think of Fiona and that day. She must have been so very, very frightened. First to have Leod whisk her away like he did, then…then to be forced into a boat. She never liked the water, did you know that?"

She picked up her cup and then returned it to the saucer, her fingers shaking. "She didn't like it at all. When we went to the beach she would clutch my hand so hard, like she was afraid the wind was going to lift her up and toss her into the waves. I keep thinking how she must have called out for me, over and over again that day, and I wasn't there to help her."

She wiped her eyes with the back of her hand, the harsh memory still as painful as an open sore. "I had always been there for her, Fen. Always. And that time when she truly needed me I wasn't, and because I wasn't, she died."

Fen was studying her with shrewd eyes. "Don't do this to yourself. There was nothing you could do."

Rosalyn tried to get control of her emotions. "I know, I know. But I still think about her fear, her terror. Poor wee darling. And don't tell me not to reflect on it, because it doesn't work."

They sat quietly for a few moments. Then Fen said, "As bad as you say the new duke is, he can't be as bad as Leod."

"You're right, of course, but I just don't know if I can go through with another marriage. When Geddes suggested it, my first reaction was anger. I railed at him for even thinking such a foolish thing. But now it's haunting me, even in my sleep."

Fen picked at her scone, popped a small piece that contained a currant into her mouth, and chewed thoughtfully. "Maybe it's not so insane. But then I haven't met the duke."

"Whether I agree or not isn't the point. He, himself, might have something to say about it."

"I think you should do it."

Surprised, Rosalyn said, "Marry the savage duke?"

Fen's lips curled into a sly smile. "The savage duke. I do like that."

Rosalyn had to laugh. "Geddes is afraid I'll call him that to his face."

"He might like it."

"Aye, he might," Rosalyn agreed, remembering his penchant for barbaric nudity.

"At first I thought the whole idea was ridiculous, but now I think you should do it. I'd absolutely hate to see you alone for the rest of your days. You deserve children and someone to love you."

"Someone to love me? That's hardly likely to happen, Fen. The man and I can barely tolerate one another as it is."

"If he's half the man his grandfather was—"

"He'll be half man, half lecherous coot," Rosalyn finished with a laugh.

"All right, so the old duke wasn't exactly a pillar of sanctity and wholesomeness. But, from what everyone says, Shamus was a good man, and it stands to reason that the young duke would be like his father."

"I don't know..." Rosalyn gnawed at her lower lip.

"What? What is it?" Fen asked.

She laughed and shook her head. "Did I tell you that he threatened to strut around the castle nude if I didn't find him suitable clothing?"

"Yes, well, if I remember right, you burned his clothes," Fen reminded her.

She recalled their heated exchange. "Aye, but it's all so ridiculous, don't you think?"

Fen shrugged. "Not really. Someone will marry him, why can't it be you?"

Rosalyn could think of many reasons, but didn't respond. "I need to get back. Thank you for the tea, and for listening."

Fen walked her to the door. "I have to take a trip to Ayr next week."

"Again?" Rosalyn asked.

"Aye, another piece of business, a loose end, to do with Ewan's affairs. It still amazes me how much I didn't know about the man even though we'd been married. But Roz, do think about marrying the duke."

I am, she thought, *I am*. Rosalyn said goodbye quickly and got into her gig. As she left the village road, she waved at Reggie, who was chopping wood. She was halfway back to the castle path when Angus MacNab blocked the road.

Concerned, Rosalyn asked, "What do you want?"

"It's ye and that woman! What I do with my Nessa is no one's business but mine."

Rosalyn felt the anger rising in her chest. "Her arm was broken. She came to us. We helped her."

"Ye stay away from my wife!" He lurched forward and grabbed her.

She fell sideways, striking her temple on the frame of the gig. She saw stars and raised her crop in self-defense.

"Stay out of my business," he repeated, and as he ran away he added, "Or ye'll be sorry!"

The threat was real, she knew. Frightened, Rosalyn righted herself and snapped the reins across the bay's rump. He reared up, almost tossing her from the seat, and took off toward home.

Her heart was still pounding when she pulled the mount to a stop in front of the castle. She fought to catch her breath. She touched her temple. There was blood on her glove. She took out her handkerchief and pressed it hard against the wound. Her hands were shaking.

"Are you all right?"

The duke's voice startled her; she quickly tucked the bloody handkerchief into the sleeve of her cape. "I'm fine, thank you."

He turned her face toward him. "You've been hurt."

"It's nothing, truly." She pulled off her gloves.

"You're shaking."

She attempted to escape, but just then Geddes bounded out of the castle.

"Rosalyn. You're hurt. What happened?"

"It's nothing." She clenched her fists to keep her hands from shaking.

"It's something, Geddes, her temple is bleeding." The duke's voice was stern. "What happened?"

Feeling trapped by the two of them, she admitted the truth. "I was attacked on the way home from Fen's."

"Who did this?" the duke demanded.

With reluctance she said, "Angus MacNab."

The duke turned to Geddes. "Who is this MacNab?"

With men on either side of her, she went into the castle. "He owns one of the pubs in the village," Geddes answered. "I told you so, didn't I? Didn't I? I knew you would get hurt. And you were coming from Fenella Begley's cottage, weren't you?" Geddes was beside himself.

"Geddes, I could have been coming from anywhere and he might have stopped me."

"But you weren't coming from just anywhere." He drove his fingers through his hair and swore. "That woman will be the death of me."

"Who is Fenella Begley?" the duke inquired.

Rosalyn hung up her cape and unwound the scarf from around her neck. "She's a nurse and my friend." She glared at Geddes. "I…I would have had her look in on you, but she herself was ill at the time."

"But, MacNab is—"

"He's just an ill-tempered sot and a bully; I'll be fine." But this was the first time she had ever been physically attacked, and she was shaken.

The duke stood by the door. "Why don't I put your gig away? But later I want more information on this MacNab."

Rosalyn nodded her thanks, and when the duke was gone, Geddes made sure he was out of hearing distance before he said, "Well, if this doesn't change your mind about marrying the duke, I don't know what will." He took her cloak and tossed it on a chair.

"Please. Not now." Rosalyn stopped at the mirror. There was a stream of dark blood on her temple, cheek, and jaw. She dabbed at her wound with her handkerchief. "I refuse to let a nasty, small-minded drunk drive me into marriage with any man, especially a stranger who is completely oblivious as to what you're trying to do to him."

"Good God, Rosalyn, this is only the beginning. Weren't you frightened? You should have been."

Her heart pounded still. "Yes. I was frightened."

"Next time he might startle the horse, and you could end up dead."

She would not admit that she'd nearly lost control of the gig as it was. "Don't be overly dramatic." But she knew he was right. Things could escalate. Some people weren't happy unless they drew blood.

And it appeared Angus MacNab was anxious to spill someone's. Fen had Reggie for protection, but she must warn them.

Geddes removed his glasses and pinched the bridge of his nose. "Rosalyn, my dear, I know all of this is quite distressing, but considering what's just happened, please, I beg you, reconsider."

But he didn't have to beg. She had been doing a lot of thinking and she was weakening. "What if he doesn't want to marry me? We don't get on very well, you know. And anyway, he just might prefer a maiden without the baggage I have."

"Baggage? What baggage?"

"Oh," she said, impatient, "I'm a widow."

With a wave of his hand, Geddes brushed the comment away. "You are a beautiful woman."

"And just tell me how you're going to approach him with this ridiculous scheme of yours? You can't saunter up to him and merely say, 'Well, old chap, you need an heir and my sister is fertile'—"

"Of course not," he assured her. He cleared his throat. "I have a plan; don't concern yourself."

Rosalyn raised an eyebrow. A plan? She didn't believe him for a minute. "But it does concern me, Geddes. I cannot simply consent; I'd feel like a lamb being led to the slaughter."

He took her hands and gave them a brotherly squeeze. "Things will work out, Rosalyn. They always do."

• • •

Fletcher wrapped the cord of the expensive silk robe around his waist and crossed to the window. It was black as pitch outside and a cold wind howled angrily, rattling the windows. Damned weather. Aboard ship, he had learned that the wind was the island's most constant visitor just as it was a ship's most welcome one. Here, it barreled down from the north where there were fjords and icebergs, with wicked glee sent with it clouds of cold mist and fog.

He shivered and poured himself a glass of whisky—his third or fourth, he'd lost count. His mind was going numb, but not numb enough. What in the hell was he doing here? For the first few weeks he'd had to gather his strength; the fever and the trip over had been hard on him. Though he had always felt he was strong and could handle most anything, he discovered he did not have sea legs and perhaps never would. And he analyzed everything. He began to wonder at the price he'd paid to get out of prison. Geddes had promised that Duncan, Gavin, and Kerry would be found, but what if they weren't? He couldn't stay here, living in luxury, when the safety of his siblings was unknown. He didn't care what he would lose by leaving, he would have to go and search for them himself.

Because he had no information about them, his mind became filled with all of the horrible possibilities. Again he wondered if Grandfather had died. If so, what would the children do? What were they doing at this very moment? Were they cold? Homeless? Ill? He swore and gripped the snifter so tightly he heard it crack.

And now, with him thousands of miles away, how would he ever know what had happened if word never arrived? It had eaten at him for weeks.

He questioned if he'd accepted the freedom Geddes had given him just to get himself out of the bind he was in. He hadn't thought much beyond that, but what choice had he had? It was either accept Geddes's offer and hope that the children could be found, or stay and be hanged, abandoning them forever. It was his fault entirely. He cursed himself for falling under Lindsay's spell.

He finished off the whisky in the cracked snifter, enjoying the buzz that blurred his brain. As he made his way back to the bed he wondered how in the hell he was going to sleep—his demons were strong, his conscience and the memories of a woman who had tempted him ate at him, and no amount of whisky seemed to diminish either one.

• • •

Rosalyn dreamed of sex. She dreamed of wanting it; she dreamed of needing it. When she woke, her fingers were at the apex of her thighs. "No." She hissed the word, making it sound like a curse. Then, slowly, she touched herself. She needed this. She closed her eyes and felt herself bloom. She lay there, satisfaction imminent.

Suddenly something, a sound, intruded upon her pleasure. She stopped and listened.

It was *him*. He was shouting.

She threw back her covers, rushed from the bed, and ran down the hallway. There was another sound, as pain-filled and frightening as the first. She flung open the door and stepped inside.

He lay thrashing on the bed, mumbling and murmuring.

Fearing his fever had returned, she closed the door and hurried to his bedside. "Your Grace?"

He was restless almost to the point of agony.

She touched his forehead. He was sweating, but he was not feverish. "Your Grace?" she said again, hoping to awaken him without startling him.

He grabbed her arm; she tried to jerk away but he was too strong.

"My fault," he murmured.

"Sir?"

"Lindsay! Don't leave me," he hissed.

"Nay, 'tis Rosalyn." Her heart drummed against her ribs.

The moon appeared from behind the clouds, the pale light gliding across the room like a stealthy shadow.

"Lindsay, please…" he said again.

Rosalyn shook him, wanting to wake him from his nightmare. His hands gripped her shoulders and he pulled her toward him. "Lindsay." He sounded relieved.

Rosalyn struggled against him, attempting to free herself.

"You're here," he murmured, threading his fingers through her long, loose hair. "You're alive!" He reached up and touched her face, running a finger along her jawline. "One last kiss before I die…"

His kiss was gentle, yet filled with a raw pain that Rosalyn felt deep in her soul. Oh, by the holy, it felt so good. She pressed her hands to his chest and gave herself up to the kiss, mindless of the consequences. All she knew was that she wanted his touch everywhere. She needed to be gratified.

His hands began to roam her body and reality came screaming back to her. "Your Grace," she whispered. "Please."

His lips found hers again and he kissed her, using his tongue, forging a path into the intimate recesses of her mouth. Unable—or perhaps unwilling—to resist, she opened for him. He tasted of whisky, tangy and sweet, his tongue wet and smooth as it circled hers. She took hold, imprisoning it, sucking on it, pulling it in, drawing on his need.

"Sweet, sweet..." He murmured the words against her lips, and his breath on her skin sent shards of want deeper and deeper into every corner of her sex-starved body. His fingers drew her nightgown up and she spread her legs, the hungry cramping she'd experienced earlier intensifying. He touched her; she nearly flew apart.

She pressed her face into his shoulder and gritted her teeth, want, need, and the urge for fulfillment so strong she bit him.

"Oh, God," he groaned. He fingered her, finding her center, briefly circling the thickened nub before dipping inside. She felt her muscles clamp down on his moving finger and she rocked with it, her hips trying to find the rhythm.

"So sweet and wet," he murmured.

She was on the very verge of orgasm, the satisfying prelude escalating.

He stopped; she felt a dash of disappointment. And then he drew her astride him. As if she'd done it dozens of times before, she straddled him. His shaft was wide and long and she impaled herself on it, biting down on her lip to keep from screaming her pleasure. He lifted her hips up and slowly down, up and slowly down. They began a rhythm. His hands cupped her buttocks and spread them wide, squeezing each cheek as he thrust deeply into her.

Rosalyn leaned forward, pressing her clitoris against him, and he took hold of her nipple through the fabric of her nightgown. An itchy, tickly sensation sprang from her breast, spreading over it, across her abdomen and down to her vagina. She cried out as the orgasm exploded and every nerve in her body quivered, from the base of her spine to the roots of her hair.

He shuddered as he came and she fell on top of him, taking in deep breaths as she tried to gain control. Her ears rang. Her body sang. She was damp with sweat and still throbbing around him. She needed this. She had forgotten how much she needed this. She closed her eyes and didn't know how long she lay like that—minutes, hours—but when she glanced at the window, dawn had come.

He stirred beneath her and was staring directly into her eyes, his expression clear and focused. Awake. Mocking? "Why, if it isn't the widow Rosalyn. What on earth are you doing in my bed?"

Chapter Six

Geddes opened the bedroom door just as Rosalyn, dressed only in her nightclothes with her hair in long tangles around her face, was scrambling off the bed.

"Rosalyn? Is he ill?" He could imagine no other scenario that made even a modicum of sense to him. His gaze went from Rosalyn to the duke, whose face was pinched into a look of amused puzzlement.

"Your Grace?"

The duke shook his head as if to clear it. "I'm sorry. I was having a dream, and suddenly it was real." He looked at Rosalyn, who was plastered against the far wall, near the door. He offered both of them a wry grin. "Normally, I'm not one to question such a gift, but—"

Stunned, Geddes said again, "Rosalyn? What is going on here?"

She huddled near the door, her fist clenched to her chest, her eyes closed, her breathing ragged, and her hair loose and wild around her shoulders. She was speechless, it seemed. He had not seen that level of panic on her face in years, not even the day before, when she'd been attacked by MacNab. Suddenly, she let out a cry of frustration and ran from the room, slamming the door soundly behind her.

Baffled, Geddes crossed to the bed. "Your Grace, what happened? Are you all right?"

The duke stared at him from the bed, his dark eyes boring deeply into him. "I'm fine, thank you. I wish I could explain what just happened here, but I'm not sure I know."

Equally confused, Geddes said, "I must find Rosalyn. Please, I shall return shortly." He strode from the room and ran to Rosalyn's suite. When he found his sister, he shook his head and sighed. She sat in an overstuffed chair in the corner, her knees to her chest and her face pressed against her hands.

"Rosalyn? What happened? What were you doing in there?"

"Oh, God, don't ask me."

"But Rosalyn, I…it's…what…" He couldn't form a coherent thought.

Rosalyn lifted her head and took a deep breath. Although he no longer saw panic in her face, he saw embarrassment, something that was not often evident in Rosalyn's demeanor.

"I woke up during the night because I heard him call out. I went to his room and he wasn't rational. He kept saying some woman's name over and over again."

"He was probably just having a nightmare."

She hesitated and then nodded. "Aye, perhaps that's it."

Relieved that she probed no further, he asked, "He got you into his bed, Rosalyn?"

She nodded again.

A strange calm settled over Geddes, replacing the shocking image of his sister scrambling off the duke's bed. Suddenly their future seemed on the verge of being quite secure indeed.

"I don't know how that happened." Slowly she rose from the chair and crossed to the window. She parted the curtains and stared outside.

Geddes tried not to sound pleased when he said, "You were compromised, dear sister. Good and compromised. I see a wedding in your future. Don't fret, Rosalyn. Everything will be fine. Just fine."

As he hastened to speak to the duke, he heard his sister's muffled cry of frustration.

• • •

Fletcher stood at his bedroom window as he mulled over the morning's curious events. Lindsay had come to him in a pristine white gown, a wide circle of bright red blood on her chest. She had hovered above the bed, a wistful, sad smile on her face. He wanted to tell her he hadn't killed her, but it was as if she couldn't hear him or didn't understand. And then suddenly she was there, in bed with him, and he knew that he had to have her one last time.

He felt a twinge at his shoulder and glanced down. Bite marks? He ran his fingers over it, remembering that in their passion, she had bit him. Rosalyn had bit him. The perfect dream had been a different reality; the widow's presence proved that. He closed his eyes, willing himself to remember more, but he could not.

She had been in his bed and they had made love. His smile turned grim. *Made love.* Hardly that. In his liquor-soaked dream it was Lindsay he pulled astride, impaling her. But in truth it had been Rosalyn.

Fletcher felt an odd squeezing in his chest, an emotion he couldn't describe. Bemused, he looked out beyond the trees where he could see the stables. Later in the morning he planned to dress and take a turn around the grounds; he enjoyed seeing what he had inherited. He made a face. But before he could enjoy himself, he had to meet with two crofters about a dispute over a goat. And then at some point he was going into the village to face the nasty pub owner.

There was a knock on the door and Geddes poked his head in, his face a study in concern. "Might I speak with you?"

Fletcher nodded.

Geddes walked toward him, wringing his hands. "It's a most unfortunate situation, my lord. My sister claims you cried out in your sleep, and when she hurried in to find out what was amiss, you, well, you dragged her into your bed."

"Dragged her into my bed?"

"Yes, Your Grace. That's what she claims."

Fletcher didn't know what he had done or what she had done. All he knew was that she was in his bed when he awoke.

Geddes cleared his throat and pulled at his collar. "Circumstances have forced me to talk to you."

"About your sister?"

"Yes, but more importantly about the terms of the will."

Fletcher lifted one eyebrow. "Terms? You told me about the will in Texas."

"Not all the terms."

Fletcher felt a great unease creep into his stomach. "So there are more conditions, other than just my being here?"

Geddes nodded. "By coming to Hedabarr, you have inherited the castle and the land, but unless you produce an heir within a year of your arrival, the MacNeil fortune will be awarded elsewhere."

Fletcher strode in front of the long table that held the ancient chime clock. "You never told me this."

"You became ill on the trip. I hadn't the chance."

"Who gets the money if I don't comply?"

"The most sniveling, self-righteous prig ever to be born, who at this moment, I am certain, is waiting to hear that I have failed in my duties to bring you here and agree to the contents of the will."

Fletcher rocked back on his heels, noting that Geddes was sweating. "Sniveling prig, huh?"

"Indeed, Your Grace."

Fletcher pinned Geddes with a level gaze. "Why do I feel that as of this morning, you now have someone in mind to carry my heir?"

A look of guilt passed over Geddes's features but was quickly gone. "I didn't, not at first."

"You mean to tell me that you hadn't given your sister a thought?"

Geddes continued to perspire. "I admit I did. But she wouldn't agree to such an arrangement and was absolutely vehement. Please, believe me. She is often stubborn and headstrong, but she is not devious. In fact, she told me she couldn't agree to such an arrangement because you could very easily disregard her as a possible wife."

"Yet I found her in my bed this very morning." He turned to Geddes once again. "Don't you find that convenient?"

Geddes looked offended. "Your Grace! You are not implying

that she and I, in any way, planned this, are you? For I assure you, Your Grace—"

"For God's sake, Geddes, will you stop Your Gracing me?"

"But, what am I to call you?"

"I don't know," Fletcher answered with an impatient swipe of his arm. "But when we're alone, like we are now, it sounds so damned pompous. If you have trouble using my name, well, then don't call me anything at all.

"Now, as to your sister. She could be carrying my heir now." He leveled another gaze at Geddes.

"Yes, she could," Geddes agreed.

"But if I ever learn that this was planned—"

"Believe me, it was not planned."

Fletcher nodded. "Make whatever arrangements you have to. I'll marry her, on one condition."

Geddes stared at him. "And that is?"

"You give me some information on my siblings. Bringing them here was part of the deal, Geddes, if you remember."

"Of course. I'll check on it immediately."

"Is there something else?"

"No. No." Geddes left.

Fletcher stared into the fire. As a half-breed living and working with the army, he'd become jaded and suspicious of people. His question about being set up quickly dissipated when he recalled the way Rosalyn had scurried from his bed and fled from the room. Geddes was an honest man and had been sincerely shocked to find his sister there. Any subterfuge would have been evident on the man's face, in his eyes. And over the years, Fletcher had become adept at catching someone in a lie. Geddes was simply not a man who could lie and get away with it.

Fletcher's thoughts went again to the early morning hours. He had been satisfied, as had she. He liked that she was spirited. She spoke her mind to him. And she was quite easy on the eyes.

His life had changed. It was as if a door to another world had opened the day Geddes came into his cell. Here he and his family could live and live well, but not without the money attached to the will. Marriage was something he had thought out of his reach, so he had never asked himself if a family was important to him.

Now all that remained was getting his brothers and his sister here. He needed them with him; he wanted to see them grow up. He wanted to try to make right the mistakes of his youth. Until he'd set foot on the Scottish shore, he hadn't realized how much he needed them. And until they were here and safe, he would not rest well.

Later, he saddled a mount and rode into the countryside to consider the question of the goat and the sheepherder.

A burly middle-aged man with his arms crossed over his chest stepped into the road ahead of him. A thick wad of tobacco bulged from his lower lip. "Ye've come about the goat, I'm thinkin'."

No niceties. Fletcher appreciated that. "You must be Douglas?"

The man nodded. "Douglas MacDougal. They call me Lum."

Fletcher raised his eyebrows.

"I clean lums," he explained. "Fireplaces."

"Where's the goat?" Fletcher dismounted and threw the reins over a long plank in front of the croft.

"Damn thing eats everything. All me prize clover and grass for me sheep, the goat gobbled up like a pig on swill."

Fletcher followed him to the back of the small house. There, on the grass next to a padlocked shed, was a tarp. He briefly noted that the shed windows appeared painted over. Douglas the Lum lifted the tarp and there lay the dead goat, a bullet hole in his head. "Whose goat is this?"

"Damn thing belongs to Bill Duncan. Bill the Goat."

Fletcher stifled a smile. "And where is Mr. Duncan now?"

MacDougal looked beyond Fletcher, who turned and saw a younger man approaching rapidly on foot, shaking his fist. "Damn ye! Damn ye to hell, MacDougal, if you shot me goat I'll sic me hounds on ye!"

"If ye kept that animal tethered it wouldn't happen, Bill," Douglas said calmly.

Bill Duncan looked down at his goat and shook his head. "He

chewed through the tether. It was a rope the size of a man's fist, mind ye, and he still ate it like it were a lamb chop."

They both looked at Fletcher, apparently waiting for him to make a decision. He remembered Rosalyn's suggestion: *use your common sense.*

"When did you shoot the goat, Douglas?"

"Dinner time yeste'day."

Fletcher didn't want to make a mistake. He didn't want to pit one crofter against another. "How about if the two of you slaughter the goat and split the meat?" He held his breath.

"But he kilt me ram," Bill said mournfully. "He coulda just led him back to me own place. Didn't have ta kill it."

Fletcher looked at Douglas for some kind of answer.

Douglas cursed and spit his wad of tobacco onto the grass. "That critter was too ornery to get close to. Nearly took a bite out o' me arse." He spat again. "I didna have no choice."

Fletcher took a breath. "Since the deed is done, gentlemen, I suggest you take my advice and split the meat. It will come in handy for both of your families come winter, won't it?"

The men studied one another. "Ye want the hide, man?" Douglas asked.

Bill cut his gaze to Fletcher, then answered, "Nah, ye can ha'e it."

The men grudgingly shook hands and Fletcher took his leave, once again relieved that he had handled the situation calmly. Of course, these were easy. He wondered how he'd handle a truly difficult or dangerous situation.

He nudged the mount east toward a stream, following it south as it burbled over the smooth stones toward the sea. A tiny cottage was perched on a rise, a small garden to one side. Out of the corner of his eye he caught just a glimpse of something red down by the stream. Moving closer, he realized it was a child, a toddler just learning to walk, in a red shirt, weaving dangerously close to the water.

He glanced toward the cottage and saw no one. Laundry rustled in the breeze from a makeshift clothesline. The garden was empty.

At that moment he heard a splash from the stream. He dismounted quickly and ran to the site to find the toddler sputtering and flailing about in the water. He scooped the child out and, with the boy coughing and crying, strode toward the cottage. At that very moment a woman threw open the door, her eyes huge as she looked at Fletcher and her soaked, wailing child.

"Clive!" She reached for her boy, trying to settle him down once Fletcher passed him to her.

"He had fallen into the river, ma'am." Fletcher watched the terror in the woman's eyes as he explained.

Once both mother and child were more subdued, the woman invited Fletcher inside. While she changed the child into dry clothing, Fletcher looked around the cottage. It was clean and tidy, with colorful patchwork quilts thrown over some of the furniture.

The woman returned, put the child on the floor, and motioned for Fletcher to take a seat at the table. "Me name's Birgit, Your Grace. Ye'll stay for a wee cuppa?"

He assumed that meant tea, so he nodded while she prepared it.

The toddler, quiet and curious, sat on the floor and rubbed his cheek against the fur of Fletcher's greatcoat and tucked his thumb into his mouth. Fletcher picked the boy up and settled him against the crook of his arm, where he sat quite contentedly.

The tea set out, the woman said, "Your Grace, I canna thank ye enough. Ye saved me Clive!" Tears threatened. "He be wandering off so much, I canna keep track of him. Some days I feel like putting him on a leash just to keep him safe."

She wasn't a pretty woman, but she was comely and the tea was strong and sweet, just as he'd begun to like it. "You know, when my younger brother was just a lad, he was the same way. Always off somewhere, scaring everyone to death with his curiosity. They put little bells on his moccasins so they would always know where he was."

She brightened. “Aye, that’s a fine idea. I’ll have Fergie get on it as soon as he and the boys return from the village.”

Fletcher slanted her a glance. “Fergie the Burn?”

She straightened, proud. “Aye, Fergie is me man. He be a good man.”

“I’ve met your husband. Yes, he is a good man.” Fletcher finished his tea and stood, and handed her the boy. “Thank you for the tea.”

“Nay, ’twas nothing,” she answered. “Ye saved me Clive, Your Grace.” Her eyes welled with tears again. “I’m grateful, so grateful.” She gave him a clumsy curtsey. “And we’ll be sure to try them bells on Clive’s shoes, we will.”

Fletcher understood small-town mentality—rarely could anyone keep a secret and everyone knew everyone else’s business. But he had no idea how swiftly the news of Clive’s rescue rumbled through the island community.

He’d barely sat down to dinner that evening when Geddes reported that the news of Fletcher’s heroism was all over the island. Fletcher could only wonder if they used smoke signals to get the message around so quickly.

Chapter Seven

In the weeks since Fletcher awoke to find Rosalyn warming his bed, he had realized she avoided him as much as possible. Hoping to amuse himself, he became acclimated to his new surroundings. He was more comfortable astride a horse than sitting in a carriage or a gig, and although he had ridden since he arrived, he had not carefully studied the horses at the stable.

One day he noticed a brown-and-white stallion, an impatient steed, frisky and anxious to run. This was the animal he wanted. He called him Ahote, which meant "restless one." He'd asked Evan, the stable boy, about the breed.

"'Tis an Irish Hunter, Yer Grace," Evan told him, and went on to explain the breed, a combination of Irish Draught mare and Thoroughbred stallion, most likely an Arabian. "Bred for jumping and racing."

So in the days afterward, man and horse flew across the sand together, soon followed by the huge, shaggy wolfhounds and menagerie of other dogs that slept in the stable. They rode into the cold, damp wind, and over the coarse grass that peppered the island. Often, at sunset, Fletcher sat astride the animal and watched as the sun slipped below the watery horizon, leaving streaks of purple, orange, and yellow.

From there he could look back and see the castle in the distance, amazed that all of this was his. His father had told him it was a small castle compared to many, but it was bigger than any damn building Fletcher had ever seen. He learned that the ivy-covered, two-and-a-half-story red stone edifice had been built in the thirteenth century on the ruins of an earlier Viking fortress. Whatever his ancestors had been, good or daft or completely amoral, the buildings and grounds were well maintained and the rooms filled with furnishings that rivaled museum pieces.

The more he walked the property, the more he understood why men settled down. He found himself bound to this place in an eerily natural way, even though it was different from anything he had ever experienced. Perhaps it was because everywhere he looked he could imagine his father as a boy, racing over the grass, peering out one of the upstairs windows, or climbing onto the roof and settling against the chimney to watch the ocean and the sky. He now lived in the stories of his youth, images that had seemed so far away back then. Here he felt less lost than anywhere else he had ever been.

He wanted his brothers and sister here. Like him, they were bound to this land by blood and bone and heritage. He smiled—he even thought of Gavin that way, for he had been his brother for many years. It had been over a month and there had been no word from the agency.

As he took the path behind the stables, he heard a woman's voice coming from inside. Curious, he stepped to the window and then pulled back quickly. He carefully looked in again and saw Rosalyn sitting on a stool, her back to the window, talking to Sima, the wolfhound bitch that had a litter of pups. He didn't find it unusual for her to be exposing her soul to a dog. At his loneliest moments he'd talked to his horse.

Rosalyn held one of the pups in her lap and stroked it tenderly.

"Everyone has an opinion about my life, Sima."

The dog looked up at Rosalyn, her tail thumping as several of her pups nursed.

"Geddes is insistent, of course, thinking he knows what's best for me," she said conversationally. "He's always been so practical. Well, not always. There was that time when he was a far younger man and we were on holiday in Vienna with our tutor. Our da had a cousin who had some connections to the Austrian court, so we'd been invited to tea." She stopped and chuckled, remembering. "There was this beautiful, fragile girl there and Geddes fell in love immediately. Unfortunately, we learned she was an Austrian princess and not at all interested in some pale, lanky schoolboy from Scotland. He was heartbroken when she rebuffed him. Sometimes I think that's why he's never allowed himself to fall in love again." She cuddled the pup close, nuzzling it with her nose. "He won't take chances with his life, but he's willing to take chances with mine.

"I know why he wants me to marry. Oh, indeed, he's anxious for an heir so the estate is secure, but he also wants me out of his hair, although he would never admit as much.

"I do wish Fen hadn't gone to the mainland. I need to talk this entire thing over with her before it's too late." She put the pup down next to its mother and it immediately rooted around for an available teat. "I don't know the duke well enough, Sima. I can't trust my own judgment. He might be as evil as Leod, but how will I know until it's too late?"

Fletcher leaned against the stable wall next to the window and closed his eyes. What reasons had he given her to trust him at all? And who was this Leod and how did he fit into Rosalyn's life?

He glanced back through the window just as she reached into her apron pocket and pulled out a griddle scone. She broke it into pieces and fed it to the bitch, who took each piece delicately, yet eagerly. And then Evan entered the stable, so Fletcher moved away from the window again.

"Good day, mistress."

"Oh, Evan, aren't these the most beautiful pups?"

"Aye, they are."

"Have you picked out the one you want?"

"Aye," he said. "The one with the bushiest eyebrows. He reminds me of my uncle Artair who lives on Mull."

"Artair means 'bear,'" Rosalyn said.

"Aye. I'll call him Bear."

"Well, he's a beauty, Evan. One of the males is spoken for, of course, but do you think we can find homes for the others?" Rosalyn asked.

"'Tis a job I'll take on happily, mistress."

"All but one," Rosalyn said. "I think perhaps I should keep one of the pups, don't you?"

"Aye," he said, pausing before he left. "You should pick the one you want to keep, mistress. Do you think His Grace would want one?"

Rosalyn paused. "All of the hounds follow him around already; I don't think he needs any more adoration."

Evan glanced at her, puzzled, but said nothing.

Fletcher smothered a chuckle from behind the stable wall.

Rosalyn sighed and picked up the pup she'd earlier held on her lap. "I've grown quite attached to this little lassie. She's found her way into my heart. I'll call her Bonnie, because she is such a bonnie little thing."

Fletcher watched Evan leave the stable, but before he left too, he heard Rosalyn speak. "Picking a loveable pup is easy; 'tis picking a good husband that's impossible."

• • •

Days later, tired of wearing Geddes's clothing, Fletcher entered the foyer, still hunched over from the early March chill. He bounded up the staircase as Rosalyn approached. "Good day, ma'am."

She looked up, surprised to find him there. "You're wearing a kilt," she said with astonishment, but no smile accompanied it.

He'd nearly frozen his balls off when he stepped outside. But he gave her a nonchalant shrug. "Yes. I felt the clothes you had Barnaby bring me were too fancy. I thought I'd save them for the wedding."

Her expression was priceless. She looked horrified. "You wouldn't. And anyway," she added hastily, "it won't be necessary. Your clothes have arrived; they're in your suite."

He bit back a grin. "Lucky for you they arrived when they did. Otherwise, what else would I have worn to the wedding?"

She finally realized he was teasing her and she appeared to stop a smile. "I had nothing to do with Barnaby finding those clothes."

"But you saw them, and you didn't discourage him from

bringing them to me." When she didn't answer, he said, "You didn't really think I'd wear them, did you?"

Her expression told him that she had hoped he would.

"As for the kilt, I like it." He glanced down at the plaid. When she didn't respond, he said, "You've been avoiding me."

"I have your household to run, Your Grace." She started to leave, but he caught her arm. She tensed.

"I'm not going to hurt you."

She seemed frozen in place, so he leaned in close, pulling her toward him. She smelled of roses and woman—a scent he remembered well. A scent he conjured up often when he was in bed alone, wishing he could remember every moment of their mating, cursing when he could not remember it at all. Her skin was pale, flawless. Her wheat-colored hair, pulled into a severe braid at the base of her neck, had a healthy shine. He wanted to see it spread out on his pillow. He longed to see desire in her eyes; he wanted to see her sated. He surprised himself when he realized he wanted her. "Do you never smile?"

She looked away. "I've had little to be joyous about of late."

"Do you dread our marriage so much, Rosalyn?"

She turned quickly and looked at him, as if her name on his tongue startled her. "I was married once, Your Grace. It was quite enough to satisfy me for a lifetime."

Evil Leod. Fletcher released his grip but kept his hand on her arm.

She didn't move away.

"Someday I would like to know more about the man who put such pain in your eyes."

She pulled her arm from his touch. When she looked at him her gaze was veiled, yet he could still see the lack of trust. "I'm afraid it's a subject I don't discuss with anyone."

He nearly said, *Not even with Sima?*, but thought better of it. "Not even your future husband?"

She studied him for a long moment, then said, "Nay, not even my future husband."

He felt a stab of disappointment that she could not confide in him, but he had given her no reason to and he was sorry. Whatever it took, he would learn why she felt as she did. He also had to assure her that he was not an oaf or a buffoon or a savage. "Rosalyn."

She turned away. "I have duties. Excuse me."

"Rosalyn," he said again.

She paused halfway down the stairs but did not turn back.

"I apologize for my crudeness when we first met."

She didn't move.

"I will try to curb my foul language. I've been among men most of my life without a woman to consider. I'm sorry if I offended you."

She hurried away and he studied her, her back straight, her chin high. There were layers upon layers of her that he had yet to discover. He realized with some surprise that he looked forward to it.

He returned to his rooms and found the clothing neatly put away in the wardrobes and dresser. It was decent enough—not like his buckskins, but it would do. He dressed carefully in casual wear—brown trousers and waistcoat and a white shirt.

It was time to stop in and surprise the pub owner with a visit.

He saddled Ahote and rode into the village. Shoppers stopped and watched him. He nodded and one woman actually curtseyed. The village was clean and well kept. Freshly painted buildings were built close together, possibly for warmth. Everything faced the water. One building stood alone. He raised an eyebrow. The brothel. Geddes had been apologetic when he'd mentioned it, as if it were his fault that sort of business was on the island at all.

A young girl with a mane of curly red hair came outside and shook a dust mop as he rode by. He greeted her warmly, but she merely stared at him and ran back into the building.

Up ahead was the sign for the Potted Haugh, MacNab's pub. Wind and weather had made it nearly unreadable. So much for a clean and sparkling village.

He was going into this blindly. He should have gotten more information from Geddes, but when he'd learned Rosalyn had been attacked by this man he felt that was enough for a confrontation—or a meeting. He dismounted and when he pulled open the door to the pub, the filthy odor of stale fish and oil that hit his nostrils was so strong it made his eyes water.

Behind the bar stood an ornery-looking man with sparse, lifeless hair that fell down over his eyes. With a hand as big as a pig's shank he wiped a gray rag over the bar top and followed Fletcher's movements, his gaze not leaving him.

"Angus MacNab?"

"I'd ask who wants ta know, but it ain't every day a savage enters me pub."

Fletcher forced a smile. "Nice to meet you, too."

MacNab studied him for a long moment, then said, "The old laird were me friend."

Fletcher raised his eyebrows. "Is that so? Did he frequent your pub?"

MacNab's laugh turned into a tobacco cough that growled into his throat. "We had other things in common."

As Fletcher waited for him to go into detail, he took in everything about the room. The floor was wood, but some boards were warped and cracked, causing the floor to slant toward the back of the room. The bar stools were sturdy, but what finish they'd had at one time was long worn off. The two small windows by the front door were filthy; Fletcher could barely make out what was on the other side of them.

A new smell permeated his nostrils, and he coughed. MacNab was cooking something, but Fletcher wasn't sure he wanted to eat it.

"Can I pour ye a pint?"

Fletcher stepped to the bar. "Thank you, I'd appreciate it." He took out the small coin purse he'd found in his dresser, but MacNab stopped him. "On the house," he said with a wink.

The ale was warm but not entirely distasteful. But there certainly was something distasteful about the place, including the owner. MacNab required further investigation.

That evening, no one spoke as they all ate their lentil soup from delicate china bowls. The flames from the candles in the tall, crystal candleholders flickered in the air, casting a glimmering glow of light over the long table.

Fletcher found the dining room both amusing and fascinating. It amused him that the three of them occupied a table big enough to seat sixteen people. What fascinated him was everything else in the room.

Two enormous globes sat on large wooden stands, one depicting the heavens and the other the world. A piece of MacNeil plaid, worn by the first Duke of Kintyre, was in a gilded frame above the simple fireplace. Other frames held portraits of family members. There was even one of his father as a young boy, and it tugged at Fletcher's heart to see him so small, almost fragile, so unlike the picture of the man he kept near his heart.

And there was always a large bouquet of fragrant fresh flowers on the sideboard, thanks, no doubt, to Rosalyn. He had noticed the enormous pot plants with exotic foliage that were tucked into many corners.

Annie came in and removed the soup dishes. Close behind her, her younger sister, Ellie, who had joined the staff recently, entered carrying a pewter platter that held salmon, boiled potatoes, onions, carrots, and turnips.

Fletcher's mouth watered. Once he had begun to feel better, he looked forward to the meals being served. He especially liked the griddle scones and porridge for breakfast, followed by the smoked fish, eggs, and biscuits.

After everyone had been served, he took a forkful of the tender salmon and put it in his mouth. As usual, it was delicious. Recalling what he'd been accustomed to eating in Texas, he couldn't help but chuckle.

"Something about the meal amuses you?" Rosalyn asked, sounding defensive.

"Not at all. I was just thinking how much better I'm fed here than I was when Geddes found me."

Geddes smiled and continued to eat. "What kind of food did they serve in the army, anyway?"

"A whole lot of beans and hardtack."

"Hardtack." Rosalyn frowned. "It doesn't sound very palatable."

"It isn't. It's a biscuit made from flour and water, without salt. When I was in the stockade, where Geddes found me, the beans were so watered down they resembled soup, and the hardtack was so tough I had to soak it in the broth." He expected a comment from Rosalyn, but she was bent over her plate, concentrating on her dinner.

He told Geddes of his trip to the Potted Haugh earlier, and Geddes recalled for him his one disastrous attempt to eat there. "I swear he used horse meat," Geddes said. After the dessert, Rosalyn got up, excused herself, and left the dining room. Fletcher followed her retreat with his gaze.

"She'll come around," Geddes promised.

Fletcher released a sigh. "I wonder." He didn't know what more he could do to convince her that he at least deserved a chance. She had been more aloof than usual during the entire meal. If her attitude continued, he wondered what sort of marriage it would be.

Just then, Fletcher heard from outside the shattering blare of an ill-tuned trumpet. He flinched, covering his ears. "What was that?"

Geddes sat back, amused. "It's Barnaby."

"What in the hell is he doing?"

Geddes tossed his napkin on the table, still grinning. "He's declaring to the entire island that the great MacNeil has finished eating, and that now everyone else may sit down to their evening meals."

Fletcher stared at him, perplexed. "Why in the hell would he do that?"

"It's an old MacNeil custom; it goes back to time when the Norsemen were here."

"No one pays any attention to it, do they?"

"I doubt it," Geddes answered. "Actually, what surprises me is that Barnaby can still climb to the roof."

"He's on the roof?"

Geddes shrugged, his eyes filled with mirth. "How else is he going to be heard all over the island?"

"I've got to stop him. He's likely to kill himself."

"Don't," Geddes said. "He has little else to do; it makes him feel useful."

True, Fletcher thought, the old man was as useless as tits on a bull. "Well, I just hope he doesn't slip and fall into the rose garden. Rosalyn thinks little enough of me as it is. Barnaby crushing her prize roses would be all she would need to hammer another nail in my coffin."

Chapter Eight

Once out of the dining room, Rosalyn had nearly run to her room. Her heart pounded as His Grace's words echoed in her brain. *When I was in the stockade.* She'd read enough history to know that was a prison.

Her gaze narrowed as she recalled the number of times Geddes had evaded her questions regarding the duke. It was no wonder he wouldn't tell her anything. The duke had been in prison.

She had rued their mating the moment it was over. She had been reluctant to marry him despite being compromised, but could see no other solution at the time. And now this.

She sank into the chair in front of her dressing table and stared at herself in the mirror. The frightening thing was she knew she was fertile. It had taken no time at all to conceive Fiona, who had come squalling into the world barely nine months from the day Rosalyn had wed Leod.

Now, she was to wed again. The duke had not charmed her as Leod had. She had been plumbing the depths of her emotions to find a way to wriggle out of this commitment, unlike the first time, when she'd rushed headlong into it.

With this new information it seemed she had what she needed to do just that. Her first husband had been like a charming placid lake. The surface was beautiful, but dive beneath and one found tangling, choking weeds and murky mud and creatures that poisoned and dragged one down for good. That, and much, much more, was Leod.

What was the duke, besides a common criminal? Again, she wondered what he had done. At first she had believed he was merely a thinly veiled aristocrat in savage clothing. Now a plethora of possibilities crammed her brain. For all she knew, he could even be a murderer.

She vowed to find Geddes and learn the truth.

• • •

After checking her brother's room and finding it empty, Rosalyn hurried down the stairs. She found Geddes sitting alone at the table.

Without preamble, she rounded on him. "Where did you find him?"

Her brother had the decency to glance away. "I told you."

"By his own admission, he was in prison."

Geddes stared at the linen table cloth.

"Why was he there?" she persisted.

"I believe that's for him to say, Rosalyn."

"No! I want you to tell me, brother." Her rage was building.

Geddes sank back in his chair. "I believe it involved the death of a young woman."

Lindsay. That was the name the duke kept murmuring in his sleep. "But why was he in prison?" A thought flooded through her like ice water. "Did he murder her? Is that what it was? He's a murderer?"

Geddes picked at his napkin, which lay crumpled on the table. "He claims he didn't do it."

Rosalyn's knees weakened. She eased herself into the chair beside her brother. "He claims he didn't do it," she repeated, although with a measure of sarcasm. "What in the devil does that mean?"

Again, Geddes frowned at her language, but said nothing. Finally he answered, "I don't know."

She rubbed her hands over her face. "Well, I guess I'd claim I didn't do it as well. After all, who wants to admit to being a murderer?"

"Rosalyn—"

"Never mind." She attempted to regain some composure.

"Perhaps I can get him to explain it to me." With effort, she stood and walked toward the door.

"Rosalyn, let me speak with him first."

She turned and gave her brother a scathing look. "Isn't this a fine kettle of fish? My first husband was a depraved lunatic and my second a murderer. What are the odds of that?"

"He's nothing like Leod, nothing at all. And you know it."

"I know nothing of the sort. You say you believe him. What if he's lying to you? Would you have me marry a murderer?"

"Rosalyn, he is not a murderer."

He said something else, but his voice was mere humming in her ears. "My God. I wonder if he used that dreadful knife. Do you suppose he killed that poor girl with a knife?"

Geddes stood, crossed to the door, and shook her. "Stop it."

"I slept with a murderer. I can't believe it."

"Stop it," he said again. "I'm sure the duke can explain everything to your satisfaction. We'll discover the truth."

Silent, she watched Geddes leave, unsure if she truly wanted to know the truth. And would "the truth" be just that, or merely what the duke wanted her to hear?

* * *

"Your Grace? Might I have a word with you in the library?"

Once inside, Geddes closed the double doors and both he and Fletcher went toward the desk, heading for the same chair. Geddes stopped, then looked at Fletcher as if he were just realizing that he was rightfully the master of this place. They exchanged a look of understanding and Geddes took another chair as Fletcher sat behind the massive mahogany.

Geddes studied him. "Rosalyn thinks you're a murderer."

Caught off guard, Fletcher said, "What? Why?"

"After you mentioned the food you were served in the stockade, she began to wonder why you were there. I guess I hadn't mentioned the exact situation in which I found you."

"And what did you tell her?"

"Only that it involved the death of a young woman," Geddes answered. "Rosalyn came to her own conclusions after that. In any case, she believes we are hiding the truth from her and she's reluctant to marry you."

So, those were her doubts, Fletcher thought. If she was reluctant before learning this, it was a wonder she would now consider marrying him at all.

Geddes leaned forward. "You must convince her that you are innocent."

Fletcher frowned, studying Geddes intently. "I am innocent. You believe me, don't you?"

Geddes hesitated. "You told me you were; I thought it best to leave it at that. I'm sure the circumstances were unpleasant."

Fletcher laughed, without mirth. "Good God, if I can't convince you, how can I convince her?"

"I suggest you try your very best, Your Grace."

"What happens if I can't?"

Again, Geddes leaned forward, but his expression changed. "Then, if Rosalyn isn't carrying your heir, the money goes to Fergus MacBean."

"Ah, yes, the nincompoop."

"Aye."

Fletcher rose from the chair and studied the wild ocean, watching the waves churn and play and finally crash against the rocks. He longed to be astride Ahote, racing across the sand.

"If you cannot convince her and you decide to leave here and return to Texas," Geddes said, "you would face the noose."

Fletcher turned. "If I cannot convince her, I might leave here anyway."

Fear sprang into Geddes's eyes. "But why?"

Fletcher strode toward the solicitor and stood close to him. "I can't stay here when I don't know what's happened to my family. If your agency doesn't find them soon, I'll leave and find them myself, the threat of hanging be damned."

Flustered, Geddes said haltingly, "I'll go directly into the village again in the morning. I'm sure there will be some news, I'm sure of it."

"I hope you're right, Geddes. I don't want to leave, but I will."

Geddes paled. "Your Grace, for my own selfish reasons, I want you to stay. Although I've managed to run things since your grandfather's death, I wouldn't want it to continue this way."

"I want to learn how to run the estate, Geddes. I want to learn what it takes to be a duke. I am pleased enough with your sister. But I promise you that if you can't produce proof that my sister and my brothers are safe and on their way, I'll chuck it all and leave you to grapple with the nincompoop."

"But you must give it more time," Geddes pleaded. "You've been here only a short while. Sometimes it takes months to get word from America."

Fletcher paused—Geddes had a point. "Maybe I've been too impatient about word of them, but if something has happened to them, I'll never forgive myself." Frustrated, he rubbed the back of his neck. "I will try to convince your sister that she should marry me. I will do this. But I'm tempted to wait and have the wedding when there is word of the children."

"The license will be here within a week. You said nothing about putting it off. I had thought we would have the ceremony as soon as it arrived."

"I'm beginning to feel boxed in."

"Perhaps I can give you an option. What I would like to propose is this: Marry Rosalyn. If, after she conceives, we still have not had word of your family, you can leave. The estate will be secure and I will stay on and manage it. Rosalyn will raise the child. I had hoped you would stay until the birth of the bairn, but…"

Fletcher paced slowly from one end of the room to the other, his hands clasped behind his back. "Are you saying that even if my siblings join me here, you're willing to let me leave after the child is born?"

"If that's your pleasure, Your Grace."

It wasn't, but Fletcher didn't say it aloud. There was no way in hell he was going to abandon another child. No way in hell. "Considering how your sister feels about me, even if she's willing to marry me, she will likely find my leaving more pleasurable than my staying."

Geddes's gaze was pleading. "So, you will stay and marry Rosalyn?"

"Yes."

"And before we have a wedding, you must have a long, honest talk with her." Geddes walked with him to the door.

Fletcher drew in a deep breath, exhaling it slowly. What kind of mess had he made for himself? He had vowed to marry a woman who didn't trust him, who thought he had killed someone, and who, in all likelihood, would resist his advances, thus making the possibility of conception impossible.

Somehow he would have to convince her that the quicker she got pregnant, the sooner he would be out of her hair.

"Where might I find her now?"

Geddes sighed. "I would wait until morning. Give her the night to work off some of her frustration. If you approach her now, I'm afraid she'll flatly refuse."

"All right. Take care of the arrangements, and I'll take care of your sister. But be warned, Geddes, I need word of the children."

As he went to his room, he wondered how he could convince Rosalyn of his innocence when his guilt held him responsible for Lindsay's death anyway.

Chapter Nine

After a sleepless night, Rosalyn rose in the morning and went where she always did when she was upset: to see Fen. She arrived at Fen's cottage, where Reggie was picking vegetables from the garden.

"Has she returned?"

Reggie nodded and Rosalyn let herself in. Fen was leaning over someone who lay on a cot near the stove. As Rosalyn got closer and recognized the woman, she couldn't hide her surprise. "Nessa MacNab? My God, Fen, Angus threatened me just the other day."

"He did? What happened?"

"As I was leaving here he stopped my gig and told me to stay away from his wife and mind my business."

"Well, then, you weren't the only one he went after." Fen gave her an angry glance. "The bastard pushed Nessa down the stairs and her arm hasn't healed from the last time. She came here after she dragged herself to that sot of a physician only to find him too drunk to give a damn. It's just as well; he'd probably have smeared it with egg white and barley meal before trying to bind it. And no doubt he told her it was her own fault for arguing with her husband."

Anger simmered in Rosalyn's stomach. She didn't want to hate all men, she truly didn't. If it weren't for Geddes's gentle nature, she might not understand how different they could be.

"Gone are the days of Brigid of Kildare and equality of the sexes," Fen said.

If ever there was a champion of the female sex, it was Fenella Begley. Once she got fired up on the subject, she could convince almost anyone to agree with her. Except a man. Rosalyn did so wish Geddes saw the same virtues in Fen that she did. She had often thought they might be perfect companions for one another, despite their differences, but they were both too headstrong by half.

Fen helped Nessa drink something from a cup, then motioned to Rosalyn to follow her. "She'll sleep for a bit, poor thing."

"How was your trip?" Rosalyn asked.

Fen settled herself into a chair. "Nothing exciting. My solicitor had sold a piece of property and I had to sign some papers. More importantly, how are things with your savage duke?"

Anxious to talk, Rosalyn asked, "Remember when I told you that I thought Geddes was hiding something about the duke's past?"

"Aye," Fen said. "What did you discover?"

Too nervous to sit, Rosalyn paced the tiny room. "I think he killed someone."

Fen gasped. "What?"

Rosalyn explained the duke's admission that he'd been in prison. She didn't reveal that during their mating, he had thought she was someone else. Someone named Lindsay.

"Who do you think he killed?"

Rosalyn plucked nervously at her skirt. "I'm sure I don't know."

"By the saints, it's no wonder Geddes was mum on the subject."

"Aye, and he still refuses to tell me anything, insisting that I go to the duke himself for an explanation. If he is innocent, why didn't Geddes just tell me the circumstances instead of changing the subject and getting angry with me every time I brought it up? And if there's a logical explanation for it all, why not tell me that, too?"

"I see your point. So, what will you do?"

Rosalyn gnawed on her thumbnail. "I don't know. I have agreed to marry him, but how can I?"

"You're going to marry him? When did this come about? The last we talked, you couldn't endure the thought of it."

"I know. I know."

"Well, it isn't written in stone that you must wed him. It's not like you're carrying his heir."

Rosalyn shot her a quick glance.

"Rosalyn," she said slowly, "what did you do?"

Too embarrassed to look Fen in the eye, she studied the round rug on the floor. "He was shouting in his sleep. I went to his room and he thought I was someone else."

"And you didn't resist?"

She continued to look down, having trouble admitting her weakness even to her dearest friend. She shook her head. "No. And now I could be carrying a murderer's heir. Good God, Fen, how can I go through with a wedding?"

"You should confront him."

"Aye, but how will I know if he's telling me the truth? Leod fooled me completely."

"Stop dragging that bastard into everything," Fen scolded. "Good lord, Roz, if he only knew how much power he still has over you, he'd rise from his watery grave and accept a bloody round of applause."

"I suppose you're right. It's just very hard for me to trust again."

Fen gave her a knowing glance. "It's obvious to me your heart says something else."

"The same heart that loved Leod."

"Roz, your brain is far too muddled with memories of Leod. Talk to the duke. See how he responds. Listen to his story. If you don't believe him, don't marry him."

As Rosalyn left Fen's cottage, she knew she had to talk to the duke face to face. She was surprised by how much she hoped she could believe his answer.

• • •

Fletcher didn't even wait to have breakfast. When he learned that Rosalyn was already gone, he remembered that Geddes had once told him that whenever she was upset, she went to see her friend. He got directions from Evan and then rode out to find her. He saw her leave the small cottage, get into her gig and take the castle road. He nudged his mount toward the small, neat structure, where a big man with a wide chest and arms the size of tree trunks stepped out from behind a shed and blocked his path.

The cottage door opened and a woman appeared. "It's all right, Reggie." The giant tossed Fletcher a suspicious glance before retreating. The woman stood, hands on hips, and studied him. She was tall and wore soft leather boots and a baggy shirt tucked into the waistband of a pair of mannish trousers that only accentuated her curves. Her dark hair was cropped short, wild curls softening her angular features. She was handsome rather than beautiful, dramatic rather than demure.

"You must be the new duke."

Fletcher dismounted. "I am."

"I'm Fenella Begley, Rosalyn's friend. You just missed her."

"I saw her leave. I'm told she spends a lot of time with you. I had hoped you could tell me something about her."

She gave him a suspicious look. "I could, if I trusted you."

"The fact that I'm here asking should tell you something."

Fenella Begley looked off into the distance. "I'm not sure it's my place to tell you Rosalyn's secrets."

"I don't want to know her secrets; I want to know her."

The widow gazed past him. "She's had a hard life, harder than most women of her station. Her father was a successful barrister and they lived very comfortably in Edinburgh. Women like Rosalyn should have their own families by this time. They should have homes, gardens, servants of their own."

"She has those things at the castle."

"Aye, but it isn't hers, don't you understand? At any moment she and Geddes could be thrown out into the street."

"I wouldn't do that. Even old Barnaby has a home for the rest of his life, and he's hardly worth the air he breathes, poor old coot."

The widow stared at him. "But that isn't a certainty, is it? Stranger things have happened to make Rosalyn's life a living hell."

"Tell me."

"Those are her secrets; they aren't mine to tell."

"Then whose is it?" He cursed. "She barely speaks to me at all, and this morning I learned that she thinks I'm a murderer."

"Are you?"

"While I feel I am probably to blame for the woman's death, I did not kill her."

She narrowed her gaze, studying him, and then motioned for him to follow her. They walked through a rose-covered trellis to her flower garden. "What do you know about her first marriage?" she asked.

"Only that it wasn't happy, and I presume the man was akin to the devil in Rosalyn's eyes."

Mrs. Begley reached into the pocket of her trousers and pulled out a small clipper. As she snipped off dead petals from the trellis roses, she asked, "Did you know that Rosalyn had a daughter?"

Surprised, he answered, "No, I didn't."

"Rosalyn and Leod—that was her husband—were living in Edinburgh. He was reasonably prosperous; I believe he managed a cannery business. Nearly four years into their marriage, they began having some problems, severe enough, according to Rosalyn, that she couldn't suffer them any longer. She asked him to leave; he would not. So, she took their three-year-old daughter, Fiona, and left him. She had little money, so she came here. We have been friends for a long time." She reached in and snipped off a dead branch.

"Before she left him he had apparently told her she could go to hell as far as he was concerned, but she wouldn't take his daughter with her."

"I presume he eventually found her," Fletcher said.

Mrs. Begley's smile was like ice. "Leod was relentless in his search. After a time, he found her here with me, and he was very charming, telling us it was all a misunderstanding. He even told Rosalyn that she could have her divorce, although he still wanted to see Fiona from time to time.

"Rosalyn knew him better than anyone; she didn't trust him. But Leod could be persuasive."

Fletcher began to get a clearer picture for the cause of Rosalyn's behavior.

"He came back the next day, when Reggie and I were gone. He brought a bottle of champagne, which Rosalyn loves. He asked her to at least think about allowing him visiting privileges after their divorce. According to Rosalyn, he had seemed remorseful and willing to set her free, yet she was still very suspicious of his motives. But as well as she knew him, she hadn't expected him to drug her, and that's what he did. He slipped something into the champagne." She stood and strode to the edge of the garden.

"Once the drug had taken effect, he stole Fiona away. When Rosalyn awoke and both Leod and Fiona were gone, she became hysterical. No one had seen them leave. Later, a search party found the boat he'd stolen smashed against the rocks. His body was floating nearby."

She paused, then looked at him, her eyes shiny. "They never found Fiona's body. The child drowned, but Rosalyn could never give her a proper burial. There is no real end to this for her. She cannot say goodbye."

She touched his arm, her gaze probing his. "I know you have inherited a grand position. Some men think that's enough to satisfy a woman. Rosalyn isn't impressed by money or power. All she wants is for someone to treat her as if she matters. She is my friend. If you hurt her, I'll come after you and cut off your manhood while you sleep, and don't think I won't. You might be handy with a knife, but I have removed the rotting limbs of soldiers with mine, and I know just where to cut to enhance your bleeding."

She gave him a look that spoke volumes. He stifled a shudder. He believed every word she said.

The look that passed between them lasted a long time. Fletcher looked away first, uncomfortable. "I will do my best not to hurt her. I gave Geddes my word on that, and I will tell you the same."

She said nothing, and the awkwardness stretched between them. He mounted his horse, looking down at the woman who seemed to see inside his head, heart, and soul. She studied him, then smiled and went back to trimming her flowers.

As Fletcher rode toward the castle he thought about his promises to Geddes and now to Rosalyn's friend. His father told him long ago that a man who kept his promises showed his worth and value and deserved trust. A man's word needed to stand for something. Rosalyn didn't trust him. He had to earn her trust—a big order. He had always been a private man, but he would have to tell her everything about his life, his past, his mistakes. He had no other choice. His life was no longer his to hide. And he definitely didn't want that Begley woman coming after him, wielding her knife at his balls.

Chapter Ten

Fletcher stabled Ahote and then took the path to the castle entrance. Geddes was waiting for him.

"She's in the solarium."

Fletcher wasn't surprised. Of all the rooms in the castle, the solarium had to be Rosalyn's favorite. Though small, it housed plants that bloomed lavish and exotic flowers, none of which he could identify. He had passed by the room on a couple of occasions and the rich, lusty aroma of plant life, heated by the sun through panes of glass, had briefly made him feel he was in a warmer clime, where lush succulence abounded and scantily clad women frolicked in the sunshine. Like Texas. He suppressed a sigh.

Perhaps, he thought, as he made his way toward the west wing, Rosalyn felt she had moral support from her foliage that she couldn't find anywhere else. Indeed, he realized that she found solace in plants, flowers, and dogs, all of which gave total devotion if handled properly.

He took a deep breath and crossed the threshold into the warm, sunny room. Amidst the rich and colorful flora sat Rosalyn, looking as beautiful and unattainable as her flowers. Sima and one of her pups were close by, the puppy playfully attacking its mother. Rosalyn stood as he entered, a book clutched to her bosom. Sunshine gleamed off her hair, catching loose ringlets, igniting them into flame. Until this moment he hadn't realized that there was any red in her hair at all.

"Rosalyn—"

She raised her hand. "Please. We must do this my way."

He nodded and looked around for a chair.

"I would rather you didn't sit," she said.

He clasped his hands behind his back. "As you wish."

She stepped forward. "I'm going to ask you some questions, one at a time, and I want your honest answer."

"Of course."

She held the book toward him. "Are you a Christian?"

He lifted an eyebrow, noting that the book she held was a leather-bound Bible. "My father saw to it that I learned his faith."

"Do you believe in it?"

"I don't disbelieve," he answered.

Her gaze was intense. "This Bible has been in your family for many generations; each birth is entered, as is each death. I must know that if you place your hand on the Bible your answers will be honest and true."

He believed that all religions, including his mother's and his father's, were intertwined. He believed that man needed religion to deal with the ebbs and flows of life. He respected any man's right to his beliefs. He certainly respected Rosalyn's.

"I have great consideration for the Bible. I will answer your questions as honestly as I can."

"Thank you." She inhaled, expelling the breath slowly, and held the Bible toward him in both of her hands.

He placed his palm on the book.

"Who is Lindsay?"

Ah, Lindsay. He hoped one day she would disappear from his nightmares. "She was a young woman I knew in Texas."

"Did you love her?"

Fletcher frowned, thoughtful. "I cared for her."

Rosalyn considered this and then asked, "What happened to her?"

"She died."

"How did she die?"

"She was shot."

Rosalyn inhaled sharply. "Who shot her?"

Old anger threatened to fester. "Her husband. She—"

"No," Rosalyn interrupted. "Just answer my questions. Please. If I want explanations, I'll ask for them."

He nodded and said no more.

"Were you with her when she was shot?"

The memory was still vivid: the blinding light from the blast, the circle of blood on Lindsay's chest, the brief look of fear and surprise in her eyes before the light went out of them and she died. "Yes."

"Why did her husband shoot her?"

"I don't think he meant to," Fletcher answered, clearly remembering the hatred in Bannerman's gaze at the trial.

"I don't understand."

"He meant to shoot me."

"You? Why?"

Fletcher took a deep breath. "Because I was in bed with her at the time."

Rosalyn blinked and glanced away, the rhythmic pulse at her throat throbbing against her pale skin. Her gaze pinned his again. "If her husband killed her, why were you in prison?"

"Because he blamed me for it."

"Why?"

"He claimed I raped her."

"And it wasn't rape?"

"No. It wasn't rape."

Rosalyn was a strong woman, revealing very little. He couldn't tell if she was relieved or distraught at his admission.

Rosalyn lowered her arms, the Bible still clutched in one hand. Her face was a study in concentration. "And you believe he meant to kill you, not her."

"I do," Fletcher answered.

"Didn't you tell someone what really happened?"

He laughed. It was an empty sound. "I supposedly had my day in court."

"But no one believed you?"

He smirked. "No one believed me. Consider it. Who is more

believable, a wild half-breed or a proper army captain? I was a dead man before I even entered the courtroom. It was very easy for the army to sentence me to hang."

"So, if Geddes hadn't come looking for Shamus, you would have been hanged?"

"Yes."

She sagged into a chair, the Bible clutched in her hands, her gaze focused on something he couldn't see, something only her mind projected. "If this is all true, then I'm sorry."

"I have sworn that it's true, and I don't want your pity, Rosalyn. I want to be your husband."

Her glance was sharp, as if, once again, her name on his tongue astonished her. She put the Bible on the table beside her and stood. "I will marry you."

Fletcher was surprised at the relief that washed over him. He wanted to drag her into his arms, hold her close, smell her hair, and kiss her. He wanted to feel the length of her against him, her softness, and her strength.

Weeks before, he would have, if only to enjoy her discomfort. But now he wanted nothing to change her mind, so he merely turned to leave her. "I understand the license will be here in a week or so."

She nodded. "I hope we can have the ceremony shortly after that, if it pleases you."

He thought he heard a slight quiver in her voice, but when he looked back at her she appeared stalwart and strong. He found himself saying, "It pleases me."

He left the solarium in search of Geddes. One hurdle had been jumped; now he had to discover if there was news of his siblings.

* * *

Rosalyn sank into a chair, closed her eyes, and leaned her head against the back. Her heart raced. There was so much more she had wanted to ask him, but perhaps there would be a time for that.

She believed him. She had to. Either that or her instincts were still all wrong and she'd learned nothing from her past experiences.

Her thoughts unconsciously went to their mating, when he'd thought she was someone else. *Lindsay. You're alive!* The words had been spoken with elation and joy. And he had touched her with such awe, finding pleasure with her body, giving pleasure in return.

And all because he thought she was someone else.

"Silly fool," she scolded. None of that mattered. What he did or what he was before he came here was no longer an issue. But still, if he had taken her in his arms and sealed their coming marriage with a kiss, she wouldn't have stopped him. She wanted to lean into his body, feel the strength in it, and lose herself, if only for a moment, in the fantasy that someone had finally come along in whom she could find safety and comfort and, eventually, love.

Indeed, in her secret heart she longed for someone to find that same such pleasure with her and for that someone to be Fletcher MacNeil.

Chapter Eleven

Geddes had never intentionally lied, especially if the lie could harm someone. He also knew he was not very good at deception. And now, as he walked from the harbor master's office, the letter tucked carefully away in his breast pocket, he rationalized that if he kept the good news to himself for just a short while, it wouldn't be a lie and it would hurt no one.

It wasn't that he didn't trust the duke to keep his promise—he did. But with the wedding mere days away, Geddes wanted everything to go as planned. News of the children would be icing on the cake, so to speak.

In the distance, the faded sign of the Potted Haugh, Angus MacNab's pub, creaked in the wind. Some found it amusing that the pub was named for a spiced, jellied meat. Geddes just found the place disgusting.

As he approached, he heard MacNab's voice raised in anger, but Geddes wasn't surprised, nor was he alarmed. MacNab was a surly, unpleasant man. Geddes could think of no logical reason why he continued to defend the bastard to Rosalyn, except that each time they argued about him, her friend Fenella Begley was in the mix. He supposed that was what got his ire up, for the mention of the woman's saintly attributes set him off and he didn't know why.

The pub door opened, slamming against the outside wall, and MacNab stepped onto the cobbled walk, snarling slurs at a customer.

Nay, not a customer. *Speak of the devil.* Geddes slowed his steps.

Fenella Begley stood nose to nose with the pub owner, hands on trouser-clad hips and breathing fire.

"You can't make her do that," she spat. "Her arm isn't healed from the last accident."

"That weren't my fault," MacNab roared. "She's a clumsy bitch, is all."

"And you are a mean son of a whore," she volleyed, appearing to egg him on.

MacNab reared back. "I'll teach you to call me names." He raised his beefy paw to strike.

Geddes stepped in. "MacNab!"

The surly good-for-nothing turned toward Geddes, his arm still raised. "This ain't your affair."

Geddes ambled toward the two of them. "Is this what makes you a man, MacNab? Striking women?"

"I said it ain't your affair." He glared at Geddes, his ham-hock hands clenched into fists so tight his knuckles were white.

Geddes realized that the man could beat him to within an inch of his life. "Go back inside and see to your other guests."

"I ain't finished with this one," he said.

"Leave her alone."

"You gonna make me?"

Geddes sighed and shook his head. Arguing with a bull like Angus MacNab would only lead to disastrous results, and although Geddes wasn't necessarily a vain man, he did value the current placement of his facial features. "You could snap me like a twig, MacNab, we both know that."

The pub owner's massive chest expanded, as if he'd taken Geddes's words as a compliment.

Geddes glanced around. A few shoppers slowed their steps but gave the two a wide berth. "Do what you wish to me, but even you wouldn't sink so low as to strike a woman, would you? That wouldn't be a fair fight."

MacNab glared at him and then lunged toward Fenella. She stepped back and expelled a surprised squeak. He guffawed, apparently getting pleasure out of scaring her, then disappeared inside the pub.

Fenella Begley quickly gathered her wits and strutted toward him, her green eyes filled with fire. "I didn't need your help."

Geddes raised a cynical eyebrow and gave her a little bow. "You're welcome, madam." He turned and started to walk away.

"Geddes Gordon," she called after him.

He paused, curious to know what she wanted.

"If you really want to help, you can open your eyes to what's happening to some of the women in this village."

He turned slightly and gazed at her. It irked him that Rosalyn found no fault with her. Nay, she praised her to the bonnie braes and beyond.

Geddes had always taken notice of her unfeminine attire. He had once thought her manly; he was wrong. As he studied her, he realized she was really quite magnificent, especially when she was fired up. Although her shirt was mannish, it was open at the throat, exposing skin that was like porcelain, white and smooth. He thought that perhaps he even saw the shadow of her breast. Her short-cropped curls were also unconventional, yet he found they softened her features, even when she frowned quite mutinously, as she did now.

"I beg your pardon, madam?"

Her gaze narrowed. "Men. Do you truly believe that you have a right to physically abuse those who are weaker and smaller than you?"

"I certainly don't—"

"Do you know that bastard, Angus MacNab, pushed his wife down the stairs and broke her arm? Do you realize that he forced her to return to work before it healed, and now she has broken it again?"

Geddes was intrigued by her passionate nature. "It's not—"

"And," she interrupted, coming closer and poking a finger at his chest, "she isn't the only wife to come to me, broken and bruised, because that old sot of a physician is too drunk to treat them, or to care, for that matter. I'm bloody sick of the way women are treated, not just here, but everywhere. But by damn, here is where I am, and

I intend to continue to do what I do until some bloody indignant bastard of a husband puts a bullet through my brain."

Fire continued to flame in her eyes and her cheeks were flushed, as if fevered. Her lips were a natural dusky shade of pale plum and she had a dimple in her chin. Why, she was a splendid creature! Why had he not seen it before? He'd been so busy listing the qualities that annoyed him, he hadn't actually seen who she really was. Hoping to mollify her, he said, "Madam, what do you expect me to do about it?"

She stood back, hands on hips once again, and studied him, her gaze roaming over him. He hoped the flush at his neck didn't rise into his face, for her scrutiny was almost sexual.

"You're not without influence, Geddes Gordon. You have the duke's ear. Surely between the two of you something will spring to mind." With an almost coquettish smile, she turned and strode away.

Geddes watched her fine behind move beneath her trousers and for the first time in years, he felt a fire in his own.

• • •

Fen strolled toward the mercantile just as Reggie came out with a fifty-pound bag of flour over his shoulder. "Is that all of it?"

Reggie nodded and frowned, gesturing toward the pub.

"It was nothing." She stepped up into the conveyance and sat on the padded bench.

He dumped the sack of flour into the back of the wagon and then pointed at Geddes, who continued to watch her from a distance. He hadn't moved. She bit the insides of her cheeks to keep from smiling. "Yes, he intervened."

Reggie nodded and then hauled his enormous bulk into the wagon next to her.

As the cart rattled over the cobbled street, Geddes tipped his hat at her. She gave him a gentle nod, but forced herself not to smile.

But as they rode home, she thought about him. Although they had sparred often, she hadn't thought much about him as a man. In fact, she'd always thought he was rather bland. But now that she had a chance to study him, she found his physique quite impressive. She liked a man who was tall and lean, yet wide through the shoulders and narrow in the hips. And now she tried to imagine him without clothes, wondering if his strategic body hair was as fair as that on his head.

He interested her—she had seen him redden as she looked at him. Perhaps he was shy; he was certainly proper. It was whispered around the island that he was a man who didn't like women. That was nonsense. He simply hadn't found one who interested him. Yet.

She settled against the seat and allowed herself a small smile.

Chapter Twelve

Two weeks later, Geddes stood helpless as Rosalyn explained where she wanted to be married. "In the garden? You want to have the ceremony in the garden?" Geddes was nearly beside himself. He had run nervous, frustrated fingers through his hair so many times that it stood on end, reminding Rosalyn of the stubs of dried wheat left in the fields.

"What could be more perfect?" Rosalyn let Annie sweep her hair up into a swirl of curls on top of her head. "It's a beautiful April day, the sun is shining, and my flowers are blooming. And, as the islanders say, *He Breeah*."

Geddes was incredulous. "A good day? You think it's a good day?"

"It's a splendid day, Geddes."

"But…but…but…"

Rosalyn gazed at his reflection in the mirror and gave him a gentle smile. "You worry too much. And what's the harm?"

"It's just never been done, Rosalyn. I've never heard of anyone getting married outside."

"But it's my wedding, brother. The chapel is cold and damp. I'd feel like I was being entombed." And she did, every time she entered the room. It had never felt all that religious to her—religion was outdoors, where God did His handiwork.

Geddes suddenly seemed calm. His features softened and his eyes warmed as he looked at her. "Why had I even thought to argue with you?"

She smiled, keeping her own demons at bay. "I have no idea. You've had a lifetime to learn not to."

He bent and kissed her cheek. “May I say that you look especially beautiful today?”

“You may, dear brother. Now, what time is Vicar Fleming to arrive?”

“In exactly two hours.”

Rosalyn’s stomach suddenly filled with dandelion fluff. “Then be gone so Annie can make me acceptable for my new husband.”

Geddes kissed her again and then left the room.

Rosalyn expelled a long, quiet sigh and sagged against the back of the chair. It had been an act for his benefit, this attempt at courage and nonchalance.

Annie fussed with her hair. “Ye look beautiful, mistress. Your gown is fit for a queen.”

Aye, Rosalyn thought, although it wasn’t a gown. It was a long skirt with a train, all of which was heavy, hand-loomed, ivory cotton. The blouse was an off-the-shoulder ivory silk with handmade lace and brown silk ribbon running through it. Some might whisper that she should be in white, as that was the preferred color for brides ever since Queen Victoria married Prince Albert, but Rosalyn didn’t care. She had worn white at her first wedding; perhaps another color would bring her better luck the second time around.

On the surface, she appeared to be a willing bride. Underneath, she was still reluctant. And who could blame her? Even though the duke had sworn on the Bible that all he had told her was true, she kept wondering if there were other surprises waiting for her once they were wed.

“There.” Annie stepped back, pleased with herself. Suddenly, she gasped.

Rosalyn’s stomach dropped. “What? What is it, Annie?”

Annie grinned at her in the mirror, picked something off her dress, and showed it to her.

“A spider? You found a spider on my dress and you’re grinning at me?”

“Aye. ’Tis for luck. Me auntie were a maid for a London lady, and she told me it's good luck for a bride to find a spider on her wedding dress."

Well, thought Rosalyn, who knew? At least it was a good omen.

She studied her hair, noting the sprig of white heather that Annie had fastened to the top of her web of curls. "Isn't the heather supposed to be in my bouquet?"

"Yes, mistress; I've made certain there is one there, too."

"You want to double my good luck, is that it?"

Annie's eyes misted over. "You've been the finest of ladies to both me and me sis, ma'am. We want all of your troubles to be little ones."

Rosalyn's attitude toward the gossipy Annie had softened over the past few weeks. The girl had become her shadow. "Is everything ready for the reception?"

"Aye, Marvella and Ellie have been cooking and baking without a break. Ellie didn't come to bed until nigh onto three this morning, and I'm not sure Marvella came to bed at all."

"They must be exhausted." Rosalyn felt a deep twinge of guilt for being the cause of so much ado, but it was useless to argue. She had noticed that the kitchen was abuzz all day; some village wives, those who were noted for their excellent culinary skills, were still stirring up aromatic wonders.

"We are your servants, mistress, and we are so happy you're marrying the duke." She was quiet a moment and then said, "Last eve I saw him outside roughhousing with one of the dogs. Every so often he stopped and glanced up at your window."

Rosalyn's heart took a leap into her throat. "He was looking up here?"

"Aye, 'twas as if he wanted a glimpse of you, like he was anxious for the morn so he could wed you."

"You're too romantic by half, Annie. You know as well as I do that this marriage is no love match."

Annie straightened Rosalyn's bedchamber, fluffing pillows and dusting tables with the corner of her apron. "It don't matter, mistress. When he sees ye all dressed up fine he'll fall in love with ye."

Rosalyn shook her head at Annie's foolishness, but once again, in her secret heart of hearts, she longed for a marriage that would give her what she'd never had before.

* * *

Vicar Fleming, a young widower who was valiantly trying to raise lively and rambunctious twin daughters, stood on the narrow cobbled path that wended its way through the garden, and smiled, inhaling deeply as he did so.

"This is the day the Lord has made, and He could not have made a finer one."

Rosalyn stood beside the duke, hoping the swift beating of her heart didn't attract his attention. She had taken Geddes's arm as she descended the steps, trying not to grip it too tightly as she pressed it to her side. The first person she saw was the duke, and from that moment on, she had seen no one else. They could have been alone or they could have been on a crowded Edinburgh street; she saw only him.

He wore a kilt of the MacNeil plaid, the overlapping flap held in place with a shiny gold brooch. She had come to admire his physique, believing that no man had ever looked as grand in a kilt as he did. He had cut his hair, although it still hung to his shoulders, and when the sun gleamed off it, there were hints of burgundy fire. He looked as if he'd just stepped from a painting, one that encompassed the Scots savage past and the beautiful pageantry of the present.

Vicar Fleming's voice broke into her reverie. Vows were spoken. A rather platonic kiss followed. She was once again a wife.

When the duke strode toward the celebration site, Rosalyn ducked into the castle to grab a few quiet moments before the festivities started. Fen met her in the foyer.

"You look absolutely radiant."

Rosalyn attempted a smile. "I feel like I'm going to jump out of my skin."

"I saw that he kissed you."

A rather unfeminine snort escaped. "It wasn't a kiss. It was a friendly peck on the mouth."

"Were you expecting him to bend you over his arm and really plant one on you?"

Rosalyn shivered at the thought. "I don't know what I expected. He continues to catch me off guard, slowly becoming someone I could actually care for."

Fen took Rosalyn's hands between her own and squeezed them. "Then don't fight it, my friend, don't fight that feeling."

Geddes rushed into the foyer, stopping when he saw the women. "Rosalyn, you should be outside, sitting next to the duke, welcoming the guests." He tossed Fen an accusatory glance.

"She's a lovely bride, don't you think, Geddes?"

He didn't take his eyes off Fen. "I imagine when you got married, you wore your trousers."

Fen's gaze narrowed. "No, I did not. There was a war on, and I barely had time to comb my hair, but I did wear my nurse's uniform, which, unfortunately, was spattered with someone else's blood."

Color crept up Geddes's neck into his cheeks. "Please, Rosalyn, the duke is waiting."

After he left, Rosalyn turned to Fen, her expression sad. "You two fight like enemies."

"Nay," Fen answered. "We're just adversaries. I don't think it's because we can't stand each other. I rather enjoy sparring with him, if you want the truth."

A spark of hope in a day filled with worry.

• • •

As neighbors toasted the newlyweds, Fletcher had heard more *Lang may your lum reeks* than any other toast. He learned that it meant "May there always be a fire in your fireplace."

As quaint as that sounded, he suspected that after numerous

draughts of ale and whisky, many of the men gave the toast a double meaning, for they all laughed and nudged one another.

He and Rosalyn stayed at the celebration until all who came could wish them well. An hour before the sun disappeared behind the gauzy sea haze, Rosalyn met his gaze, quickly looked away, then announced that she was going to retire.

Now, Fletcher stood near the stable and smoked a cigar, watching the villagers celebrate. All afternoon there had been dancing: four reels, Mairi's Wedding, and various jigs. It was evident that a wedding was just an excuse for the people to make merry, but then, in that respect they weren't any different from Texans. Even old Barnaby had performed, doing an agile jig that Fletcher would not have thought possible, considering the decrepit nature of the old valet.

Ah, but he was avoiding the real issue of why he was standing outside, rather than hustling his new bride to their bridal chamber. He had no idea how to proceed.

And wasn't that comical? Fletcher, Maker of Arrows, who had seduced saloon girls and trollops, housewives and maidens, didn't know how to approach the only woman who now mattered. His wife.

As she had walked toward him on Geddes's arm earlier in the day, her hair wreathed in heather and her gown shimmering around her, he had felt as though someone had punched him in the stomach.

It wasn't just that she was beautiful; that was almost a given. He had found her comely from the beginning. It was the look in her eyes that had hit him like a blow.

* * *

Rosalyn stepped to the window and drew back the curtain just enough so she could watch her new husband. He appeared as uncertain about this entire escapade as she was, smoking and pacing.

Angry with her musings, she swung away from the window and crossed to her dressing table. The fact that she was now a titled woman should have given her some pleasure. It did not. As far as she was concerned, the title meant as little as the marriage that had granted it to her.

She glanced at her reflection, eyeing her own figure in her nightgown with the tucks that extended down the front and the back and the handmade eyelet lace she had stitched on the cuffs and placket. It was her finest nightgown, and it was soft and comfortable, but at this moment it could just as well have been a hair shirt, for her discomfort went that deep.

The lord savage stood just inside her door, tall, dark, and dangerous. He crossed his arms over his wide chest and leaned casually against the doorjamb, studying her.

"I didn't hear you knock." She touched her lace collar and discovered the pulse at her throat pounding. She felt alive, raw, aching with a new wonderment.

"That's because I didn't." He stepped into the room and closed the door.

Before he got too close, she said, "We will not share bedrooms."

He crossed the room, stopping just behind her. "We won't?"

She tried to laugh. "Of course not. It isn't as though this were a real marriage."

"The ceremony was real enough."

She caught his gaze, suddenly feeling naked and vulnerable and nervous. "You know what I mean."

He chuckled, the sound like silk on her bare skin. "Oh, I know what you mean. But if we are to produce the required heir, Rosalyn, we must spend at least a minimal amount of time alone together."

She straightened and picked up her brush, gripping it tightly as she ran it through her hair. "Perhaps I'm already pregnant."

He took the brush from her and continued the task, sending frissons of shock through her. "Maybe you are, but if you aren't, your return to celibacy will only drag this marriage out."

"My return to celibacy? What about you? Do you intend to bed every available wench on the island if I don't submit?"

One corner of his mouth turned upward. "Would you care if I did?"

She crossed her arms and stared at him in the mirror. It was on the tip of her tongue to say she wouldn't care one whit, until she saw the look on his face. For the moment, his roguish air was gone. His cavalier attitude didn't exist.

She considered carefully how to respond. "Whether this marriage is an emotional fraud or not, it is still a marriage. It binds us together for a specific purpose. If it were not for that purpose, we wouldn't be in this room, talking about it. But it's still a marriage, and yes, I would care if you went out and satisfied yourself with every trollop on the island."

"Because of how it would make you look?"

She glanced away, her discomfort palpable. "In part, I suppose."

He ran a finger along her cheek. For some odd reason, her nipples pebbled.

"For what other reason, Rosalyn?"

"Because it is still a marriage."

"Does this have anything to do with your first foray into wedded bliss?" he asked.

She turned on him swiftly. "It has nothing to do with Leod, if that's what you mean."

His gaze narrowed. "Was Leod not a faithful husband?"

She laughed in spite of herself. "I cannot and will not begin to tell you what Leod was or was not, Your Grace. To speak of him at all will only make this day worse. Suffice it to say that whatever this marriage becomes, it will undoubtedly surpass my first one in every conceivable way, and I won't necessarily even have to like you very much to achieve that."

He pulled her up from the dressing table and drew her close to him. "Then we had better set down some rules, wife, if this marriage is to achieve its one main goal."

Her fingers fluttered nervously over the neck of her nightgown. "What do you mean?"

"I mean," he began, "I will want access to your body at all times."

"You what?" Her eyes grew big and her heart drummed erratically. He spoke so casually one would have thought he was speaking about accessing the pantry or the root cellar.

"I'm sure you'll agree, Rosalyn, that the quicker you become pregnant, the sooner we can stop dancing around one another so cautiously."

She stood in the circle of his arms, fighting the urge to lean into him, fighting the need to feel satisfied once again. "Surely you don't mean that whenever you want me, I must submit, no matter the time of day."

"That's exactly what I mean, Rosalyn."

Frantically, she said, "I must have one day. I must have one day to call my own. A day that you cannot touch me, a day that will be mine to do what I wish without wondering when you'll stalk me."

He tipped her chin up so she was gazing into his dark eyes. She saw humor there, a hint of merriment, and it annoyed her.

"Considering what we've had together, I would think you'd be more receptive."

"We've had nothing together."

"Was it so terrible, Rosalyn? Was it so unpleasant?"

"It was an accident. But for the circumstances, it would never have happened."

"But it did happen, Rosalyn."

His fingers grazed her cheek, the gentleness throwing her off balance. "I still need a day to myself."

"I can live with that. What day do you wish to escape me?"

She swallowed; she couldn't deal with this today. "Sunday. Every Sunday you will not touch me from midnight to midnight."

"Today is Sunday," he reminded her.

She gave him a triumphant smile. "I know."

He smiled too, but she wasn't certain she liked the dare behind it. "Then I'll leave you, ma'am. Good night."

After he'd gone, she couldn't explain the feeling that came over her. She should have been happy to have outsmarted him. But had she? In truth, her free day was almost over. She could expect him to return at the stroke of midnight, and she wasn't ready. Or was she? By the holy, she was becoming a mess of nerves, and this folly of a marriage had just begun.

* * *

She didn't sleep; she kept waiting for his footsteps. Once the clock had struck midnight, she had been certain he would barge in on her and expect her to submit to him. When he didn't, the reasons why kept her from falling asleep.

She had even gotten up, lit a candle, gone into the hallway, and crept toward his room. She had stood outside his door briefly, but of course it was not like the first time, when he'd cried out and she had gone in all innocence because she'd thought he was in pain.

In the end, she had returned to her room, blown out the candle, and crawled back into bed, wide awake, nervous as a caged wild bird, anxious for morning.

Now, in the gray light of dawn, she struggled from her bed, stiff, sleepy, and irritable. In truth, she had expected him to come. She had waited for him. She would have submitted. She might even have enjoyed it.

Who was she kidding? She had wanted him to come. She had lain there, imagining the moment, wondering how she would respond when she saw him standing beside the bed. Dampness had gathered between her legs as she had envisioned him there, warm and naked. She had remembered his manhood well. Thick and strong, hot and hard, and she had impaled herself on it, feeling it press so deep inside her she had thought she might faint from the pleasure of it.

But to admit she wanted him was to submit, and that was very, very hard for her to do.

She had wondered if he would be a gentle lover. She thought he could be, but she also felt he could be rough and demanding. And what were they, anyway? Who set the standards for how people should act in the bedroom? Some pious, self-proclaimed virginal queen?

Although Rosalyn's marriage to Leod had deteriorated into something dreadful before she had known what he was, she had been an enthusiastic partner.

Perhaps she would be again. Perhaps. In fact, in a way, her new husband's savage past excited her in some insane, exasperating fashion.

She had been ready to shed her nightgown, if he had wished it. She had been waiting to touch his warm, brown skin, feel the scars, the bumps and indentations she had seen on him that first morning when he had arrived.

Perhaps she was not happy in her celibacy, but she had been content. At least until it was shattered by that one moment when she could stay celibate no longer.

And now, although she would admit it to no one, especially her husband, she wanted him. Her needs and desires had been awakened, and like a wakening beast, they were hungry to be fed.

But to admit this would be like opening herself to pain and heartache. She had done that once; she didn't intend to do it again.

* * *

Fletcher had slept, eventually. He had gone downstairs to retrieve another bottle of whisky to replace the one he had drunk the week before, and as he came up the stairs he saw the flickering of a candle slanting shadows against the walls of the long hallway.

The indistinct silhouette of his wife appeared not far from the door to her bedroom. He took a few steps back to stay out of her sight.

She had stopped near his door, paused, and then turned and hurried back to her room, a wraith in her pristine white gown with her wheaten hair flowing down her back.

Even now, in the dim morning light, it made him smile. He had ignored her intentionally. He knew she expected him to return after midnight and claim his rights as her husband. He wanted her, yes, but he wanted her eager and willing, not reticent and unwilling. Her venture to his bedroom door was encouraging, but he didn't think she was ready. Yet.

There were other thoughts on his mind as well. He loved riding and he had enjoyed getting familiar with the castle and the village. Although he'd been on Hedabarr only a short time, he already knew most of it well. He wasn't one who could sit idly by and do nothing; he had worked for a living from the time he was a boy of ten. He was bored.

He desperately needed a project, something to throw himself into. Something besides the seduction of his reluctant bride, although that certainly could become a full-time and very pleasurable endeavor.

But he needed something else, something to make him feel useful. This life of ease wore thin.

Chapter Thirteen

In the week that followed, Fletcher rose early each day, saddled Ahote, and rode around the island. One morning he rode north. He passed numerous small huts, all with thatched roofing and small windows. A woman bent over a steaming wash pail, and when he rode by, she straightened and stared at him. He bowed his head and smiled, but she gave no response. At another hut, a woman dug in the earth, a trifling pile of potatoes beside her. A number of small children, at least five, dressed in sparse and ragged clothing, ran toward him as he came closer, gleeful and excited, laughing and shouting.

The woman raised her head, looked at Fletcher, and then gave them a sharp order, and they all scampered away like so many frightened puppies.

Further on, he drew Ahote to a halt as a herd of sheep crossed his path, driven by a shaggy dog and a grim shepherd. Fletcher watched as the dog obeyed the shepherd's whistles, forcing the sheep to stay together and hurrying them along, out of Fletcher's way. Again, Fletcher smiled and again got no response from the native.

As he came to the far end, the landscape, desolate and craggy, reminded Fletcher of a world yet to be discovered. But as he approached a grassy plain, his heart beat faster as he viewed a magnificent surprise.

A few dozen wild horses pranced and played, running and rearing up with abandon. The sight thrilled him. Beneath him, Ahote shivered, perhaps with anticipation or excitement.

Fletcher rubbed the stallion's neck. "Easy, boy."

The animal's answer was a throaty whicker as he pawed at the ground.

Gathering the circle of rope in one hand, Fletcher gently nudged his mount's belly and, with stealth and purpose, headed toward the herd.

* * *

"Mistress! Mistress, come look!"

Alarmed by Annie's voice, Rosalyn dropped her spade, dusted off her apron, and followed her maid from the garden.

Annie ran toward the stable, her skirt to her knees and her pale calves exposed above her worn boots.

Curious, Rosalyn followed. And what she saw filled her with wonder.

There, in the wide fenced circle, was her husband and a horse she had not seen before.

Her husband's movements captivated her. With a looped rope, he stepped slowly toward the skittish animal, all the while talking to her under his breath.

Rosalyn studied her savage. He wore no shirt and the thick, rope-like muscles of his brown arms bunched as he worked. Sweat glistened off his shoulders and even from where she stood, Rosalyn could see it running in rivulets down his broad, smooth back. Tall and strong, he was very, very appealing indeed.

An unfamiliar pride of possession sluiced through her and she felt a peculiar need, one she couldn't explain and one she had never felt before.

He coaxed the mare, speaking in low, seductive tones. Rosalyn imagined it was how he would seduce a woman, and the mare began to respond, whinnying and prancing before him as if she, too, could play his game.

Rosalyn watched as he approached the mare, rope in hand. He reached out and touched her nose, his motions gentle. She jerked back, and then forward, finally allowing him to stroke her.

As he would a woman, Rosalyn thought, imagining the gesture on her own skin. Gooseflesh rose on her arms.

But she saw something else. There was happiness on his face that she had never seen before. A look of pure bliss, almost, certainly satisfaction. And she realized that this was a man who could not sit idly by and do nothing. He needed a purpose and he had found one. She was happy for him, almost envious.

"It's one of them wild horses from the north end," Annie said, excited.

"I see that."

The duke turned briefly and caught her gaze. Again, something fluttered in her stomach.

"Why didn't anyone tell me about the horses?" His words weren't accusatory, but filled with reverence.

"How were we to know you'd be interested?"

He stroked the mare's nose. "How did they get there?"

Rosalyn watched him, still envious that something should bring him such unfettered joy. "I heard they had been on board a ship, bound for Ireland, from Sweden, I believe. At one time I believe there were as many as fifty or sixty, maybe more."

Her husband frowned. "I know there weren't that many, maybe a few dozen at the most." He stroked the mare's nose.

"Are you going to ride her?"

Her husband continued stroking the mare. "In time I will." He turned toward her again, a cautious yet mischievous gleam in his eyes. "Like any woman, she's reluctant to be forced."

Rosalyn glanced away, "And you're certain she will eventually capitulate?"

"I, personally, have never met a female who didn't eventually surrender." His hand did not stop caressing the mare, yet his gaze was on Rosalyn.

She had to force herself not to look away. "You rate your skills very highly. Perhaps you have yet to meet your match."

He gave her a roguish grin. "In horses or in women?"

She felt the flush creep up her neck into her ears. "Perhaps in both," she answered, then turned and strode purposefully toward the castle, her heart still beating an erratic tattoo in her chest.

* * *

Fletcher watched her leave, her head high and her back straight as a board.

As engrossed as he had been in the mare, he knew the moment Rosalyn stepped to the fence; he felt her presence the moment she came near. He could also detect her scent, which was like smelling a breeze that had just blown through a succulent rose bush. She was a remarkable woman, and, like a good mare, difficult to tame, which only made him determined to do so. But when he decided the time was right.

The mere fact that she had understood his innuendo meant she was closer to capitulation than she had been the day before.

Chapter Fourteen

Fletcher found Geddes in the library. "What haven't you told me?"

Geddes looked up, guilt written all over him. "Well, I meant to, but—"

"It's almost like they're angry with me. Why is that?"

Geddes frowned, puzzled. "Who?"

"Those poor crofters who live north of here."

Geddes sat back in the chair and removed his spectacles. "What makes you think they're angry with you?"

"Well, they might not be angry, but they sure as hell aren't friendly."

"They know their place," Geddes said, straightening some papers on the desk.

Fletcher paced in front of him, his hands behind his back. "Tell me everything about them."

With a casual shrug, Geddes said, "There's not much to tell. You already know that crofts are actually little parcels of land worked by the farmers. Those who live north of here have the poorest land on the island. As with all the crofters, some raise sheep, some fish, and some collect kelp."

"Kelp? You mean seaweed? What for?"

"It's collected to make alkali."

"Why do they have such poor land? There's plenty of fertile land on the island, I've seen it myself."

"Aye, that's your land."

Fletcher stopped pacing and stared at Geddes. "You mean, all the arable land is mine, and what's left belongs to those crofters up north?"

"It's been that way for a long time, sir."

"Do they at least own it?"

Geddes glanced down. "I'm afraid not. They pay you rent."

Fletcher dropped into a chair beside the desk. "They actually pay me for that? That's terrible."

"It's always been that way, probably from the beginning of time."

The elation of finding the horses was quickly diminishing into self-loathing, something he was quite good at. "Good God, it's no wonder they hated the sight of me."

"It's not your concern, sir."

"Of course it's my concern." But Fletcher had no idea what to do about it. He had so much to learn about his new station in life. "Surely something can be done."

"If that's what you wish," Geddes answered.

"You mean it's up to me to change it?"

"Of course. You're the duke."

Fletcher laughed quietly. "You say that so easily. It isn't easy for me to believe I actually have the power to do something. You must realize I've never had any power before. When you found me I was two days away from being hanged."

"What do you want to do?"

Fletcher steepled his fingers in front of him. "Do we really need rent from those poor people?"

"No, it's just always been that way."

"Then stop collecting it."

Geddes gave him a cautious look. "As your solicitor, I don't recommend it."

"Have you any idea how much rent we've collected, say, in the past ten years, for example?"

"I have very complete records, sir. I can look it up."

"Would you say that in the past ten years, we have collected more rent from that land than it's currently worth?"

"I'm sure we have."

"Then don't you think it's about time we stop? Good God, man, I couldn't live with myself if I took any more money from them."

"Sir, this is highly unorthodox."

"But I can do it, right?"

"Yes. You can do it."

"Then make the arrangements, Geddes, and no fanfare. Just get word to them somehow that they no longer owe me rent for that paltry land." Fletcher got up to leave.

Geddes mouth lifted into a smile. "I will get right on it. And sir?"

"Yes?"

Geddes cleared his throat and tugged at his collar. "I'll be gone for a spell, sir. Business in Edinburgh, I'm afraid. I've…ah, notified the station master to keep you posted on your siblings. He will be in touch with you weekly, if you wish."

"Thank you, Geddes. That will be fine." Fletcher left the library, an uncomfortable weight gone from his shoulders and a pleasant sensation in his stomach.

• • •

"It's been almost a bloody month since we wed and he hasn't so much as touched me on the chin." Rosalyn morosely took a sip of tea, then placed the cup on the table.

"What did you say to him?"

Fen's voice was accusatory, and Rosalyn bristled. "Are you saying this is my fault?"

"Yes," Fenella said without hesitation. "You must have said something, or he wouldn't have backed away."

Rosalyn exhaled sharply, recalling the exchange the night after their wedding. "Well, I did tell him we would not share a bedroom."

Fen glared at her. "Why on earth would you tell him that?"

"Because he came into my bedroom like he belonged there. He didn't even have the decency to knock first."

"God, but you're a stubborn woman, Roz. You're your own worst enemy, I swear."

Rosalyn broke a honey cake in two, biting into one of the halves. "I just didn't want him to think he could do whatever he pleased."

"Good lord, Roz. He's toying with you, love. You set the rules, and he's playing by them, knowing that eventually you'll give in. I would bet you a bottle of good champagne that he's doing this intentionally, reveling in the fact that he's making you squirm."

Rosalyn thought about their conversation regarding the mare. "I do believe you might be right, Fen."

"Of course I'm right."

"But, what shall I do about it?"

"If it were me, I would crawl into his bed and surprise him. And I wouldn't have a stitch of clothing on."

Rosalyn, desperate during the past week, had even thought of that, but she hadn't done it. "Oh, Fen, I don't know."

"It's probably what he's waiting for you to do. He's tasted your wares, Roz, and he wants them again. No red-blooded male alive could resist that, and he's certainly a red-blooded male, your savage."

Rosalyn chewed on her thumbnail. "I just don't know if I could do it."

"Take a drink to fortify yourself, then. What harm could it do?"

"Nay, that's your medicine, not mine. Remember, when I drink I get sleepy and intimacy is the furthest thing from my mind."

"Aye, that might be so, but things can't go on this way—you know that as well as I."

She had to do something; she was actually getting desperate.

* * *

Geddes carefully packed a satchel. God, he hated lying! But he wanted the duke and Rosalyn to have some time alone, some time to get to know one another without the anticipation of the children's arrival. And they would be here soon enough. That was his mission. He was going to collect them himself.

There was a soft knock on the door.

"Enter."

Rosalyn opened the door and stepped into the room. "Where are you going?"

He fussed with the clothing in his wardrobe so he wouldn't have to look at her. She always knew when he was lying. "I have some of the duke's business in Edinburgh. I'll be back in a few weeks."

"Is he going with you?"

He turned from the wardrobe at the hint of concern in her voice. Her face was carefully masked, but he knew her, too. She was worried. "It isn't necessary. I didn't think it was a good time to tear him away from here."

Her gaze dropped to the floor. "Because of me."

"Rosalyn, you need some time alone with him. I haven't seen the two of you together other than at meals, and frankly, I'm beginning to worry."

She picked at her apron. "He hasn't come to me, brother."

Geddes knew this was a hard thing for her to admit. "Then perhaps it's time you go to him."

"That's what Fen said, too."

"Good God, Rosalyn, is there nothing you don't discuss with that woman?"

Rosalyn met his gaze, hers resolute. "No. She's my friend and I trust her with my life."

He crossed to where she stood and lifted her chin. "Whatever you think the duke is, he's a fine man. Aye, he has a lot to learn, but he is intelligent and, above all, he is fair. You will not believe what he has asked me to do."

Her eyes were wide, eager. "What?"

"He learned that the poor crofters pay him rent for their pitiful plots of land and has told me to stop collecting them."

Rosalyn's face expressed shock and surprise. "Can he do that?"

"Of course, he can do whatever he wishes. It's a most generous idea, but the more I think about it, the more I feel we should come to a compromise. Simply giving them the land seems irresponsible. I believe they should pay something, perhaps just a pittance."

"Aye," she said. "They are poor, but they are also proud. Will you explain this to him?"

"Perhaps you can." He lifted an eyebrow. "It will give you an excuse to go to him."

She opened her mouth as if to argue, but instead said, "I wonder what brought him to that decision."

"It undoubtedly goes back to his roots. He's quite aware of how it is to live in poverty. I assume the thought of him having so much and the crofters having so little appalled him."

She moved toward the door. "It will be quiet around here without you."

"All the better. When I return, I will expect things to have changed between you, Rosalyn. Don't disappoint me."

She bristled slightly. "Remember, what you expect takes two—I cannot do it alone."

"Then do something about it." He picked up his satchel and followed her out into the hall. He left her, went outside, and called for his gig. He needed to let someone know his mission, and since he didn't want to tell either Rosalyn or the duke, he took the worn path to Fenella Begley's cottage. Oddly, his heart beat fast in anticipation of seeing her again. Her remark about someone else's blood on her uniform the day she was married gave him pause, and he'd thought of her frequently.

Chapter Fifteen

Fenella had just finished tending a youngster with a deep gash. She had sent him on his way when she spotted Geddes's gig coming up the path. Never one to particularly care about her appearance, she astonished herself by rushing to the mirror and running her fingers through her hair. His surprise appearance rattled her, but by the time she heard him at the door she was calm. Or she appeared to be, at any rate. She could not imagine what he wanted.

She opened the door and nodded a greeting. He still looked very good to her. No, she hadn't imagined it. It pleased her that she had to look up at him. She adored tall men. He wore traveling clothes, a smart thigh-length, single-breasted, gray-and-white wool coat, and gray wool trousers. He held his black top hat in his hand. He looked very fine, indeed.

"Might I have a word with you?" he asked.

He could have more than that if he wanted to, she decided. She swung the door wide, allowing him to enter. "We can talk in here." She extended an arm toward the salon. As she followed him, she smelled a hint of soap. My, she thought, not only is he finely made, he's clean as well.

"I'll come directly to the point," Geddes said, accepting a cup of coffee from her and taking a biscuit. "Are you aware of the duke's siblings?"

Fenella frowned. "No. He has siblings?"

"He has two younger brothers and a sister whom he has been waiting for since his arrival." Geddes put his cup on the table beside him and tugged at his collar. "We had no word, not until the day before the wedding, and then I was informed that they were aboard the *Sea Mistress* and, should the weather prevail, would arrive at the end of May."

Fenella thought a moment. "That would be in less than two weeks."

Geddes nodded. "I have not yet informed the duke that they are coming." He scrubbed his face with his hand and then looked at her. "I do not tell lies, nor am I in the habit of keeping good news from anyone, especially the duke. But…I wanted Rosalyn and him to have some time alone together, some time to adjust to one another without the anticipation of the children."

"And Rosalyn doesn't even know these children exist?"

Geddes shook his head. "But I don't think it's because the duke doesn't want her to know, I think it's merely because they haven't been intimately involved in any sort of meaningful conversation since the day he promised to tell her the whole truth about his past."

Fenella understood. There was a strain between the newlyweds brought on by Rosalyn's stubbornness and her miserable history with Leod. "Why are you telling me this?"

"Because I had to tell someone where I was going, and I thought perhaps you might keep my secret. And should I not return in a timely fashion, at least there would be someone who would know what I was up to."

"So you're going to simply surprise everyone when you return, is that it?"

He frowned. "I shall have His Grace notified, of course. I couldn't very well simply spring them on Rosalyn."

"No, not if Rosalyn is unaware of their existence before they arrive on her doorstep. I can't imagine that she would be upset having the duke's siblings there, but she might be puzzled that she wasn't told they exist."

He shook his head and gazed toward the window. "I truly feel they need this time together without any disruptions, but perhaps I've erred in not telling the duke."

"I should think he would overlook your negligence once he saw his family," she said.

"That's precisely my hope." He stood. "Then I can count on your discretion?"

"I won't tell Rosalyn of your secret errand, but I just may intercede on her behalf if I learn that, in another week, she still doesn't know."

"I hadn't thought to mention that to him, and now the ferry to Edinburgh is due and I have no time to return to the castle to explain."

She walked him to the door. "I think perhaps you're doing the wrong thing for the right reasons."

He turned and gave her a warm smile, one that reached his pale blue eyes. "I thank you for understanding, Mrs. Begley. Oh, and I believe they are sending a chaperone with the youngsters. A woman from some agency that protects children."

She enjoyed watching him walk away. He was so tall, so fine. So unattached. She would have to work on that. Although she had been a widow for more years than she was married, she realized that she no longer prized her solitude. It was time to share it. And she planned to share it with Geddes Gordon.

• • •

Rosalyn searched out the duke, finding him in the stable. He glanced at her briefly and then went back to his chore. He had shed his shirt and was bare to the waist as he curried his steed. Lord, but he was finely made.

"To what do I owe this honor, madam?" The stallion's muscles shivered with delight as the grooming continued.

Rosalyn swallowed. "Geddes tells me you wish to eliminate all the rents from the crofters."

He paused in his chore. "You don't agree?"

"I think it's a fine thing to think of, but these are proud people. Poverty stricken, yet proud, nevertheless."

"Yes, but haven't they been paying for this land forever? I merely feel it should come to an end. It should be theirs to do with as they wish. I don't need any of it; I'm disgusted about the fact that all of the decent land is apparently mine. I can't let this continue. For God's sake, they've probably overpaid for the land. It may not be a wise decision, but it's the one I want to make. It's the very least I can do."

Rosalyn was constantly surprised by the duke. She reached into her apron pocket and pulled out a sugar cube, placing it on her palm beneath the stallion's nostrils. He took it, his soft mouth brushing her skin.

"You'll spoil him."

She chuckled. "I think you've already done a fine job of that, Your Grace."

"When are you and Geddes going to quit Your Gracing me?"

She blinked, her nerves beginning to thrum. "What would you have us call you?"

"How about My Savage Duke? Or is it My Lord Savage?"

She gasped as he turned to study her, one eyebrow and one corner of his mouth lifted in wry amusement.

"I…I mean…it didn't…I didn't…" She felt the flush stain her cheeks and neck.

"You what? You didn't mean to call me that?" he interrupted, stepping closer.

"Well, I…" She drew in a breath and decided she couldn't lie, for apparently he'd heard from someone, God knows who, about how she'd talked of him that first day. She expelled the breath and straightened her shoulders. "Yes. I admit I called you that. Do you know why?" She didn't give him time to answer. "Because when you arrived, you were wild and savage looking. You had braids down your back nearly to your bum and you wielded a knife big enough to flense a whale. You swore like a sailor and your clothes were unspeakably filthy. You flaunted your big, naked body in front of me like someone who had no sense of decorum. How else would you have me address you?"

"You have seen a whale flensed, madam?" He was calm, unperturbed.

"I don't have to. All I have to know is that it takes a bloody huge weapon, and yours was bloody huge."

He gave her a salacious grin. "Why, thank you, ma'am. I'm happy you noticed."

She blushed further. "I meant your knife, you oaf."

He drew the stallion to his stall, making sure he had feed and water before closing the door. "Did you really? I mean, there we were, just the two of us, and you had stripped me of all my worldly possessions, leaving me naked. Are you really telling me you didn't notice my bag of tricks?"

Oh, God. That damned trick bag again. She caught her gaze before it wandered down the length of him. "Are you always this crass?"

He shelved the curry comb, briefly turning away from her. "Not always."

"Then why with me?"

He turned and gave her a smile, his teeth white against his skin. "Because I enjoy seeing you flustered. It makes your cheeks pink and your eyes glitter, putting so much life into your face that I can hardly keep myself from kissing you until you faint."

She stood there, mouth open, unable to respond to his words. But her body responded, sending her blood soaring through her veins.

He looked around them, his gaze casual. "You know, the stable is one of my favorite places."

Was she supposed to answer? God, she didn't know. "Wh… why is that?"

He moved a bit closer. "Because I love horses. I love the smell of the stable, the earthy, damp scent of a horse after he's been ridden. It reminds me of sex. Stallions are very sexual, did you know that?"

She couldn't answer. It didn't matter.

"Stallions get one whiff of a mare in heat and they're ready to mate. To lunge and bite and thrust, every male animal instinct is magnified in a stallion."

She was able to gather her frazzled nerves about her, although she wasn't sure how she did it. "And you're comparing yourself to a stallion?"

"I've been compared to worse," he answered.

"I'll just bet you have," she almost whispered, trying to imagine him in his rough days as a youth in the West, where, she imagined, everything was wild and untamed.

Either he didn't hear her, or he was simply ignoring her comment.

"Do you know how a stallion woos his mare?"

"With flowers and song?" she answered dryly.

He chuckled and shook his head. "He tempts her with loud, insistent whinnying. Then, with neck curved high and nostrils flaring, he comes near her, his trot jaunty. He struts." The duke paraded around her, almost preening. "He dances around her, bites her, nibbles at her," he added, coming dangerously close to touching her cheek with his lips, "and finally, when he's sure she's ready, or perhaps even if she's not," he said, standing so close their bodies nearly touched, "he mounts her."

Her mouth was dry and she took a step backward. "I have seen horses mate."

"And it didn't affect you at all? It didn't make you quiver in places you'd though were long dead? It didn't send your heart bounding into your mouth so swift and hard you could almost taste the heat of the occasion?"

She briefly glanced away, recalling the thrilling bite of raw pleasure she'd had the one time she had, by accident, watched a mating. Truth? Nay. "How did we get off on this subject?"

"You were reminded that you called me a savage."

"And at times I believe you still are," she countered.

He laughed softly. "Perhaps I am. But actually, we were talking about the crofters."

"Oh. Oh, yes." She had meant to tell him that they should pay him something, a pittance, for their pride, but after hearing his opinion of the situation, she kept quiet. "Well, I do see your point."

"So, we can tell them to stop paying me?"

"I guess we can do as you wish, but perhaps we should wait for Geddes's return."

He crossed to the water basin, splashed his face and chest with water, then lifted a towel off a post by the tack room and wiped himself. "I'll wait for him, then. But no longer. I won't sleep comfortably until this whole thing has been put to rights."

"What would you have them do in return for their land, then?"

He stepped close to her, so close she could smell his maleness and feel his heat—again. "Ye're a clever lassie," he said, affecting a thick brogue. "Ye'll think of something." He got as far as the stable door and then turned. "By the way, tomorrow is Sunday."

And then he was gone.

She stared at his retreating form and shouted, "What in the devil does that mean?"

He glanced at her over his shoulder and then laughed, continuing on toward the castle. Aye, she thought, tomorrow was Sunday, and the way their connubial bliss had been going, it mattered not one whit, for he hadn't even attempted to touch her, so what difference did it make?

• • •

She stewed about his statement the rest of the afternoon, carrying the words with her as she did her chores, allowing them to gnaw at her insides. Did it mean he would finally visit her tonight? She stopped dusting the dining room table, her cleaning cloth held suspended midair as she imagined him coming to her, speaking to her in his low, sultry voice, perhaps saying something like, "It's time, madam. It's time we make perfect love together, beautiful, blissful love. I'm ready to make you my wife in every sense of the word."

She snorted a laugh. Not likely. It was more like him to say something savage, like, "Are you wet for me, wife? Do you ache in that place between your thighs?"

She snorted again. "You're daft, Rosalyn, that's what you are."

"Madam?"

She turned as Barnaby wobbled into the room, his stockings sagging on his chicken legs.

"Did you say something?" he asked, his face puckered like a dried apple.

"No, I'm just ranting to myself, Barnaby. All is well."

He bowed. "Very good, madam." He continued on past her to the kitchen and she noticed that his breeches were askew, as if he'd put them on backward or in the dark. As he went through the swinging door, he broke wind, not even bothering to excuse himself.

Poor old sod, she thought, smiling sadly. She glanced at the long, gleaming dining table and sighed. With Geddes away, the evening meal would be just the two of them—her and her husband. That ought to be a jolly affair, she thought, frowning.

Well, jolly affair or not, she had to get ready for it. She looked down at her gown and bit her bottom lip, trapping a smile. Perhaps it was time to do something drastic.

* * *

She studied her reflection in the mirror, posing this way and that, trying to decide if her gown was suitable. She stifled a laugh. Suitable for what, she didn't know, but it certainly was not one she would have worn on a normal work day. Cut low, it exposed more of her breasts than it ever had before. She tugged the bodice upward, but it made little difference. Odd—this gown had always been more comfortable than this. Of course, she hadn't worn it in a long time.

With a sigh, she said softly, "You've done it now, Roz, go through with it." What was it Fen had said to her? Take a drink? Perhaps she would. Perhaps this one time she would.

Giving her hair one final pat, she left her room and moved swiftly down the staircase. She stopped short when she stepped into the dining room, for the table had not been set and there was no sign of either the duke or the kitchen help. But on further inspection she noticed a small table with a long white cloth that reached the floor and two table settings upon it in the corner by the window. The silverware shimmered with light from a single long, tapered candle that was sitting in the middle of the table.

"What is this?" she murmured, sincerely taken by surprise.

The kitchen door swung open behind her, and the duke came into the room. "Ah, there you are, madam. I thought it foolish to sit at that big table, especially since it's just the two of us. I hope this suits you."

It was actually very thoughtful and quite intimate. "'Tis a very fine idea."

He pulled out her chair, and when she was seated he leaned toward her and whispered low in her ear. "You look absolutely delectable tonight. I could eat you up." He added, his voice even softer, "And I just might."

She blushed, sensing his meaning but not understanding how she knew. "You are not a proper gentleman," she scolded, but the thrill of her tone said she didn't much care. This just might be the best night of their marriage, so far.

He poured them each a glass of wine and she took a sip, then another.

"Don't drink too fast, madam. It will go straight to your head."

That is my intention, she thought, taking another deliberate swallow.

They talked of small things, table talk, really, and all at once she realized he was filling her glass again—and she felt a warm glow all over.

Annie brought out the soup, and when she had disappeared into the kitchen again, Rosalyn felt the duke's knee touch hers under the table. Believing it was an accident, she said, "I'm afraid the table is a wee bit small for a man of your size."

"On the contrary," he replied, "it's perfect." And once again, she felt his knee touch hers, but this time he rubbed against it.

It was as if she wore nothing at all, for the touch was electrifying. Her soup was getting chilled, and she couldn't even think to bring a spoonful to her mouth. The wine had addled her, robbing her of logical thought. What in the name of heaven was he doing?

The girl returned and removed the soup plates and came back with the stew. She made a swift curtsey and left them again.

"Madam," he began.

She looked over at him, wondering if he could see the pulsing at her throat. "Yes?"

"May I ask you a question?"

She smiled at him. "Of course. Anything."

He sat back and studied her. "Are you wearing underdrawers?"

Her jaw dropped and her spoon clattered to the table. "What?!"

"It's a simple question, madam. Are you, or aren't you?"

Her mouth worked a little before she was able to speak. The warmth from the wine continued to soar through her blood. "Why would you ask me such a thing?"

"Because I'm interested."

"I…don't think I have to answer that question." Yes, he was a savage, indeed. Why, then, didn't she just get up and leave?

"All right."

She gave him a look of surprise. "All right?"

"Yes. That's all right. I'll just have to find out for myself."

She gasped as she felt his foot slide up her calf to her thigh. When had he removed his boot, for God's sake?

Just then Annie came in and the savage's foot stopped, just at the top of her thigh, making her skin shiver and her womanhood throb.

"Is everything all right here, ma'am?"

She gave the girl a wobbly smile, praying that she would not titter like a silly unschooled milkmaid at her savage lord's antics. "All is well. Thank you." She glanced at him, and he was buttering a roll, appearing completely innocent of his actions.

When the girl retreated once again, her husband's toe worked its way to the split in her drawers. The ache gnawed at Rosalyn, and she spread her legs, feeling wanton. *It's the wine*, she told herself. *It's just the wine.*

He looked across the table at her, his expression hot and dangerous. "How nice that there's a place for me down there."

She closed her eyes and allowed the thrill of his touch to wash over her. Oh, this was going to be some night, it was. When his toe left her, she felt bereft, and her expression must have said as much. She opened her eyes to find him watching her. And then he knocked his knife to the floor and kicked it under the table.

"I suppose I should get that."

He rose, pushed his chair back, lifted the long linen table cloth, and disappeared under the table. She bit back a cry of surprise when she felt him raise her gown above her knees and spread her legs apart.

"My dear sir," she whispered, frantically looking around her, a bubble of shock rising into her throat, "what are you doing?"

From beneath the table, he answered, "I'm having dessert, madam."

The moment she felt his tongue probe her opening, she began to shake. There was such an exquisite sensation radiating through her, she thought she might faint. "Oh, my," she said on a breath. "Oh, my!"

"Mistress?"

Rosalyn hadn't heard Annie enter. She tried to trap her husband's head between her legs to stop his assault, but it only gave him closer access to his goal. She blinked and smiled nervously at the girl. "Yes, Annie?"

Annie frowned. "Are you all right?"

Rosalyn giggled, sounding daft, like a woman gone mad. "Fine, dear. I'm fine."

"His Grace. He's gone, ma'am?"

Gone off the deep end, Rosalyn thought, *gone right out of his head.* "He…ah…he had a brief errand. It's fine, run along, then."

Annie seemed to study the table for a long moment, a quizzical expression on her face, and then finally disappeared into the kitchen.

Rosalyn thought she heard the servant chuckle behind the door, but that thought slid from her mind when she felt the hot breath against her wet, swollen flesh as her husband said, "I have an errand, all right. But it won't be brief, wife."

The wine was truly getting to her, for she bit back a laugh.

She could only imagine what it must look like under there, her legs splayed, her skirt up around her hips, and her husband's dark head between her thighs.

She tried to relax and enjoy it, truly she did, but she kept expecting someone to walk in and discover her husband under the table, doing things to her with his tongue that she had no idea could be done.

"Perhaps we should continue this another time." He moved away slightly, and then she felt him touch her with his thumb and she jumped. "Your Grace, please," she pleaded.

"Oh, all right, if you insist," she heard him say.

As he was crawling out from under the table, Annie came through the door with their dessert. Rosalyn looked up, saw Annie's surprise, and suddenly couldn't speak.

Her husband had no such problem. "Well," he said as he picked up his fallen utensil, "so that's where the knife went." With all of the poise of a gentleman, he slid onto his chair and rested his arms on the table. "Now, my dear, where were we?"

"About to have dessert, I believe," she said, hoping her voice didn't betray her.

The savage gave Annie a long, pleasant look. "Annie, just serve up some dessert for the lady. I've already had mine."

Rosalyn pressed her lips together to keep from making a comment of any kind as Annie placed a tulip-shaped glass filled with pudding in front of her. When Annie was finished, she once again disappeared into the kitchen.

Then, truly then, one could hear her laughing, practically whinnying like a horse.

Rosalyn gave him a dark look. "You do know that whatever she thinks she saw or heard will be all over the island by morning, don't you?"

He leaned back into the chair and crossed his arms over his chest. "Then everyone will know that all is well at the castle, won't they, Rosalyn?"

He pushed his chair back and rose. "Are you really hungry for that pudding?"

Her heart leapt against her ribs. "I…no, not really."

He came around pulled her chair out. "Then I think it's time to go upstairs, don't you?"

Her head was dizzy from the wine and from the anticipation of what was to come next. She could feel every nerve in her body pulsating, her blood coursing hot through new veins. It was as if she was aware of her entire being for the very first time, and every feeling she had was centered down there between her thighs, radiating everywhere.

They climbed the stairs together, his arm around her shoulders, which was a good thing because she was a wee bit unsteady on her feet. "I feel a bit dizzy."

He drew her closer. "It's the wine, no doubt."

"Aye, I rarely drink at all."

"And you thought you had to fortify yourself tonight?" His voice had a slight teasing quality to it, but underneath, she thought she heard a touch of wariness.

She nodded. "But not for the reason you think."

"What reason would that be, Rosalyn?"

She wasn't sure how to put it, so she just blurted it out. "It isn't because I find you unappealing or unattractive."

He laughed quietly beside her as they arrived on the landing. "Well, I'm certainly glad I'm not repugnant."

"You are far from repugnant, Your Grace."

He stopped and swore. "Will you and your brother quit Your Gracing me? I will never get used to that. My name is Fletcher. Please, Rosalyn," he said, adding softly, "please call me by my name. Now, say it."

She turned to him in the upstairs hallway, his face in shadows except for the gleam of his dark eyes. She would do it. She wanted everything to be perfect tonight. "Fletcher." It sounded so fine rolling off her tongue. She imagined crying out his name in passion, and it only made the fire within her body all the more urgent.

His fingers touched her chin, and he lifted her face toward him. "Was that so hard?"

"Nay, not when we're alone, but when the servants are about, I'd rather be more formal, if you don't mind."

"As you wish." His fingers dove gently into her hair, pulling some of it loose from its pins. "Your hair is the color of Texas wheat," he murmured against her ear.

Another shudder raced through her. Between the wine and her anticipation, she was nearly flying apart. When he pulled her to him, he touched his mouth to her forehead, her nose, and her mouth, their breaths mingling oh, so gently. Her knees went weak and she leaned against him.

He pulled away; she let him go reluctantly.

Touching her elbow, he steered her toward her room. In front of her door, he said, "I'll let you get ready, Rosalyn." He lifted her hand to his lips and kissed it.

Feeling giddy and a bit nervous, she went into her room and began preparing for bed—or for whatever it was her husband had in mind, she thought, her heart still drumming in her chest. After she had changed into a light cotton dressing gown, taken down her hair, and brushed it until it gleamed, she sat and waited.

After a few minutes she rose from her dressing table and went to the window. It was dreary and black outside. Not wanting the bleakness to spoil her mood, she strode purposefully to the door, opened it, and looked down the hallway toward her husband's room. Nothing.

Puzzled, she crossed to her bed and crawled into it, pulling a light cover over her. What was he doing? What possible reason could he have for taking so long? She began to have a nagging feeling in the pit of her stomach, not wishing to believe he wouldn't come, not after what he'd put her through at dinner.

She was about to blow out the candle by her bedside when finally, finally, she heard a soft tapping at the door. Finally! "Please, come in." She lay on her side, her breathing suddenly shallow with expectation as he watched him come through the door—but wait! It wasn't her husband at all.

Alarmed, she sat up in bed. "Barnaby? What is it?"

He shuffled over to the bed and handed her a note. "From the master, my lady."

Frowning, she relit her candle and took the note from him. "Thank you, Barnaby. I'm sorry you were bothered so late. Good night."

He bowed, tilting precariously to one side, and then hobbled out, shutting the door behind him.

"What in the world," she said to herself. She opened the note and read:

I know you are ready for me. I, too, am ready for you. However, due to the lateness of the hour, I didn't want to start something I couldn't finish properly. After all, tomorrow is, as you know, Sunday.

Just then the clock in the foyer chimed and she sat in her bed, the note crumpled in her fist, as she counted to twelve with the resonating gongs.

Suddenly she began to feel the rage building up inside her. Gone, gone was the fire of need and passion, replaced by anger, humiliation, and pummeled pride. Without a thought, she threw the covers aside, stormed out of her room, and stomped down to her husband's chambers. Not bothering to knock, she flung open the door. He was in bed, reading.

Oh, the gall of the man!

"You did this on purpose, didn't you?" she said without preamble. "You purposely whipped me into a state of frenzy and then simply dropped me like a bucket of rotten haggis."

He gave her a bland look. "Now, why would I do that, Rosalyn? Why on earth would I want to punish you? Haven't you been through enough?"

She was not assuaged. "You're bloody right I've been through enough. And now, don't go thinking you'll get into my bed any time soon, savage, because I can play this game as well as anyone. Especially you. You haven't seen determination until you've seen mine." With that, she tore through the door and slammed it. Hard.

Chapter Sixteen

Fletcher woke up before the sun. He stretched under the covers, flexing his legs and raising his arms over his head. Sunday. Blessed Sunday.

He threw back the covers and bounded out of bed, sprinting to the commode where he washed his face. He checked his beard, deciding he wasn't in need of a shave. His dressing gown lay draped over the back of a chair, but he ignored it and left his room, ambling casually toward Rosalyn's.

He met Barnaby halfway down the hallway. "Good morning, Barnaby."

The old servant nodded and said, quite matter-of-factly, "So it's naked day today, Your Grace?"

Fletcher bit back a laugh. He had to wonder what sort of folly his grandfather had been up to if "naked day" didn't even give old Barnaby a start. "All day, my good man, all day."

When he got to Rosalyn's door he rapped on it with his knuckles.

"Yes?" she answered from within.

"Would you like some breakfast?"

There was a long pause, then she answered, "Only if you have coffee. Otherwise I don't want to see you at all today."

He opened the door, slipping inside as he closed it behind him. When he turned toward the bed, she was gaping at him.

"What on earth?"

He yawned and stretched, flexing his muscles again. Noting her stunned puzzlement, he said in a most serious tone, "Oh, didn't I tell you? I often laze about nude on Sundays. It gives my body a chance to breathe from all those scratchy, uncomfortable clothes you've provided for me."

Her gaze went from his groin to his face and then back again before she looked away. He forced himself not to become aroused, focusing on things that kept him level, like his escape from the stockade or hunting, for that would defeat his purpose, at least for now.

His wife scooted out of bed, wrapped herself in her dressing gown, and marched past him to the door. She flung it open with a flourish. "Out."

"But I just got here, Rosalyn."

She was breathing hard and her eyes glittered angrily. "I don't know what you think you're doing, but whatever it is, it won't work. Not with me. Not now, not ever."

He frowned. "But I didn't mean anything, Rosalyn. I simply explained to you that I often spend my Sundays exactly like this."

"If you don't get out of here right now, I'll call for…for…"

"For who? Barnaby? Or the master of the castle?" He put his fingers to his lips and inhaled sharply. "Oh, that's right. I'm the master. I don't think anyone would dare throw me out of my own home, do you?"

She made a loud, exasperated noise in her throat. "Fine." She stepped to her wardrobe and pulled out a day gown. "The place is yours. I won't stand in the way of your debauchery. Obviously, this is something you have inherited from your grandfather. Maybe, like him, you'll end up deader than a rodent killed by a cat and we can cart you out of here on a slab."

He bit the insides of his cheeks to keep from laughing. "You've threatened that before, madam."

"And I'm threatening you again, you savage. Now get out!"

He raised his hands in defeat. "As you wish, madam. I suppose we won't be breakfasting together, then."

Her expression was priceless. Her mouth dropped open and her eyes were huge blue orbs of fear and disbelief. "Not even you would let the servants see you like this."

He stroked his chin and said, "Well, maybe I'll wear my dressing gown when I'm out and about, but," he added, smiling slyly, "when it's the two of us, Rosalyn, this is the way I'll be dressed—or undressed—all day long."

"Out!"

He bowed low and let himself out, feeling the breeze from the door as it slammed soundly behind him. He allowed himself a wicked laugh as he went back to his own chamber.

* * *

Rosalyn was already halfway out the door when Annie called after her that her breakfast was ready. "Give it to His Grace," she said, then added to herself, "and put some rat poison in it."

She walked so fast to Fen's cottage that by the time she arrived she was perspiring and breathing as if she'd run all the way.

Fen opened the door and took a step back. "My God, Roz, what's wrong?"

Rosalyn pushed her way into the cottage and began to pace.

"Roz?"

She turned to Fen, her arms crossed over her chest. "Do you know what that savage just did?"

Fen drew her into her small salon and forced her to sit down. "Tell me."

Rosalyn pressed a hand to her heart and breathed in deeply to catch her breath. "He showed up in my bedchamber this morning, stark naked."

Fen expelled a sharp laugh. "What? Why?"

"Oh, he's a clever bastard, he is. Just last night he practically wooed the britches off me. He got me so ready for him that I went to my chamber and prepared myself for him. Prepared to finally give myself to him like the good wife I am."

"And then what happened?"

"Nothing happened! Absolutely nothing."

Fen thought for a moment. "That is odd, I'll grant you that."

"He's simply throwing my own words back into my face."

"What do you mean?"

"We were married on a Sunday, remember? That night, I told him I would have one day a week to myself. One day when he couldn't pressure me into having relations."

"You mean, having sex?"

Rosalyn made a face. "Of course that's what I mean."

"And what day did you choose, Roz?"

She exhaled sharply. "Because I wanted time to grow accustomed to the entire situation, I told him we would not have any sexual relations on Sunday. Any Sunday. All day long."

Fen threw back her head and laughed. "So, if I'm hearing this right, he seduced you madly last night without consummating your marriage, and this morning he honorably did your bidding."

"But he paraded around me naked, Fen. He was teasing me."

"Well of course he was teasing you, you naïve thing." She gave Rosalyn a sly look. "And what did you observe?"

Rosalyn felt herself blush. "He is finely made."

"Ha! I'll just bet he is. And did it arouse you?"

"No, not really, I was too angry to be aroused."

"But I'll bet it wouldn't have taken him long to thaw you out, dear," Fen mused.

"Not today. I'm too angry and, if you must know, humiliated."

Fen gave her a warm smile. "Oh, my dearest. This is the kind of courtship that should go into a novel."

"Ha! Who would read such a thing?" She followed Fen into the kitchen where Fen had made up a cot with a pillow and soft blankets. On the stove sat a huge pot, steam rolling from it that had the odor of something medicinal.

"Did you know that our fine doctor has left the island for good?" Fen asked.

Rosalyn glanced at her. "Really? Whatever possessed him to leave?"

"I heard he was offered something on another island where he was promised a finer house with servants. Good riddance, I'd say."

"So that means you'll be busier than ever, doesn't it? Oh, good," Rosalyn answered. "I'll help you all I can. After all, I don't really want to spend any more time in my husband's company than I have to."

Fen bustled around the kitchen, preparing them coffee. She motioned to the small kitchen table and Rosalyn took a seat. "There's something I need to tell you."

Rosalyn felt an immediate wave of discomfort. "About what?"

Fen didn't answer immediately, but studied Rosalyn a long moment before she said, "Has His Grace told you about his siblings?"

Something like a fist hit Rosalyn in the stomach. "His what?"

"Oh, dear," Fen answered. "So he hasn't told you that he has two brothers and a sister. I thought he would have by this time."

Rosalyn threw her hands up and yelped, the sound filled with frustration and astonishment. "He has siblings? And how is it that you know this, Fen?"

Fen screwed up her face. "Your brother stopped here on his way off the island. He said that after his business was done in Edinburgh, he was going to pick them up. Apparently they're landing soon."

Rosalyn fought a building sense of panic. "And when was I supposed to learn of this?"

Fen sighed. "Geddes thought His Grace would have mentioned them to you by now so that you would be prepared, both emotionally and physically, when they arrived. I suppose either he or I could have told you, but your brother truly felt it was His Grace's responsibility."

Rosalyn paced. "I don't know how to react to this." She stopped and stared at Fen. "When do you suppose he was going to say something? When they were at the castle doorstep? And how old are these children, anyway? Will they need special care?" She expelled an exasperated huff.

"Your brother didn't tell me, Roz, I don't know. I do know there is also a chaperone with them, someone who travels with them to secure their safety."

Rosalyn plopped down at the table again, stunned. "By the saints, if anything could take the wind out of my sails it's this news.

Oh, don't get me wrong. I'm still angry with him, but this rather changes a lot of things, doesn't it?"

"I know you'll make all the right decisions, dear. You always do, you know?"

Rosalyn gave her a wan smile. "Aye, so you tell me. But this time I haven't got a clue as to how to proceed."

• • •

Fletcher was in the study, wrapped in his dressing gown like he'd promised, when the door flew open and banged against the wall. Rosalyn stood there, and if he had had to describe her stance, he would have said she was battle ready.

She closed the door and strode up to the desk, her hands on her hips. "You have siblings."

Fletcher grimaced. "I suppose I should have mentioned it."

"Well, when were you going to tell me? After they arrived?"

"Sit down, Rosalyn."

She ignored him and continued to stand in front of him, breathtakingly beautiful in her ire.

"Sit down, and I'll tell you the whole story, all right?"

She exhaled deeply and took a chair in front of him, crossing her arms over her chest. "I can't wait to hear this," she murmured.

He told her the whole story. How he felt he had abandoned them, how he had threatened Geddes that he wouldn't go with him unless they were found and brought over. How he worried every day that some ill had happened to them, and if it had, it would be his fault and he would pay for it in eternity.

"How old are they, and what are their names?" Rosalyn's voice was softer now that she understood.

"Duncan is the oldest—he's my half-brother. He is nearly fifteen. Gavin is fourteen. My father took him in after his family's ranch was burned to the ground. He found him hiding in a root cellar, nearly starving. The youngest is Kerry." He smiled, thinking of that sweet girl, his baby sister, his lifeline to the others. "She's twelve and beautiful."

He paused a moment and then said, "If anything should happen to them, not only would I be devastated, but my guilt at my behavior during the years after my father died would kill me. I lived my life my way, Rosalyn. It wasn't the best way, it wasn't even the way I really wanted it. I became self-destructive. Maybe I even willed my own arrest, I don't know." Suddenly he asked, "How did you know about them?"

She raised a sardonic eyebrow in his direction. "Apparently you were supposed to do that. I had to hear of their existence from Fen, who, I'm told, heard it from Geddes. And also, it appears that Geddes is on his way to retrieve them from the ship."

Fletcher's heart soared and he stood. "They're going to be here? How soon?"

"That I don't know," she answered, and then rose from her chair as well. "But since we are to have three more people in the castle, I should guess it's time to air out the west wing and prepare bedchambers for all of them, don't you think?"

Fletcher blinked hard, trying to keep the moisture from collecting in his eyes. God, he was so happy he didn't know what to do with himself. Without a thought, he came out from behind the desk to where Rosalyn stood and pulled her into his arms.

"They're coming here, Rosalyn. Oh, God, how I've worried about them. You have no idea what remorse I've carried around since I was imprisoned and lost contact. If something had happened to them, I don't think I could have ever forgiven myself."

She looked up at him and brought her fingers to his cheek. "You're crying, Your Grace."

"Hell, yes," he admitted. "I'm happy. The happiest day of my life will be when I see their beautiful faces again. You will love them, Rosalyn, I know you will."

"But will they take to me?"

"They will love you as well. Especially Kerry. She needs a woman around, I would think, after all the years of watching out for her brothers."

"Why didn't you tell me sooner? Did you think I wouldn't warm to the idea?"

He thought for a moment. "No, I never believed that. When you're treated properly, you have a generous heart, Rosalyn."

"And when you're not acting like a savage, you act almost human, my husband." She gave him an impish smile.

Arousal rose up, deep and hard, and his heart began to pound. He bent and kissed her, tasting her sweetness, his thirst for her unbearable. She responded by pressing her palms flat against his naked chest.

She shuddered against him. "'Tis Sunday, Fletcher."

"Are you going to put up a fight, my dear wife?" he murmured against her ear.

Her breathing was erratic. "I'm not sure I have much fight left in me." Her hands were at his waist and she fumbled with the tie of his dressing gown, finally releasing it. It fell open and she pressed herself against him.

"I could take you right now, right here," he threatened.

"And you had better do it, for I am on fire, and if you don't do something about it, I might burst into flames and burn the place down."

He took her hand and nearly dragged her to the chaise lounge. "I want you astride. I want to feel myself deep inside you." He laid down, his head resting on the back, and started to pull her to him.

"Wait." She shimmied out of her drawers.

Before she straddled him, he lifted her gown and petticoats and gazed at the luscious patch of wheat-colored fur at the apex of her thighs. "I knew you would be fair here," he almost whispered. He dipped a finger inside, finding her ready, and before her knees buckled, he lifted her onto him.

They rode together and he watched as she threw her head back, her face bathed in a light sheen of perspiration and her cheeks pink. She was spectacular and she was his. He grabbed her hips and guided her, gathering the rhythm, and not until he saw her mouth open in rapturous pleasure did he allow his own seed to be released.

Chapter Seventeen

Over the next week, Rosalyn and the maids prepared the three bedchambers for Fletcher's family. They brought clean blankets out of storage, scented with lavender, cloves and pepper between the folds to keep them fresh. They scrubbed floors, walls, and brass bedsteads, shook rugs, and put an oil lamp in each room. Annie and her sister chattered incessantly, wondering what the children would be like, if they would be handsome like their brother, if they would take to the island girls (the boys, of course), and if the girl would be as beautiful as an Indian princess.

Rosalyn hadn't had time to dwell on such things; she was still thinking about the escapade in the library. So much for her staunch vow and her angry threats, she thought. There was much about her husband she didn't understand, but she was discovering a depth of character she had only imagined might be there, under all of that wild and reckless behavior.

One week after the lovely library liaison, after a light meal, they said goodnight on the landing. Disappointed, Rosalyn went her chamber and prepared for bed. She didn't know what she had expected, but for her, the evening had ended too quickly.

After she had changed into her nightclothes, she sat in her wing chair with her feet tucked under her and began to read.

There was a knock at the door. "Come in," she called softly.

Fletcher entered.

"Is something wrong?" she asked, laying her book down on the table beside her.

"Rosalyn, I want you to tell me about your life." He stood before her, tall, handsome, and serious.

Surprised, she asked, "What about my life?"

He glanced down and then met her stare. "I can't understand you if I don't know about you, about your marriage and...everything."

Her gaze dropped and she felt the old anguish. "Oh, that."

"Yes, that. Let me hear it one time, Rosalyn, and then I promise you I will never bring it up or ask about it ever again."

She drew in a breath, expelling it loudly. "I suppose you deserve that."

"I think I do." He took her hand and gently rubbed his thumb over her knuckles.

Rosalyn took another deep breath. "I met Leod Marshall in Edinburgh at a charity function. His family owned a cannery and was moderately wealthy. He was also very handsome and charming."

She closed her eyes briefly against the memories that washed over her. "He wooed me and we married within six months." She gave Fletcher a rueful smile. "Not against my better judgment either—I was eager to wed."

Things had gone well at first. Leod worked hard and was often gone in the evenings. She had prepared herself for that, because the cannery was now in his care since his father died.

"I got pregnant quickly." She glanced at Fletcher and gave him a sad smile. "Which should be good news for you, I suspect."

He squeezed her hand but said nothing.

Rosalyn went on to tell him about how, after a few months, Leod became secretive. She couldn't reach him at the cannery when she needed to, and she didn't know where he was or what he was doing.

"We had trouble keeping help, which I didn't understand because I tried very hard not to be overly critical or demanding." She shook her head. "But the girls, some of them very young and others with babies of their own, rarely stayed more than a couple of weeks. Except for our cook, Marvella."

She noted Fletcher's frown. "Yes, it's the same Marvella who works for you now. Geddes brought her here after—well, you'll find out."

"Why? Because Leod had died? " he asked.

"You'll understand in a while," she answered cryptically.

About six months into the marriage, Rosalyn discovered that Leod often lied to her about his whereabouts. Quite accidentally she learned he spent time with a mistress. Although she wasn't happy about it, she realized that many men did similar things and she was pregnant anyway, so it caused her little real concern.

"Doesn't sound very promising for a newly married couple, does it?"

Again he said nothing, but continued to stroke her hand.

It wasn't until her daughter was born that she learned of some truly heinous things about Leod, things she had never believed one person could do to another, and that she even thought about leaving him. But he was strong and controlling and attempted to convince her that she had driven him to such depths, although he couldn't tell her why. Rosalyn wasn't easily controlled, and had she not had a baby to think of, she might very well have left him.

"Oh, Fletcher, what I learned is so monstrous I can barely abide saying it aloud." Nausea rose in her throat.

He took her hand to his lips and kissed it. "This once, Rosalyn, and then never again."

She took a deep breath. "Marvella came to me one day, distraught. She had been bringing her young daughter to work with her, as she had no one to watch her." Rosalyn bit down on her lip, the memory bringing tears to her eyes. "Poor thing, she was so very distressed and I could see she didn't want to tell me what was amiss, but I could also sense she simply had to tell someone." Rosalyn took in a deep breath, letting it out slowly.

"She told me that her little girl, who was perhaps six or seven years old at the time, had begun to resist accompanying her to work. I thought that was odd, because the child seemed to have a wonderful time helping me care for the baby. But there were many times, when my little Fiona was sleeping, that I wouldn't see the girl at all, sometimes for hours. Still, I thought nothing of it." Rosalyn put her face in her hands.

"I learned that at first, Leod had been taking her for little walks and buying her sweets, probably to gain her trust. In the end, he had—oh, God, I hope he's burning in hell—he had been… molesting her." She sobbed on a shuddered breath, and put her head on Fletcher's shoulder.

"Every time I think about it I feel soiled, dirty. And I ache for every wee lassie who had the misfortune to come in contact with him."

He drew her close. "You aren't to blame; you know that, don't you?"

"In theory, I suppose you're right. But why didn't I notice anything? Why didn't I probe deeper into the reasons our servants kept quitting? I was certain I hadn't been to blame, but with Leod gone so much, how could I have thought it was he who was to blame? I was so naïve. You see," she added, "we had many young girls with us, some as young as twelve, and I always encouraged the others to bring their young children to work. At least then I knew they would come. So, when it comes right down to it, it was my fault."

Fletcher drew her closer. "Leod probably had had this fondness for little girls long before he ever met you, Rosalyn. I don't think there's anything you could have done to prevent his behavior."

She didn't answer, but said instead, "It took a long time for me to gather the courage to leave him. And then when I did, he found me and kidnapped my daughter, and then they both died." Tears welled, spilling over onto her cheeks.

"Leod was selfish to the core—he couldn't simply kill himself, he had to take my daughter with him."

They sat in silence for a long moment. Rosalyn was glad she'd bared her soul.

"My dear Rosalyn," Fletcher whispered against her ear. "I'm sorry you had to live that life."

"I had my beautiful daughter for such a short time, yet I think of her every day. Every day."

"You've had so much to do lately, getting ready for the children." He stood and pulled her up. "Go to bed, love. Try to get some rest."

She held his hand. "Only if you'll join me."

He looked skeptical. "We can just sleep, Rosalyn."

She smiled at him. "Why don't we go to bed and find out just what will happen?"

• • •

Geddes paced, rubbing his hand over the back of his neck, hoping to ease the tension that had settled there. The *Sea Mistress*, the ship carrying the duke's siblings, had encountered rough seas and would be delayed at least a week, perhaps longer. Geddes was not necessarily a religious man, but he prayed that whatever power there was would keep those children safe. He had no idea how he would tell the duke if something happened to them. He shuddered at the thought. He coughed, the sound coming from deep within his chest, and he swore. Now was not the time to fall ill.

He crossed to the window of the room he had rented and gazed at the fishing port where dozens of boats were docked, some waiting to unload their catches. The smell from the waterfronts had never bothered him; he prided himself at being an islander, never having lived in the highlands.

He checked his pocket watch and shook his head. What was he to do now? With another curse, he put on his hat and drew his coat around him against the chill. He left in search of a pub. Maybe a pint of ale could conjure up a picture of the widow Begley; at least then he'd have something pleasant to think about.

• • •

When Rosalyn woke the next morning, her husband was gone from her bed. She gave herself a lazy smile and stretched beneath the covers. Aye, it was nice to have a man in bed next to her. It felt right.

There was a knock on the door.

"Yes?"

Annie poked her head around and announced, "His Grace

asked me to give you this." She crossed to the bed and handed Rosalyn the note. What was it with him and notes?

Annie rocked back and forth, waiting for a response.

"Is he waiting for an answer?"

"He didna say," Annie said.

Rosalyn shook her head and opened the note. Immediately upon reading it she felt a frisson of fear. *Wife—please come to the stables immediately. I am in need of your help.* Frowning, she glanced up at Annie. "No, that's fine. I'll take care of it."

After Annie left, Rosalyn hurried to dress and rushed down the stairs, truly concerned that her husband might somehow in jeopardy. Or perhaps he needed her to help with one of the horses. She all but ran to the stables. "Your Grace?"

"Back here," he answered from the tack room. He sounded as if he were in pain.

"Is something wrong?" Rosalyn's concern spread, for he didn't turn to face her. "Your note said you needed me."

He slowly turned to her and smiled. "Indeed I do."

She glanced down and saw that his trousers were tented over his groin. She felt a thrill followed by a stab of annoyance. "You mean you made me rush out here because of that? I thought there was something seriously wrong with you."

He gave her that grin that melted her. "My dear Rosalyn, there is most definitely something wrong with me, and only you can help." He started to undo his leather breeches.

Rosalyn glanced surreptitiously around, as if someone would walk in on them. "Here? You want to do it here?"

He continued to grin at her. "Do what, Rosalyn?"

Her pulse began to throb and she ached between her legs. "You know very well what."

He continued to undress. "You have to say it. And while you're thinking of the right answer, slip out of your drawers."

She went back and peeked out the door. "Where's Evan?"

"I sent him on an errand," he said behind her.

She turned and found him naked. Beautiful, proud and naked. "Why here?"

"Why not?" he said, starting toward her. "It's earthy. I love doing it in places that remind me of raw animal heat."

She gave him a saucy look. "Do what?"

"You know what."

Feeling brave and a bit indecent, she said, "You'd better say the words before I slip out of my unmentionables."

He moved close, his erection dangerously close to her arm, and whispered something in her ear.

Her knees nearly buckled with raw desire. "I guess that'll have to do." She kicked her drawers away from her and stood before him.

"Now undo your bodice," he ordered. "I want to see your breasts."

She accommodated him, wincing just a little when her clothing raked over her nipples. Although her breasts were a bit tender, she allowed him to fondle them, for he did it so very gently. When he bent and took one nipple into his mouth, she gasped and held onto his arms, for otherwise she would have fallen to the tack room floor.

"Come, sit on my lap," he said.

They made their way to the bench along the wall and he pulled her onto him, inserting himself inside her. They sat that way for a while, neither moving nor barely breathing. She squeezed him with the muscles she had down there, and he sucked in a hiss of air. "If you continue to do that, this will be over before it gets started."

Although she shook with yearning, she said, "Is that all it takes?"

"Under the right circumstances, yes." His voice was deep and husky.

"And what are they?" She sounded breathless.

"This. Being inside you. Here, in a room full of leather and harnesses and the smell of sex as it radiates from our bodies like heady perfume. The fragrance of sex; nothing is more heady." He spoke against her ear; his breath moved the fine hairs along her hairline.

She could only agree. The feeling began, that itch, that unattainable feeling that spread through her blood with a hotness and wetness that was like no other she'd ever known. She whimpered against his neck. "Your Grace…I…it's…" And there it was, opening her, taking her breath away, digging deeper and deeper into an intoxication that she'd only felt with him.

He thrust deeper, growling into her ear, and then he took her mouth and swallowed the scream of pleasure that told him she was satisfied.

She sagged against him, her face wet with sweat and tears. "Oh, my." She felt him chuckle against her. "Oh, my, indeed."

They stayed like that, as if melted together as one person, until Rosalyn heard a noise. She sat up with a start and put a finger to her lips. Someone moved around in the stable.

"Aye, Ahote," Evan crooned. "Where be your master?"

Rosalyn clamped her lips together and her eyes widened. She looked at his lordship, her expression alone asking him what they should do.

His lordship drew her close and whispered very softly into her ear. "It's all right; we're married."

She opened her mouth to say something, then clamped it shut again, gave him a stern glare, and quickly buttoned up her bodice.

Bringing her close again, he whispered, "You're no fun." Then he slowly and quietly helped her off his lap and pulled on his breeches.

Suddenly Evan was at the door, his mouth open and his eyes wide. "Oh! I didna know you were here, Your Grace." He turned to Rosalyn and nodded.

Rosalyn furtively kicked her drawers under a worktable.

"It's all right, Evan," the duke said, "I was just showing her ladyship something."

Rosalyn rolled her eyes as she hurried from the stable. Indeed, he had showed her something. She would deal with him later. How could she have allowed him to put her in such a position? *Easily*, her little voice said. *Oh, so easily*. She took the stairs to her room, her breast brushing against the edge of the door as she entered. She winced again as she had earlier with Fletcher. Slowly, she made her way to her dressing table and sat down, working through the weeks and months since he had arrived. How long had he been here? It had been over three months since his entrance into their lives. And over two months since.... She put her hand to her mouth and closed her eyes. Yes, she could certainly be pregnant. It would be her secret for now, if it were true. Time would tell all.

• • •

Rosalyn had noticed the tension in her husband's stance for the past week, ever since he'd heard that Geddes would finally arrive any day now with his siblings in tow. So when the messenger rode up with the news that they would all be arriving later in the afternoon, Fletcher relaxed visibly. "I can't believe they're really here, Rosalyn. Finally, after these many months. I'm too antsy. I think I'll take Ahote out for a run."

Rosalyn watched him go and then went upstairs to make sure each of the bedchambers was in order. Yes, these many months, indeed. It was already May, she was pregnant, and there was peace at the castle. Everything seemed so perfect. But perfection never lasted forever. When she was satisfied, she checked with the kitchen staff to ensure the evening meal would be special. When she had done everything to prepare for Fletcher's siblings' arrival, she retired to her room and attempted to do some hand work.

She must have dozed for some hours, because when she woke long shadows crept along the floor. And the hounds were baying. Then she heard the carriage. When it stopped in front of the castle, Rosalyn rose from her chair and pulled aside the gauzy curtain.

Part of her wanted to rush downstairs immediately, throw open the door, and greet the children as if she'd known them all their lives. Another part of her held back, waiting, instead, to watch as they exited the carriage.

The first out was a tall lad, finely built and handsome, like Fletcher. The next lad out was fair as she was. His hair was the color of wheat and very curly, clinging to his scalp like a cap. He squinted, as if the brightness bothered his eyes. He took in his surroundings, then bent down and scratched one of the young hounds behind its ears, not taking his eyes off the castle. His gaze rose to the window where Rosalyn stood and she stopped herself from stepping back into the shadows. He gave her a brief smile, one she returned with a small wave of her hand. Gavin, she thought.

Geddes stepped out next, then reached back and helped the young lassie to the ground. Rosalyn nearly gasped at the girl's beauty. Her dark, almost black hair hung in long, soft curls over her shoulders and her face was so striking Rosalyn blinked repeatedly, for she didn't believe anyone could be that perfectly made.

But it was her demeanor that drew Rosalyn's attention. She didn't smile like the other two and she didn't even give Geddes a glance after he'd helped her exit the carriage. She hugged herself and stood, looking around her as if she would rather be somewhere else. Anywhere but here. But it was too early to make judgments, and really, wasn't Rosalyn being a little presumptuous? After all, the child had been dragged from her homeland. How else was she to feel?

The last to get off the carriage was a rather dour-looking young woman whose pale, lifeless hair was pulled back severely and whose clothing was drab and unremarkable. Rosalyn shivered. The chaperone.

Fletcher raced from the stables and reached the carriage, where he drew his sister in his arms. She hugged him and smiled and that beautiful face lit up, making her seem almost angelic.

Turning from the window, Rosalyn pulled in a deep breath and made her way toward the door, eager, yet anxious, to meet her new family. There was a tiny feeling that they might resent her. She wasn't so naïve to believe that everyone liked her; she'd learned years ago that it took very little for some people to actually dislike others.

Whatever the outcome, they were here and she would do her very best to make them feel at home.

Chapter Eighteen

Rosalyn need not have worried about the boys. They were exuberant, with a mixture of the boldness of colts and the strength of young stallions.

After introductions had been made, Fletcher grabbed both boys by the shoulders and hugged them gruffly, his own enthusiasm bubbling over, as youthful as theirs.

Kerry had given Rosalyn a cautious look, as if she wondered exactly how she was to respond to this woman who had married her brother. And she was a little distant, but Rosalyn chose to overlook that. The girl needed time to adapt. That was all.

Kerry clung to Fletcher. When he suggested that she go inside and find her bedchamber, she said she'd rather be with him. He had given Rosalyn a look that said, *Don't worry, she's just shy*, and the five of them, including the chaperone, left for the stables. Rosalyn and Geddes were left alone in front of the entry to the castle.

"So tell me, dear brother, how did you fare with the three of them? Did they obey you?"

Geddes chuckled. "Obey might not be the right word, I'm afraid. They certainly are spirited youngsters, I'll give you that. But the boys are easily amused. Although they are as different as two lads can be, they are inquisitive and amiable. They got on well with the ship's crew."

Rosalyn hid a small smile. "And Kerry?"

Geddes drew in a sigh. "She and the chaperone stayed to themselves much of the time." He shook his head. "Dorcas Blessing. Not much of a blessing, in my mind."

Curious, Rosalyn asked, "Why do you say that?"

"It's just a feeling I have. She seemed to want to keep Kerry separated from the boys; I can't imagine why. Maybe it was my imagination. But I can tell you, sister, Kerry is smart as a whip. Everything she learns and sees seems to be stored like an image in her mind, for she can repeat a conversation word for word, days after it was spoken. And just to test my theory, I gave her twelve objects to study for only a few seconds, and without any hesitation she rattled them off in order. She even repeated them again later for me." He shook his head in wonder. "She even knew how to calculate fathoms. What kind of child knows such things?"

Rosalyn watched as the chaperone returned from the stables and instructed the servants as the luggage was unloaded. She didn't always agree with her brother's intuitions, so as she watched Miss Blessing, she decided she would wait and judge for herself the kind of young woman she was.

It didn't take her long to realize that her brother's suspicions were right.

Dorcas Blessing walked up to her and, without preamble, said, "I don't know what accommodations you have for me, madam, but I will have to insist that I stay with Kerry in her bedchamber. She's frightened, she's alone, and she needs my support."

Rosalyn drew in a breath. *Well*, she thought, *that didn't take long.* "I have prepared a nice suite for you just down the hallway from Kerry. I should think that would be sufficient. You would both have your privacy, yet you could keep in touch with her at any time."

The woman began shaking her head before Rosalyn had finished speaking. "No. I'm afraid that won't do. I must stay with her. Surely it doesn't matter to you. It would be one less room your servants would have to keep clean."

What harm could it do? In truth, it would lessen the load on the servants.

"Are you truly that worried about Kerry?" she asked. "Surely she will settle in once she feels a bit more comfortable."

Miss Blessing stepped closer. "I know you aren't aware of how the children were found or what the circumstances were, but I assure you, Kerry does not like to be alone."

Rosalyn frowned. How the children were found? Their circumstances? That sounded very distressing, indeed. She would have to ask Geddes about it. "I will send one of the serving girls in to prepare the spare bed in Kerry's chamber," Rosalyn offered.

Dorcas Blessing emitted a sigh of relief, and her shoulders relaxed somewhat. "I apologize for sounding high-handed, madam. The children have been in my care and have been my responsibility since before we embarked. I've grown quite fond of them, especially Kerry. The boys have had each other for company but Kerry has been quite alone. You can understand my need to protect her."

Rosalyn raised her eyebrows a fraction. Perhaps Geddes had been wrong about her after all. "Of course. We all want what's best for them, and anything we can do to make their transition here easier is our ultimate goal."

Dorcas smiled at her. "Thank you."

Evan arrived, driving the small, two-person carriage, reining in the steed in front of them. He hopped down from the seat swiftly and stood before Rosalyn, his hat in his hands.

"Yes, Evan?"

"Ma'am, I was passing by Miz Begley's and she stopped me and asked that you come see her right away."

Alarmed, Rosalyn asked, "Did she say why?"

"No, ma'am. She seemed a mite upset, though."

Rosalyn threw a glance at the stables and then toward the castle. She couldn't just leave without alerting someone as to why she was gone.

"Miss Blessing," she said, turning to the chaperone, "would you please explain to everyone that I have had to answer an emergency? I'll return as soon as I can."

The chaperone nodded, but said nothing.

Rosalyn went inside, grabbed her cape and her gloves, and returned to the carriage, and she and Evan were off.

• • •

She heard the noise before they even stopped in front of Fen's cottage. Wailing, bawling children.

Hurrying inside, she called, "Fen?"

From the kitchen, she heard Fen's reply. "In here."

Rosalyn rushed into the kitchen, where she noticed two little ones clinging to Fen's chest like animated bookends.

"What's this?"

Fen was clearly frazzled. "In all my days as a camp nurse, I never had this much frustration with my patients."

Rosalyn lifted one of the children off her and brought the bairn to her own chest. A sudden jab of pain sliced through her, and for a very brief moment, she remembered holding her darling Fiona.

"What's wrong with them?"

Fen shushed the child, bouncing him up and down, trying to calm him. "They both have fevers and have been wailing since their mother dropped them off. Twins, they are."

Rosalyn rocked the child gently, patting his back. "Whose are they?"

"They belong to the parson's sister. She's come to visit, and they arrived with this fever. The mother was no help at all, wailing louder than the bairns. I sent her home."

Rosalyn sat and held out her free arm for the other child so Fen could prepare cool compresses. After they had gotten the fevers down far enough that the little ones could sleep, Fen and Rosalyn collapsed on the settee in the parlor.

"Thank you for coming, dear. This all happened so suddenly, and I wasn't prepared. I guess I had better learn to be now, since our drunken sot of a doctor has left the island permanently."

"You're going to need me more often now than you did before," Rosalyn mused.

Fen glanced at her, appearing to note hesitancy in her voice. "Is that a problem?"

Rosalyn shook her head. "No, I've always assumed I would help you. It's just that…"

"What?"

"His Grace's siblings arrived today."

Fen gasped. "Oh, blast. Why didn't you just send Evan back with that news? I would have managed this somehow, you know that."

"No, it's all right. I should get back, though, if you think things will go smoothly from now on."

"Of course. Go. But before you do, tell me what you think of them."

Rosalyn drew in a long breath. "I haven't really had time, Fen. But the boys, Duncan and Gavin, are energetic and curious. His lordship took them to the stables straight off and I believe they will each have chosen a pony before dinner."

"They sound delightful. And, what about the girl?"

Rosalyn's smile was rueful. "Ah. Kerry. That may be another story altogether. The chaperone, Dorcas Blessing, whom Geddes is quite certain has slanted the truth about everything to Kerry, is a mild, stark-looking woman. She insisted right off that she stay in Kerry's room, not wishing a room of her own. I'm trying not to rush to judgment, but…" Rosalyn rubbed her forehead. "Oh, I don't know. It's all so new. We'll see how things work out."

"You sound unsettled."

"Well, the girl wasn't exactly friendly, but maybe I'm just sensitive. I don't want to think the worst of someone. I'll give it some time, I guess, that's all I can do. And Fen, she is the most exquisite young lass I have ever seen. Such beauty! And when she saw her brother, you could tell that in her eyes, he hangs out the moon."

"Aye, he could have that effect on women." Fen stood. "We can talk later. You'd best get back before you're missed. I don't want to be responsible for your absence."

Rosalyn stood as well. "I did tell the chaperone where I was going. I hope she passed the message along."

Rosalyn stopped at the door. She had to tell someone her little secret—who better than Fen? "Fen?"

Fen was beside her immediately. "What's wrong?"

Rosalyn shook her head. "'Tis only that…I think I'm pregnant."

Fen pulled her around to face her. "Are you sure?"

Nodding, Rosalyn said, "I've been through this before, remember?"

"And how do you feel about it?"

Uncertain excitement fluttered in Rosalyn's stomach. "I don't know yet. It's so early."

"You think it happened right off?"

"Aye, I'm certain of it."

"Well, if it's so, then you must let me check you regularly. Will you promise?"

With a nod, Rosalyn hugged her friend and left.

But when Rosalyn walked into the roomy castle foyer, Geddes and His Grace were there, both apparently loaded for bear, so to speak.

"Where in the devil have you been?" Geddes glared at her.

Fletcher, his arms crossed over his chest, simply stood there, waiting for her answer.

Surprised by their behavior, Rosalyn hung up her cape and answered, "Fen had an emergency. I asked Miss Blessing to tell you where I was going."

"And Mrs. Begley's 'emergency' was more important than making His Grace's siblings feel comfortable their first moments here?"

Rosalyn frowned. "Actually, yes. Since the doctor has left the island, Fen is alone in treating the ill. But had she known His Grace's brothers and sister had just arrived, she would never have asked for my help, you can be sure of that. So don't go blaming Fen for my absence. The blame, if there is any, is entirely mine."

Geddes scowled. "I swear—"

"Don't," Rosalyn interrupted. "Perhaps it was a poor decision on my part to leave for a while, but don't blame Fen. Now that she's alone, treating everyone and anyone who needs her, and possibly even those who don't want her help, I'll be assisting her more often, and I don't intend to shirk any of my duties here. So I don't want either of you complaining, do you hear me?"

"She's right, Geddes," Fletcher began. "The children and I have just returned from the stables as it is. Rosalyn has prepared everything so well she didn't need to hang around until we came back inside."

"But," Rosalyn said, "didn't Miss Blessing tell you where I'd gone?"

"Neither of us has seen her since she went up to her bedchamber," Geddes informed her.

Well, thought Rosalyn, perhaps Geddes was right about her after all. She studied her brother, really looking at him for the first time. "Geddes, you look awful. Are you ill?"

Geddes coughed. It was a cavernous sound, hoarse and raspy, one that came from deep within his chest. "It's nothing, just something I picked up on the trip."

Startled, she felt his face. "You're burning up!" Now she felt guilty because she'd been ranting about the necessity of her trip to Fen's when she should have been paying attention to what was going on right under her nose.

Geddes seemed to shrink. "Yes. If you two don't mind, I think I'll skip supper and go straight to bed." Without waiting for a response, he slowly took the stairs to his bedchamber.

Rosalyn watched his ascent. "How could I have been so blind?"

"You've had quite a bit on your mind, Rosalyn."

"I know, but…" She gasped and turned to face him. "Oh, about the children! They seem like lovely young people, really they do."

He gave her a boyish grin, one that reached inside and continued to thaw her. "They are, aren't they? Of course," he added, his face changing, "I can't take any credit for that. Had it been up to me, they all might well have been hoodlums."

She thought about what Miss Blessing had said about their condition when they'd been found, still determined to discuss it with Geddes. "Nonsense. I watched them when they saw you; their eyes and their smiles expressed how they feel about you."

"I hope you and Kerry can be friends," he said.

"Well, of course," she answered, carefully hiding her misgivings. "Why wouldn't we?"

"She's never really had a woman to look up to, you know. She was just a little girl when her mother died."

"She's still a little girl, Your Grace."

"But a beauty, wouldn't you say?"

Rosalyn touched his arm, feeling his strength. "Aye. She's the most beautiful child I have ever seen."

Rosalyn recalled what Geddes had said about Kerry and the chaperone, how they had been nearly inseparable on the voyage. She wasn't ready to share with her husband Geddes's opinion about the woman. "She and Miss Blessing seem quite comfortable with each other."

"The chaperone won't be here forever. I don't want Kerry getting so close to her that she'll grieve when the woman leaves."

Rosalyn thought that perhaps it was already too late for that, but she said nothing.

They walked past the library and Rosalyn saw a light under the door. "I wonder who's in there."

Fletcher pushed the door open, and Dorcas Blessing turned quickly from in front of the desk. "Miss Blessing? Can we help you?"

"No. Well, actually, I was looking for some notepaper; I must write a letter to my superiors."

Rosalyn crossed to the desk, pulled open a drawer, and handed the chaperone the materials she would need to post a letter. For a brief moment Rosalyn thought the woman might have been snooping, but she scolded herself. After Geddes's warning, Rosalyn would probably see goblins in every corner.

The three of them left the library and Fletcher and Rosalyn watched Miss Blessing take the stairs to Kerry's room.

"My goodness," said Rosalyn. "It didn't take her long to make herself at home, did it?"

"She'll be leaving soon enough," Fletcher answered.

Rosalyn remembered Geddes's warning. "I wonder how that will affect Kerry in the long run."

Fletcher turned to her, surprised. "Why should it bother her? Oh, she may miss her at first, but she'll have you. Trust me, if there was a choice to be made, you would win, hands down." He pulled her close and they mounted the stairs together.

Rosalyn wasn't so sure, but she refused to argue. This was only the first day, and considering everything, she thought things had gone quite well. They could only get better. Or not.

Chapter Nineteen

Fen had just finished her morning coffee and had sent her tiny patients back to their mother when there was a knock at the door. She opened it to find Evan standing on her doorstep. Studying him briefly, she realized that he had begun to grow up. His scraggly hair had been cut and combed, his face was scrubbed clean, and he was really quite handsome. He showed great potential, she thought.

"Yes, Evan?"

The lad shifted nervously from foot to foot, his hat in his hand. "The mistress asked that I fetch you because Mister Geddes is ill."

A surprising tenseness grew low in her stomach, as if she'd eaten something not quite ripe. Evan waited outside with the carriage while she collected what she would need to take with her. "Leave it to that man to provide me with a bellyache."

As they rode up the drive to the castle, Fen saw the girl, Kerry, sitting on the steps, eyeing them with skepticism.

As Fen stepped from the carriage, a brisk wind picked up her cape and swirled it around behind her.

The girl looked up at her, one eyebrow raised. "Are you a witch?"

Fen studied her. She was, indeed, ravishing. Fen gave her a wry smile. "Some might think so. But today I'm here to check on Mr. Gordon. I hear he's ill." She noticed that the girl moved her gaze to Evan, settling on him with interest.

"So, who are you, anyway?"

"I'm a friend of Rosalyn's. You know—your brother's wife."

"I know who she is," the girl replied, sounding disinterested and annoyed.

"She's been very excited about your arrival."

"What could she possibly want me here for?" The girl absently gnawed at a fingernail.

Fen raised an eyebrow. "I'm sure you'll have to ask her that, but I know she's delighted that the three of you are here."

The girl harrumphed, rose from the steps, and sauntered toward the stables.

Hmmm, thought Fen. *That went well, didn't it?* Kerry was going to need some special handling. Not the kind with kid gloves, but perhaps the kind with a firmer hand.

She was about to lift the huge metal door knocker when the door opened and the old valet stood looking at her. "Yes?"

"Hello, Barnaby. I'm here to see Mr. Gordon. I hear he's unwell."

The old man gave her a gallant, if somewhat unsteady, bow, turned, and said, "This way."

She followed him up the stairs as he broke wind all the way, sounding every bit like a poorly tuned piccolo.

She rapped lightly on the door she was shown to and heard a raspy voice telling her to enter.

Stepping inside, she stopped herself from gasping out loud, for Geddes lay on his bed, propped up with pillows, looking as gray as death.

He gave her a lazy, glassy-eyed glance. "What are you doing here?"

She strode to his bedside and put her basket of goodies on the table beside him. "What do you think? I've brought you a picnic and we're going to spend the day at the loch."

He coughed and drew in a heavy breath. "I dare say you'll probably poison me."

Smiling gaily, she said, "Don't tempt me. Now unbutton your shirt."

"Why?" he groused.

She reached into her basket and pulled out a poultice. "Because I'm going to put this on your chest."

He coughed again and made a face. "It smells like something died."

"It does not. It smells like mint. Now open your shirt or I'll have to do it for you."

He sighed and began unbuttoning his shirt, revealing, to Fen's surprise and delight, a chest full of tawny hair so thick she was tempted to sink her fingers into it.

Deftly, so as not to linger too obviously, she pressed the poultice over his chest and covered it with a length of flannel and then buttoned his shirt over it to keep it in place.

She then reached into the basket and drew out a flask. "Now I have some tea for you to drink."

"Tea!" He nearly spat out the word. "Some nurse you are. Why do women think tea cures everything?"

She raised her eyebrows and poured him a cupful. "Just taste it."

He did, under duress, and drew back, surprised. "There's whisky in it."

"Of course. I think you need a good shot of it every few hours, but don't overdo it or you'll simply have a hangover."

He took another sip and then another as he studied her. "How long have you been a widow?"

"Longer than I was married," she answered.

"Who was your husband?"

Fen straightened the remainder of the items in her basket as she spoke. "Ewan Begley was an army man. He fell in the Caspian."

"I'm sorry," Geddes said. "Were you very much in love?"

Fen thought the whisky was loosening his tongue, but didn't remark on it. In fact, she rather liked this softer side of him. "I was. I never do anything casually, Mr. Gordon. I didn't enter matrimony casually either. I had thought I could do quite nicely without a man in my life until I met him. It will sound clichéd, but the moment I laid eyes on him I knew I would marry him."

"It must be wonderful to be that certain of someone else." His voice was slurred; the whisky had mellowed him greatly. "Do you still miss him?"

Fen paused, running her fingers over the piece of lamb's wool she often used for padding a broken limb. "Interesting question. We were together for less than three years and in that time, we never lived together in the conventional way. He was always at war, and I was always patching up the wounded. But yes," she said, "I do miss him. Not like I did at first, but there's a level of emptiness that never seems to completely disappear."

Geddes drained his cup and handed it to her, gesturing for more.

Fen shook her head. "No refills for you, not yet. I'll see that Rosalyn gives you another cup before bedtime. Until then, I suggest you sleep."

He smiled and it was the first time she had ever seen him totally unguarded. And he was beautiful.

• • •

Rosalyn met Fen on the stairs. "How is he?"

"He'll live. It's probably just some kind of croup. He has no fever this morning, but that doesn't mean it won't crop up again tonight." She dug into her basket and drew out the flask.

"Give him a cup of this before bedtime, but not before. It will help him sleep."

Rosalyn uncapped it and sniffed. "Whisky?"

"Partly. That's why he shouldn't have any more until he's ready to retire, else he'll just suffer the rest of the day."

Rosalyn slipped the flask into her apron pocket.

Adolescent laughter erupted from downstairs.

Fen took Rosalyn's arm as they descended. "They seem to be making themselves at home."

"The lads, aye. They are strapping and handsome and full of life."

Nodding, Fen answered, "I met Kerry on the steps as I rode up." She raised her brows and shook her head. "You're right; she's a beauty, but you've got your hands full with that one."

"I know. But I think she's merely protecting herself. You know how children can be, better to act tough than to show your vulnerabilities."

"I hope you're right and that's all it is."

"As do I," Rosalyn responded. They arrived in the foyer. "I'll have Evan take you home."

Fen shook her head. "No need. The walk will do me good."

As she started down the road she turned back and briefly glanced up toward Geddes's room. Her heart gave a little bump when she saw him standing there, watching her leave.

* * *

Rosalyn worked through the wave of nausea, the second one of the day. If she weren't absolutely certain of it before, she knew for sure now: she was pregnant. But it would still be her secret. And Fen's. Her husband had enough on his plate; he didn't need to worry about her.

She went to Geddes's room and found him resting in a comfortable chair by the window. He glanced up. "Good morning."

She responded with the same, and went to sit on the hassock in front of him. Recalling her discussion with Miss Blessing, she said, "Tell me what the conditions were in which the children were found."

"Conditions? Well, indeed their grandfather had died."

"And they were left alone, to fend for themselves?" If Fletcher ever learned that, he'd never forgive himself. Ever.

Geddes frowned. "No, not at all."

"No? Then…"

"They were—well, Gavin and Kerry were staying with some of her Comanche relatives. I learned that it is not unusual at all for orphaned children to be taken in by family."

"So, they were fine?"

"Yes, mostly. Kerry was concerned because Duncan had declared himself an adult and had gone off alone. He was found working on a nearby ranch. It seems it took some doing to get him to agree to accompany the other two."

Rosalyn nibbled at her lower lip. Odd that Miss Blessing would make it sound like the children had been in danger. "Well, I'm happy about that. Do you need another of Fen's potions?"

He smiled. "No whisky this morning."

As she descended the stairs she met Kerry and Miss Blessing, their heads together, speaking in near whispers.

Rosalyn pasted on a smile to mask her unsettled stomach. "What have you two got planned?"

Kerry gazed off, looking beyond Rosalyn's shoulder, not meeting her eyes. Miss Blessing bent her head slightly in acknowledgment and then said, "I thought we'd take a stroll around the grounds. Would you care to join us?"

Immediately Kerry nudged the chaperone with her elbow and frowned.

Rosalyn got the picture. "Oh, no, thank you. But if you're going to walk along the seashore, I suggest you take a wrap. It's colder than you think down by the water."

Again, Miss Blessing nodded, but the two of them disappeared outside, neither wearing a cape.

Rosalyn shook her head, wondering why she bothered to be civil when it was obvious those two didn't care a whit. She went to the solarium, settled into a comfortable chair, and picked up her sewing. Sima and her pup, Bonnie, were already there, napping. Rosalyn studied the bunting she was making, quite sure no one would wonder what it was. She had kept it to herself, not wanting to explain to anyone else why she was doing it. She felt so very protective of this child that grew within her. It was almost as if she feared something would happen to it if the news were made public.

She thought back to Geddes's suggestion that she get pregnant to replace her sweet Fiona. She frowned and shook her head as she continued to make tiny stitches in the soft fabric. Men did not understand that there was no such thing as a replacement for a child.

Hearing the sound of horses beating a path over the lawn, she glanced outside just in time to see His Grace and his brothers racing over the grass—oh, no! Racing over the grass toward her rose garden!

She stood, her sewing falling to the floor, and raced from the room. "Oh, no. No, no, no!"

By the time she got outside they had ridden out of sight and her roses…She stifled a sob. Her rose garden was in shambles.

She crossed to the patch that she had spent so many hours cultivating. Falling to her knees, she surveyed the damage, and damage it was. Great clods of rich earth were strewn everywhere. Rose petals were flung wide, scattered like refuse over the ground.

The devastation was like a death. When she no longer had a child to rear, she had turned her love and attention toward her gardens, particularly her roses. She spoke to them. They listened and they thrived.

Another sob forced its way into her throat, and she did not swallow it back but allowed it to come forth, with her tears of anger and disappointment.

She knew it was not logical, but she bent over and cried, mourning her loss.

The return of the horses penetrated her sorrow. She looked up to find the three of them, His Grace, Duncan, and Gavin, smiling gaily—until they saw her face.

Just then, Kerry and Miss Blessing rounded the side of the castle as well, and it was as if Rosalyn now had an audience for her grief.

"My garden! Look what you've done to my roses!" And now she could stop neither her weeping nor her fury. "Oafs! Great, clumsy oafs! Auch! Don't you have enough land to gallop over? Aren't there acres upon acres upon which to ride your blasted horses? Did you have to ride right through the only thing out here that is mine, and mine alone? That makes any difference to me?"

Still fuming—and still crying—she marched past all of them into the castle, taking great pains to slam the mighty door behind her.

• • •

Fletcher dismounted and handed the reins to Duncan. "Stable him. And make sure they all have oats and water."

Duncan glanced at the castle. "She was really mad, wasn't she?"

"Truthfully, I've never seen her so angry before. And she's had reason to be so, believe me."

Duncan and Gavin led the mounts to the stable.

Beside Fletcher, Kerry gave a little snort. "Why would she get so upset over some dumb flowers?"

When Fletcher didn't answer, Miss Blessing did.

"I imagine she has worked hard in her garden. I will say it's quite spectacular. Or…at least it was."

"But," Kerry argued, "flowers aren't people. Shouldn't she be more concerned about people?"

Fletcher drew Kerry close; she burrowed against him. "Rosalyn takes pride in her gardens, Kerry. The boys and I got carried away. They aren't to blame. I, of all people, should have known better than to ride so close to the flower beds.

"And now," he said, "off with you two. I must go find my bride and mend some fences. Or, plant some gardens, as it were."

He went first to the solarium, which was where he knew Rosalyn took solace. She wasn't there, but he noticed something on the floor by her chair. He picked it up and studied it, his heart racing. He might be a great oaf, but he knew what it was. He laid it on the chair and strode out into the chilly hallway, intent on going up to his wife's bedchamber.

Instead, he went to the stables and prepared the rig that could take him into the village and leave some room for purchases.

* * *

Rosalyn was not a person who could stay angry for long. Yes, she could explode quite readily, but after the explosion, she usually came around and rued her prior behavior.

Such was the case now. Oh, she certainly was angry that they had so cavalierly trampled her roses. That had been quite thoughtless. But she also realized that when she had seen the destruction, something inside her cracked and weeks of anguish and frustration had poured out of her. Once again she was reliving the pain of losing Fiona. Once again she wanted to destroy Leod before he destroyed her family. Once again she railed at having no control over her past or her future.

People had told her that if only they could have found Fiona's tiny body, perhaps Rosalyn would have had a sense of finality, of laying her sorrow to rest, once and for all. What foolishness! Her sorrow would always be with her. Perhaps it wasn't as acute as it had been, but the hole was still there, the jagged edges of her grief merely softened over time.

She brought her hand to her stomach, certain she'd felt a fluttering, but knowing it was too early for that. Or was it? She counted back to that morning and decided it indeed was possible the bairn had moved. "I wonder what's in store for you, wee one," she mused. "Your father may be a great oaf, but he is a kind and good man. He will not forsake you." But, she wondered, will he abandon her once the heir is born?

Chapter Twenty

Rosalyn awoke late. It had been two weeks since the children had arrived, and Rosalyn had kept busy, making sure everything went smoothly. Although she hadn't seen much of the duke, she had been making a mental list of things she wanted to talk with both him and Geddes about, one of which was the children's schooling. She guessed that they would have to hire tutors or send the children to Ayr, but she was certain her husband did not want that.

She hurried from her bed as the queasiness rose in her throat and just made it to the commode before she experienced her first nausea of the day.

Fletcher hadn't shared her bed since the arrival of his siblings, and although she was curious as to why he hadn't, she refused to dwell on it when she had so many other things to worry about. At any rate, her sleep had been interrupted with wild dreams that awakened her frequently, so it was just as well that she was alone. Or so she told herself.

She stood at the commode and studied her reflection in the mirror. She was pale and there were mauve smudges under her eyes. She knew that these things would pass as they had before. And she also knew that Fletcher had gotten her with child that very first night when, in his fevered sleep, he had believed she was someone else.

Once her morning ailments had passed, she dressed quickly and hurried to Geddes's room. She knocked and he told her to enter.

She poked her head in. "How are you this morning?"

He was in his dressing gown and trousers, sitting in a chair by the window. Two weeks of rest had done him the world of good. "I'm fine."

She stepped into his room. "Do you want some breakfast?"

"A biscuit and jam would be nice," he said.

"I'll bring it right up." She turned to leave.

"Rosalyn?"

She glanced back at him. "Yes?"

Geddes appeared to weigh his words carefully. "Is it true that we now have no physician on the island?"

Rosalyn closed the door and walked toward him. "It's true. The old sot left while you were away."

"Then Mrs. Begley will be quite busy, won't she?"

"I dare say she will," Rosalyn answered, cautiously hopeful. "Why do you ask?"

"I was thinking…well…" He coughed and cleared his throat. "I, that is His Grace and I were thinking that perhaps she needs a bigger space to treat her patients."

Feeling a bump of anticipation, Rosalyn eased herself into a chair beside him. "You…and His Grace?"

"Well, yes. I dare say the doctor's old office space is empty, and it seems a pity to let it simply sit there, unoccupied. Do you…um…do you think she would consider using it, instead of her own home? And even if, at some time down the road, we get another physician, the space is quite ample for both of them."

"And whose decision will that be?"

Geddes looked at her, puzzled. "His Grace's, of course. And perhaps Mrs. Begley's, considering she'll be the only healer on the island for a while."

Rosalyn felt a surge of excitement, but contained it. As if mulling it over, she tapped two fingers against her lips. "Would she be required to pay rent?"

"I…we haven't discussed that yet. First we wanted to see if she was amenable to the situation," he answered, his voice gruff.

Rosalyn wanted to yelp for joy, jump up and down; instead she said, "Perhaps you should talk it over with her, as you have with me. I can't say what her reaction would be, but I can't imagine what reason she would have to turn down such an offer."

Geddes cleared his throat again and scraped a hand over the stubble at his chin. "Yes, well. I'll get on it soon."

Rosalyn stood and moved toward the door. "I'll bring you some breakfast."

Once she was on the stairs she nearly flew down them, her entire demeanor changed from earlier in the morning when she'd felt so wretched. But when she went into the dining room, she found it empty and one of the kitchen girls was clearing the table.

"Everyone has eaten already?" Rosalyn asked, surprised.

The girl curtseyed. "Only His Grace and the boys, mum. Can I get you some breakfast?"

Rosalyn waved her off. "I can get it myself, dear. Thank you. But could you put together a tray for Mr. Gordon? He's hungry for biscuits and jam this morning."

The girl curtseyed again, removed the tray of dirty breakfast dishes, and disappeared into the kitchen.

Rosalyn poured herself some coffee, took a sip, and felt her stomach lurch. No more of that for a few months, she decided.

After preparing a cup of tea, she heard laughter coming from outside. With her cup and saucer in hand, she went to the window. The sight that met her eyes surprised her so she nearly spilled her tea.

Her husband, Duncan, Gavin, and Evan, were planting new rose bushes in her garden! They all worked feverishly, as if they had a timetable to which they adhered. She watched them work, recalling her horrid behavior nearly two weeks before. Until now she had avoided the subject, her nerves as scattered as the ground they had destroyed. How would she apologize? She had ranted and raved like an asylum lunatic. Now, here they all were, planting and digging, hoeing and raking, and even if the plants weren't precisely where she would have put them, she couldn't fault them for trying.

She turned from the window just as Kerry and Dorcas Blessing descended the stairs. The two of them had, Rosalyn decided, become as close as peas in a pod. Perhaps it was time for the overprotective chaperone to say her farewells. Rosalyn would look into it, and happily so. Once out from under Miss Blessing's wing, Kerry might just turn to Rosalyn, and Rosalyn thought it couldn't be too soon. The longer the woman stayed, the harder it would be for Kerry to adjust to life on Hedabarr.

Miss Blessing nodded to Rosalyn as they passed, but Kerry breezed by her as if she were invisible.

"Do you two have plans today?" Rosalyn asked politely.

The chaperone gave her a rare smile. "We had hoped to go into the village. I'm running out of a few essentials and thought I could replenish my supply."

Yes, thought Rosalyn, it was time for the dear woman to bid the island and all its inhabitants farewell. "I would think you would be anxious to return to America, Miss Blessing. Surely you have family there who miss you."

Miss Blessing unfolded a napkin and placed it on Kerry's lap. "No, I'm quite alone." She looked up abruptly as the serving girl entered. "Bring us a full breakfast, and make sure it isn't cold. Yesterday I nearly got a chill from the shirred eggs."

Rosalyn bristled.

The young girl glanced at Rosalyn, her eyes wide.

"Lucy, go ahead. I'm sure what you bring them will be fine."

The girl curtseyed and left the dining room. When she was gone, Rosalyn said, "I don't appreciate your tone with the help, Miss Blessing."

The woman scoffed. "She's just a servant."

"She's a young girl in training. It's hard enough to keep these girls from running off to the mainland. We don't need them leaving because they're treated poorly."

"I beg to differ. It seems to me that if they work under a stern hand, they will learn never to take advantage."

Rosalyn pressed her lips together and then said, "So, you have experience in training servants?"

Dorcas Blessing backed down. "Well, no, but—"

"Then I would appreciate it if you would not attempt to train mine."

Rosalyn left the dining room, and as she was making her way upstairs, she heard Kerry say, "She's mean."

Rosalyn stormed into Geddes's room, taking him by surprise.

He had just finished shaving and was wiping his face with a towel. She exhaled loudly. "When is that woman going back to America?"

Her brother frowned. "The chaperone? We haven't booked passage yet—"

"Well, you'd best do so before I take a broom to her backside," Rosalyn interrupted.

Geddes appeared confused. "What has she done?"

"What hasn't she done? She's taken to bossing the servants and I won't have that. Not here, not ever. They answer to me and certainly don't need a sharp-tongued upstart telling them what to do."

Cautious, Geddes asked, "What else?"

"Kerry is completely dependent on her. The girl doesn't make a move without her, and she ignores me like I don't exist. This morning, the woman even placed Kerry's napkin on her lap, as if she were four years old instead of twelve."

"I'll speak with His Grace—"

"Please do," Rosalyn interrupted again. "The way I'm feeling at this moment, I wouldn't want to approach him on the subject."

She marched toward the door.

"Rosalyn?"

Turning, she snapped, "What?"

"Where's my breakfast?"

Exasperated, Rosalyn said, "Lucy is bringing it up. And for heaven's sake, don't shout at her if your biscuit is cold."

"Can I shout at her if my biscuit is too warm?"

Rosalyn raised one eyebrow. "Sarcasm doesn't suit you, brother, it never has."

• • •

Later, after she had checked all of the bedchambers to make sure they were in order, she went downstairs and stepped into the library. To her surprise, Gavin sat in the overstuffed chair by the window, reading. He looked up when she entered and gave her a shy smile.

"I hope you don't mind if I'm in here," he began.

"Certainly not," Rosalyn said. "This room doesn't get used enough and I don't believe half of these books have ever been off the shelves."

Changing the subject, she said, "Gavin, I must apologize for my awful behavior—over the roses, I mean." She shook her head and gave him a wan smile. "I shouldn't have overreacted. I'm so very sorry. You must have wondered what kind of shrew your brother had married."

Gavin gave her another shy smile. He had a crescent-shaped dimple in his left cheek and his eyes were a startling shade of blue, even indoors. Because he was so much more subdued and never seemed to have cause to complain, he hadn't drawn a lot of attention to himself. But Rosalyn could see now that he would become a very handsome man. "You had every right to be mad. Fletcher was sorry the minute it happened and told us afterwards that he had deserved your anger. He said he knew better, but was so happy to have us here, he didn't think about anything else."

She went to where he sat and perched on the arm of the chair. "Oh, Gavin, I'm happy you're here, too. Really, I couldn't be more pleased, and I want you all to feel comfortable here, for this is your home. I insist on that," she added, smiling slyly.

"I think we do—at least Duncan and I do. As for Kerry, well…"

Rosalyn nodded. "I understand. Can you keep a secret?"

His eyes brightened. "Sure."

"I can't wait for Miss Blessing to board that ship and be on her way back to America."

Gavin chuckled, amused. "She has a way of making Kerry believe every word she says. And that surprises me because Kerry usually has a mind of her own."

"I think…I hope that once the chaperone is gone, Kerry will begin to warm up to me a little bit," Rosalyn murmured.

"She's kind of headstrong, I guess, but she's okay. Before Grandfather died, he taught her to cook. She was only nine. After he died, she somehow kept us fed until we moved in with her relatives."

"Where did you learn to read?"

"In school. Fletcher insisted that we go, even if he wasn't there. That's what Grandfather told us, anyway. Duncan and I went, but Kerry didn't go after her third year. She was busy caring for Grandfather. And us. That didn't keep her from stealing my books from time to time. I'd find them in her bed, under the bed, and once I even found my *History of the Roman Empire* in a dry dishpan under a shelf with a cloth over it, like she was hiding it from me."

"She had a pretty big burden for a little girl," Rosalyn mused, her feelings for the child softening.

"But I don't think she resented it," Gavin answered. "She would do anything to make Fletcher happy."

She left the boy to his reading and stepped out into the hall. She checked the noon and evening menus with the kitchen staff and then felt the need to lie down. The pregnancy was wearing her out and she had months to go. She thought she might see her husband around somewhere, but everything was quiet and his rooms were empty. Not that she expected him to be lolling about inside, but they had never been as far apart as they were now, with the children here. She had certainly been relegated to fourth on his list of priorities. Not that she blamed him for that. She knew what they had together wasn't what fairy tales were made of.

She stepped into her chamber and closed the door behind her. So, then, why was she even thinking about it? It was probably because of her mood swings. One minute she wanted to throw herself into his arms, and the next she wanted to throw something at him. Or throw up. One day all she thought about was the way he had seduced her and made her feel wanted, and the next day she knew it was all probably just because he was a man and had needs and he was legally allowed to bed her.

She crossed the room and drew the heavy curtains against the afternoon sun. Yawning, she slipped off her shoes and lay down on the bed, drawing a warm comforter over her. Within moments, she was asleep.

* * *

Fletcher stepped into the dimly lit room and saw his wife curled up on the bed. He went to the bedside and stared down, studying her. She had smudges of color beneath her eyes, as if she hadn't been getting enough sleep. Her sweet mouth was open slightly as she breathed, and one hand was curled into a fist, under her chin.

This was not like her at all. She never slept during the day; she was always busy with one chore or another. And he believed he knew why this had changed. He put the gift box he was carrying on the table and then sank into one of the chairs near the bed.

After discovering the bunting, he had begun to watch her carefully. At one point, Rosalyn was talking with one of the housemaids. Her hands automatically went to the small of her back as she spoke, as if there were discomfort there. He continued to study her, and saw how little she ate, only picking at her food. He had noticed her paleness, too, and the tiredness in her eyes.

Since he'd come here, she'd done everything for him. Married him to keep the fortune in the family. Kept his household together. Welcomed his family into her heart as if it were her own. And lastly, carried his heir. Was there anything in this for her, except a child to love?

Maybe that was enough, considering her tragic history. He wanted it to be more, but how could he do that if all she felt for him was gratitude? And there were days when he felt she didn't even have much of that for him.

She stirred and sighed, rolling onto her back, exposing the soft white flesh at her neck.

He felt his own stirrings and wished he could crawl in beside her and draw her to him, make her want him. But he was so conflicted. Now that Duncan, Gavin, and Kerry were here, were he and Rosalyn to have a companionable relationship and nothing else?

He couldn't force her to care for him, much less love him. But he knew there was something in her that made him want to protect her. And maybe he already loved her, he didn't know. Anything other than familial love wasn't something he'd had much experience with.

Geddes had told him about Rosalyn's need to get the chaperone off the island, so Fletcher had made the arrangements immediately. He, too, had noticed how the woman guarded Kerry, keeping her from getting too close to Rosalyn. Or so it appeared. As much as he loved his sister, he knew she needed a firm yet loving and honest hand. That person was his wife, not some paid-for chaperone.

Like it or not, Dorcas Blessing would be out of Kerry's life by the end of the week.

Chapter Twenty-One

Rosalyn found Dorcas Blessing in the dining room, having a cup of tea. "May I join you?" she asked.

Dorcas smiled. "Please do."

Rosalyn fixed herself some tea and took a seat across from the chaperone. "I feel that sometimes we haven't gotten on well together, and I want to apologize for that."

Dorcas blinked and studied her cup. "No, it's not entirely your fault. I've become overly protective of Kerry even though I know there is no reason to now. And I do understand that I must leave here for her to begin to grow." She gave Rosalyn a wan smile. "I've been her protector for a long time. It's hard to let go."

"And Kerry would prefer that you stay here indefinitely, I imagine."

Dorcas nodded. "I warn you that once she learns I'm leaving, there will be hell to pay, so to speak. I'll talk to her, though; she's just at a difficult age. I've been in the employ of other families who had daughters Kerry's age, and somehow, as awful as they seem at the time, they eventually become wonderful young women."

Rosalyn smiled at the thought. "I hope you're right."

• • •

Kerry stormed into the stable, her face pinched with fury. "She made you do it, didn't she?"

Fletcher continued grooming one of the horses. Unflappable, he asked, "What are you talking about?"

Kerry stamped her foot. "You know what I mean. Your wife

talked you into getting rid of my friend, my only friend on this stupid island." Her voice cracked with the threat of tears.

Fletcher stopped and narrowed his gaze at his baby sister. "It's time for Miss Blessing to return to America."

"Then I want to go with her." Kerry stood before him, her arms crossed over her chest, her gaze threatening.

Fletcher had had enough. Setting the grooming brush on a stool, he turned to give her his full attention. "You are going to stay here with your family."

"I don't want to!"

His own temper rising, he said, "That's enough, Kerry. That's quite enough. I don't know what's going on here, but we're all quite tired of the way you're treating anyone who doesn't do what you want them to. Miss Blessing is going back to America, and you're staying here and becoming a part of this family."

Tears sprang into Kerry's eyes. "She doesn't like me."

"Who doesn't?"

"You know very well who."

"If you mean Rosalyn, you're wrong. She wants very much to be your friend. You just have to give her a chance, and that will happen once your chaperone is gone. And," he added, "you're going to start helping the nurse with her patients once she's settled into her new office. It will give you something worthwhile to do, along with your studies."

Kerry was breathing hard. She appeared to want to say something more, but instead she turned on her heels and stomped out of the stables.

Fletcher watched her go, wondering how that final decision had entered his mind. Mrs. Begley had taken Geddes's offer eagerly, so that wasn't the problem. The problem was that no one had even suggested that Kerry work for her. But the more he thought about it, the better he liked the idea.

He shook his head. She was only twelve; what kind of trouble would she cause him when she turned sixteen? He shuddered to think.

• • •

Rosalyn was returning from one of the neighboring women who had picked some herbs for her, now beside her in the one-horse buggy. She was still thinking about the wonderful news regarding the new clinic. Last week, Fen had been struck speechless when Geddes had made her the offer, which was surprising enough since Fen rarely was found without something to say on a subject.

Immersed in her thoughts, Rosalyn didn't see Kerry until the girl jumped out from the scrub bushes along the side of the road, causing the horse to skitter and rear up on its hind legs. Rosalyn had trouble settling him down—in fact, she was thrust sideways and her temple smacked the wooden brace. She briefly saw stars.

"You did this! You're to blame!" Kerry screamed.

Rosalyn shifted upright, drawing on the reins to settle the horse. Fortunately, she knew how to handle this particular animal. "What is it, Kerry? What's wrong?"

"Don't pretend you don't know. Why don't you want me to be happy? And don't think my brother really cares about you. He doesn't. And I'm not going to work for that witch in her hospital, either. I'm not. I'm not!"

Kerry stumbled away, bawling and wailing into the wind.

It wasn't until Rosalyn was at the castle door and Evan took the rig that she understood the full meaning of Kerry's rage. Obviously she'd been told that Miss Blessing was leaving, and in Kerry's mind, it was Rosalyn's fault. Which was true enough.

Fletcher met her at the door. "What happened?"

"Why? What's wrong?"

"Your temple is bleeding."

She touched it and came away with some blood on her fingertips. "Oh, it's nothing." Now was not the time to start blaming Kerry for the near accident, even though it was the girl's fault.

He gripped her wrist. "It's something, dear wife, and I want you to tell me what it is. If you're going to be traipsing around the countryside carrying my heir, I want you safe."

Rosalyn's heart skipped a beat and she automatically placed a protective hand over her stomach. "How did you know?"

He gave her a wry glance. "It would have been nice if you had told me, but I figured it out without your help, Rosalyn."

"How?"

"Little things, like you napping during the day, for one thing. And you've grown pale; you aren't eating. Before this, nothing has slowed you down."

She flushed and glanced away. "I would have told you, but the children came and things got hectic and, well, I guess there just didn't seem to be time." When she looked back at him, she saw a rare tenderness in his gaze.

"And now you've gone and hurt yourself," he said softly. "What happened?" he asked again.

She hung her cape on the coatrack. "Really, it was nothing."

"Rosalyn, answer me."

It sounded like an order.

"Well, if you must know, Kerry inadvertently startled the horse—"

"Damn it!" He strode off.

Rosalyn went after him and grabbed his sleeve to stop him. "Fletcher, please. She resents me enough as it is; she'll really hate me if she thinks I ran to you and tattled on her."

"But she can't go around scaring horses and almost maiming people." He raked his fingers through his hair. "I impetuously told her she was going to work for Mrs. Begley. She needs to understand that she's not so terribly put upon. That there are many others in this world who are far worse off than she is."

"You told her she would work for Fen? Does Fen know?" Rosalyn asked, curious.

Fletcher heaved a sigh. "I hadn't gotten that far yet. I'll ask Geddes to do that for me."

Rosalyn smiled at him. "I think it's a brilliant plan. Fen can use the help and she doesn't put up with children who have tantrums. I think it will do Kerry a world of good."

Fletcher returned her smile. "Evan said he heard Kerry call Mrs. Begley a witch."

"If she is, she's a good witch. And maybe she can cast some sort of spell over Kerry and bring back the wonderful little girl I know is in there somewhere."

"I hope you're right, and I haven't just loosed a twelve-year-old plague upon the island."

Chapter Twenty-Two

Fen stood in the middle of the largest room and studied her surroundings. As much as she wanted to complain about some little thing, she couldn't. It was the perfect place for her to treat her patients. The doc had left all of his larger items behind, including a wood-burning stove, a treatment table, and a cupboard full of paraphernalia she would go through and sterilize as soon as she had the time.

Geddes came in with an armload of wood and dumped it into the woodbox by the stove. "So," he said, "is this going to suit your purposes?"

She breathed in a deep, contented sigh. "Aye, it's going to be perfect." She turned and gazed at him. "Was this your idea?"

Geddes colored. "His Grace and I came to the same conclusion."

Fen crossed her arms over her chest and continued to study him. "You've never really cared for how close Rosalyn and I are, have you?"

Geddes frowned. "To be honest, no."

"And why not?"

"I always felt the doctor was the one who should do the healing," Geddes admitted.

"Even though he used more outdated and obscure methods of healing that often didn't work anyway, plus the fact he was in his cups most of the time?"

Geddes nodded. "I will admit to being a bit stubborn where you were concerned, Mrs. Begley."

"Oh, please. My name is Fen, and if you can't get that personal, call me Fenella." They watched each other for a moment and then she said, "I've always thought you were a very handsome man."

He colored again, but said nothing.

"And what of me, Geddes? What do you think about me?" She was pushing him, but she couldn't stand it any longer.

Geddes pulled himself up to his full height and straightened his waistcoat. "I was going to say I hadn't given it any thought, but that would be a lie."

Fen's heart bumped her ribs.

"Actually, ever since I found you arguing with MacNab outside his bar a while back, I've thought of you quite differently than I had in the past. You aren't a delicate beauty; you are quite a classic, and I find that I'm drawn to you, short hair, trousers and all."

Fen was so pleased she was rendered speechless.

"I believe you are blushing, Fenella," Geddes observed.

She placed her palm against her cheek. "I believe you're right."

The sound of the door opening and the bell tinkling over it broke the spell.

"Fen? Are you here?"

Fen rushed toward the entryway. "Rosalyn! How good of you to come." When His Grace followed her in, Fen was once again mute.

Rosalyn frowned. "Fen, are you all right?"

Fen cleared her throat. "Of course I'm all right, why do you ask?"

Rosalyn scrutinized her friend. "You look a little flushed."

"Well of course I'm flushed," she rushed to say. "I've been working like a madwoman on this place."

They all went into the big room where Geddes was stacking wood very precisely in the woodbox.

"Oh, good. You're both here. Fletcher and I have something to tell you," Rosalyn announced. "Your Grace?"

Geddes came and stood beside Fen, his arm brushing against hers. Once again she felt her heart go bump.

His Grace cleared his throat. "I made an impulsive decision, one I hope you, Mrs. Begley, can live with."

Fen glanced at Rosalyn and then back at the laird. "You've made a decision that involves me?"

Rosalyn put her hand on her husband's arm. "Kerry was being particularly bad-tempered, having just learned that the chaperone was going back to America, and His Grace decided, quite impetuously, that she should work with you here, in the clinic."

Fen automatically moved closer to Geddes and quite innocently put her arm through his. The motion was not lost on Rosalyn, who raised her eyebrows.

"I think it's a wonderful idea," Fen said. "She will see all sorts of things here, things that perhaps no youngster should see, but I can put her to use doing simple things, and she can watch the flow of island humanity come and go through the door."

"Good," His Grace answered. "The sooner she starts, the better."

"If anyone can bring her around, Fen, it's you," Rosalyn said warmly.

"Bring her by tomorrow. Nessa MacNab is bringing her little ones in to have their ears checked. She says they've been pulling on them and waking at night, screaming their heads off. No doubt they have some sort of infection."

Rosalyn studied her brother and her friend once again. "Well, I guess that does it, then, doesn't it?"

"Yes," Fletcher said. "It's time for us to go. Thank you, Mrs. Begley, for your generosity. You have no idea how much I appreciate it."

Fen watched them leave, noting how carefully the laird handled his wife, her very dear friend, and she began to feel that perhaps their relationship just might work after all.

She turned from the doorway and found Geddes watching her. "Would you like to have dinner with me, Fenella?"

"I'd like that. Why don't we have dinner at my cottage? I think I can whip up something for the two of us."

He gave her a broad smile. "As you wish."

Fen's life was changing so fast she was almost dizzy. She was giddy, too, but that had nothing to do with her new clinic, she was very certain of that. Before she lost her nerve, she said, "Geddes, I've been alone a long while and I've been perfectly content. But ever since you came into my life, my feelings for being alone have changed." At his look of confusion, she continued, "I'm too old to be coy. I want to spend more time with you. I know this isn't the proper thing to do, but then, I have never been one to give a rat's behind about propriety. Would you be interested in calling on me?"

Actually, she wanted to drag him into her bed, but she knew that would scare him away. *Wee little steps*, she told herself. *Wee little baby steps.*

Geddes flushed; his ears turned red, but he cleared his throat and said, "You, madam, have seen me nearly naked. I think we're beyond the calling stage, don't you?"

She remembered his glorious furry chest and felt a fluttering, a swelling and heat deep in that place that had been dead for so very, very long. Picking up her cape and her gloves and pocketing the key to her new clinic, she answered, "Let's not waste any more time, shall we?"

• • •

Geddes raised his arms over his head and stared at the ceiling, quite satisfied with himself. "I don't know why we didn't do this sooner."

Fen chuckled softly and nuzzled him. "Because you were fighting so hard to dislike me, I suppose."

He rolled onto his side and cupped her small, firm breast, causing the strawberry-colored nipple to pebble. "Your skin is perfection." He splayed his fingers over her ribcage and then traveled downward, across her navel. "Who would have thought you would be as delicate and succulent as cream under all that mannish clothing?"

Fen stirred beneath his touch and reached over to run her fingers through the tawny hair that covered his chest. "When I applied that poultice to your chest weeks ago, it was all I could do to keep from touching you exactly like this." She continued to move south, found him, and made a satisfied sound in her throat. "You are quite ready again, aren't you?"

He groaned with pleasure. "Madam, I haven't been with a woman for so long, I may need to thrust my sword into your sheath until you die of either weariness or boredom."

She actually laughed. "Not likely boredom. Not likely at all. And I find your sword very, very ample, my dear man, big and hard and robust. And as far as being celibate, I may have you beat." With that, she continued to stroke him until he tested her readiness, finding her as wet as she was when he took her the first time.

Geddes discovered he liked it when she talked so blatantly—it made him feel as randy as a boy. He whipped back the covers, exposing her nakedness, and she shifted her legs so they were slightly parted.

He ran his fingers over her dusty curls and then slid one finger inside, prompting her to spread her legs further to ease his entrance. He bent and placed a kiss over her slightly protruding clitoris, drinking in her scent, and she shuddered so deeply he wondered if she had had another orgasm.

He briefly looked up at her and said, "No matter who was celibate the longest, at least we are celibate no longer."

With that, he eased himself into her and they rode together toward another brilliant explosion of pleasure.

Chapter Twenty-Three

After they left the new clinic they took a drive around the island so Fletcher could once again see the land that belonged to him. They went north; he wanted to see the horses again. Perhaps he'd been mistaken about the number.

As the herd came into view, he counted only what he had counted before. "Can they be grazing somewhere else, do you suppose?"

Rosalyn studied the herd. "I've never heard that they were anywhere but here. There certainly don't seem to be nearly as many as I'd been told."

"The other day I asked around to see who might be familiar with the herd. Fergie the Burn said that when he arrived on Hedabarr, he was told the herd was nearly one hundred." Fletcher shook his head as he glanced at the few dozen remaining horses. "I don't understand it."

As they rode back toward home, it seemed that word had gotten out that the crofters were no longer to pay for their land, and those who were outside bowed and waved as they rode by.

"They adore you," Rosalyn said.

"I'm happy to see them more content," he answered. "There's more than enough for everyone here." He pointed toward a small row of buildings. "That's the new distillery. There was some at our wedding celebration and I had never tasted anything quite so smooth. I want them to succeed."

They rode along in silence and then Fletcher glanced down at Rosalyn's stomach. "When do you think you conceived?"

Feeling a little self-conscious, she said quietly, "I think it was that very first night, when you…you were having the nightmare."

"That was months ago," he calculated. "How are you feeling?"

"Actually, I'm much better. I did have a bit of queasiness at the beginning, but that's to be expected."

Fletcher put his arm around her and she leaned into him. "I don't want you taking any unnecessary chances, Rosalyn. I don't want you going off on your own anymore. If I can't go with you, take one of the boys or Evan. Under no circumstances are you to wander off on your own."

She cocked her head and looked up at him. "That's rather high-handed of you, isn't it?"

"Absolutely. I don't want anything happening to you or to our child." He turned and kissed her hair, gently rubbing his nose against her skin.

It was almost more than Rosalyn could stand. The gentleness, the tenderness, the concern…did it mean that he might actually learn to love her?

"Can we still…be intimate?" he asked cautiously.

She bit the corner of her lip to keep from smiling. "That's rather a sedate way of putting it, don't you think? After all, you've made love to me in some very bizarre places and only twice in a bed, and one of those times you didn't even know it was me."

He dropped his gaze to his lap. "How you must have detested me."

She felt such a rush of feeling for him, she wondered if she could speak. "Believe me, I wanted to. I knew it wasn't me you had been so passionate with, and to have Geddes walk in on us like that made things oh, so much worse. But I dreamed about you often after that, and you truly had awakened something that I'd long thought was dead."

He stirred next to her and placed his hand on her thigh. "You're getting me all worked up, wife. I may have to take you right here in the buggy."

"And frighten the poor horse? He'd probably take off at a gallop and we'd end up in the bushes."

Her husband glanced around. "Ah, the bushes. Even better."

• • •

A week after Kerry started coming to the clinic, things were no better. Fen was examining Nessa MacNab's two-year-old girl when Kerry slouched into the room, her eyes darting about, her mouth in a perpetual pout.

"Good morning, Kerry," Fen greeted her. "Would you mind straightening up the medicine cabinet? I have my hands full here." She watched as the girl slunk over to the cabinet where Fen kept her medicines.

Fen fed small amounts of warm oil into the child's ear, causing the little lass to scream. "It's all right, lassie," Fen said soothingly. She glanced at Nessa, who was trying to quiet her youngest boy while the older one, Clyde, ignored her. With her arm in a sling, Nessa had difficulty handling one of her children, much less three.

Suddenly Kerry was at her side. "What's wrong with her and what are you doing to her?"

"She has an earache. The oil will hopefully ease her discomfort." She glanced at Kerry, noting her concerned expression.

"But she's still bawling." Kerry frowned, her dark, shapely brows pulled into a furrow.

"Aye," said Fen, "and she may cry until the pressure eases up." She watched as Kerry studied the child, taking in her ragged clothing, chafed cheeks, and snarled hair. Then she saw the girl glance at Nessa and the two boys, all of whom were in ragged clothing. Both of the boys had red and runny noses and both sniffled and coughed, wiping their noses with their fists.

There was no chance to chat the rest of the day. One patient after another came to Fen with anything from boils ready to burst to broken arms to bruised ribs. She kept Kerry busy boiling water, bringing her clean cloths and unguents, and cleaning up after the patients.

At the end of the day, Kerry stood by the window, just as quiet as she'd been all day.

"You've been a big help today, Kerry," Fen said. "I hope you'll continue to help me."

Kerry turned, her face creased with distress. "How did that girl get those bruises on her ribs?"

Fen straightened the medicine cabinet and closed the glass door. "Her da was unhappy with the meal she prepared for him."

"But she wasn't even as old as I am."

"Aye," said Fen, "but her mam died some time back, and the lassie is the only girl in a house with four brothers. It's up to her to carry on where her mam left off."

Kerry's frown deepened. "But it's unfair of him to hit her. She's probably doing the best she can."

Fen remembered Roz telling her that Kerry, too, had cooked for her family. Obviously she had not been abused. Thank God. "Fairness has nothing to do with life on the isle, Kerry."

Kerry chewed on her thumbnail and returned to staring out the window. "And the little boy with the broken arm?"

Fen smiled sadly. "I'm sure you want me to tell you he fell from a tree while playing with his brothers, or while sneaking apples from a neighbor's yard."

Kerry turned toward her again. "How did he break it?"

"His uncle broke it for him."

Kerry gasped. "Why?"

Fen wondered how much to tell the girl. She decided that the truth, as harsh as it was, was what Kerry needed. "The little fellow didn't bring home enough money."

"Doing what? He couldn't have been more than seven or eight years old."

"He's a pickpocket, Kerry. Do you know what that is?" Fen crossed to the alcove near the door, picked up a broom, and began to sweep the floor. "His uncle sends him out every day, especially when ships come in and the crew rushes toward the pubs. He isn't to come home until he has stolen what his uncle thinks is enough."

Kerry swallowed hard. "And he broke the boy's arm because he didn't come home with enough? What good does that do? Now he won't be able to do anything."

"Life is hard here, Kerry. Money is scarce. Children are often just possessions. Merchandise. Something to be used and bartered with." She stopped sweeping and gave Kerry a solemn gaze. "It's not pretty and it's not fair, but it is life on this island." She didn't mention the children who were turned out into the streets to whore for their fathers, and sometimes even their mothers.

• • •

Kerry left the hospital, not quite believing everything the woman had said. After all, Rosalyn had probably told her to put a scare into her, trying to make her realize just how easy she had it. She missed Dorcas. Even though Dorcas had sat her down the night before she sailed to tell her that all would be well, she hadn't wanted to lose her. She had no one to confide in, no one to share her pain with, and even though adults probably didn't believe children felt emotional pain, they really did. How was Kerry to cope if she had no one to talk with? Where were the girls her age?

She would find them. She didn't need any help. She would walk into the village and find someone her own age who could become her friend. And even though she had seen some bad things at the hospital, the children with their bruises, breaks, and ragged clothes, she still wasn't convinced that she hadn't seen the worst of it today.

She would do it tomorrow. Who would know? Rosalyn would send her off to the clinic once again, and she would leave the castle and pretend to go in that direction. Or maybe she would actually show up and hang around the clinic for a few hours, then leave. But when she was sure no one was watching she'd hike into the village. Or maybe she'd take a pony. She could ride as well as the boys. It would sure beat hanging around the depressing monster of a fortress as well as having to look at any more sad, sorry children.

Chapter Twenty-Four

The next morning, Rosalyn, who was attempting to keep down a breakfast of boiled egg and oatcake and not having much luck, glanced up as Kerry came into the dining room.

"Good morning, Rosalyn," Kerry said, smiling at her.

Hmmm. This is a switch, thought Rosalyn. Maybe the time with Fen had done the trick. "Good morning, Kerry. How are you enjoying the days helping Fen?"

Kerry took a seat across from her, unfolded her napkin, and placed it across her lap. Rosalyn studied the girl, recalling how the chaperone had once done that for her, as if she were a child of three or four instead of a young girl on the verge of womanhood.

"It's interesting," Kerry answered as one of the kitchen girls placed a bowl of porridge in front of her. "She's really busy, isn't she?"

"Yes, she is extremely busy since the doctor left the island."

Kerry poured cream on her porridge and stirred it. "Why did he leave? Shouldn't there really be a doctor for all those people?"

"He left because he got a better offer, but God help those he is supposed to heal," Rosalyn answered.

Kerry dug into her porridge. "What was wrong with him?"

"Well, if you must know, he was a drunken sot. Maybe I shouldn't speak so of him, but 'tis the truth and we're all better off without him. Do you know that he told a patient that if he bathed his bald head in dog urine every day, his hair would grow back?"

Kerry laughed and once again Rosalyn saw the beauty she would become.

"That sounds like Wandering Eye."

"And who is that?"

Kerry put a spoonful of cereal into her mouth, closed her eyes with pleasure, and swallowed. "He's an old man at home who claimed he could cure everything. Even the medicine men don't claim to cure everything. But Wandering Eye put together the oddest concoctions. Beetles and rosemary. Skunk spray and wild cherries. Grandfather always said to be nice and patient with him, because he had—you know—that one eye that wandered all over the place. And I felt kind of sorry for him, especially when other kids teased him and made fun of him behind his back.

"One day," she continued, "I had made a big pot of squirrel stew for supper and Grandfather suggested I take him some. I think he almost cried when he came to the door and saw me with it."

Suddenly aware of how much she had exposed of herself, she stopped talking and dug into her cereal.

"It was a nice gesture, Kerry." Rosalyn wanted to take the girl into her arms and hug her, but she didn't think that would go over very well.

Kerry merely shrugged and finished her cereal. "Well, should I keep on going to the clinic?"

Rosalyn bit off a piece of oatcake and chewed it slowly. "If you don't mind, I think she'd really appreciate the help. And if she doesn't need it, you don't need to stay if you don't want to."

"I don't mind. And Fletcher said I could ride one of your ponies over today. I'm a good rider, really I am."

"I'm sure you are, Kerry. Make sure Evan gives you a hand with the tack. Have a good day." Rosalyn watched the girl leave, still surprised at such a quick turnaround in her behavior. It would be so peaceful around here if Kerry had actually changed this quickly, but somehow Rosalyn doubted that was the case. She would have to talk with Fen later today, after Kerry had returned home, to see just how things were going. She hoped she had the time—it seemed like every chore she used to do in minutes was now taking her hours.

* * *

Kerry sauntered to the stable and out of the corner of her eye she saw the stable boy. Evan. Of course she had noticed him right away that first day. He interested her. A lively pup with bushy eyebrows pranced and danced around him. The boy had watched her carefully every time they were together in the stables, but he never spoke to her.

She turned to him, hoping she appeared grown up. "Evan—that is your name, isn't it?"

He gave her a sly yet quite charming smile. "'Tis."

"I need a pony. Pick one out for me, would you please?"

He slowly came toward her, one eyebrow lifted over his clear blue eyes, the dog following, a bundle of energy. "You be needin' a pony, young miss? Do ye have the duke's permission to ride?"

She bristled. "I don't need his permission; I can ride as well as any of you boys. So saddle one up for me." The pup loped up to her, sniffed her legs, then jumped up on her. She bent down and gave its ears a rough tug. "You are a happy little thing, aren't you?" She was rewarded with a wet kiss. It made her laugh. She could never ignore a dog of any kind. They were one of her weaknesses. Once she had discovered a book that described dog breeds and where they were first bred. She had memorized them all. She could still rattle them off—if anyone had asked her to. "What's the pup's name?"

Evan appeared to study her. "Bear." The dog's ears perked up at his name.

"He's got big paws. I read in a book about a dog like this. It's a wolfhound of some kind, isn't it?"

"Aye, 'tis a wolfhound. An Irish wolfhound." Evan nodded toward the castle. "His mum sticks close to her ladyship. You've seen her?"

"You mean Sima?" She had fallen in love with the dog and her pup the minute she saw them. "It's the first time I've seen a real one." She continued to scratch the pup's ears. "At home—I mean, back where I came from—we had a lot of dogs roaming about, most of them friendly, especially if you fed them the smallest little thing, but I've never seen one as big as Sima." She frowned. "You named your dog Bear? That's an odd name for dog that's so wiggly and funny."

Evan swaggered closer. "What would you call him, then, if he were yours?"

Kerry took a step back and studied the pup. He was gray and shaggy and made her want to laugh. "I don't know, maybe I'd call him my little clown."

Evan gave the pup a thoughtful look. "Aye, I suppose, but he won't always be so, you know. He will grow to be a fiercely huge animal, one that could fell a sheep or even a larger animal."

"When you look at it like that, I suppose you're right. Anyway, can you suggest a pony for me?"

"I ain't yer personal servant." His words weren't mean or threatening.

She gave him a look of mock surprise. "Well, you are the stable boy, aren't you?"

He gave a low whistle and the pup raced to his side and sat, tail moving so hard it nearly moved the dog. "Aye, I am. But…" He stopped and slid his cap off, revealing a shock of curly black hair, hair so black Kerry wondered how it could be darker than her own. "I only do what the duke tells me, otherwise I need to be asked nicely, sweetly, if you please."

Kerry rolled her eyes and heaved a sigh. "Please saddle me a pony."

Evan gave her a sly look and shook his head. "Not very sweet, lassie. I'll prob'ly need a wee kiss, too."

Kerry made an impatient sound in her throat and stomped toward the stalls where the horses were kept. She pointed at a pretty little paint with a bushy tail. "That one. I'll take that one, and I can saddle her myself if you're too stubborn to do it for me."

"No kiss, then?" He had a wicked look in those blue eyes, and when he smiled, his teeth were white.

Kerry felt a little giddy, but hid it well. "I don't go around giving my kisses away, especially to a stable boy."

"Yer loss, lassie." Evan relented, saddled up a pony, and within minutes, Kerry was off on her adventure. She felt a wonderful freedom atop the mount, which, she learned, was named Mariah. Kerry reached down and stroked the filly's soft, velvety neck. It felt so good to be on horseback again.

She saw a little church up ahead, and in the yard next to it, in front of a tiny white house, two girls played with hoops. They looked close to her age. She reined in Mariah, slowing down their pace. The girls looked up as she approached. And stared.

"What's the matter, haven't you ever seen a girl ride a horse before?"

Both girls continued to stare at her. One of them, the prettier one with the curly reddish hair, put her fists on her hips and took a few brave steps forward. "Oh, we've seen girls on horses before," she began, "we've just never seen a savage lassie in pants."

"Birdie!" the plainer one scolded. "Da would put a switch to you if he heard you talking like that. You know he always preaches that the Lord doesn't care about skin color. Don't mind her," she said to Kerry. "She always talks before she thinks."

The pretty one, Birdie, responded, "Oh, pooh on Da's preaching."

The other one gasped. "Birdie! You'll go to hell!"

Appearing undaunted, Birdie answered, "Well, it's true, isn't it, Robbie? We've only seen pictures of them in books that the tutor lets us page through."

Kerry was too intrigued by their language to be hurt by the insult. She knew they spoke English, but she had to work hard to understand them.

The plainer one, Robbie, stepped forward. "Are you the girl living at the castle?"

"How many other 'savages' have moved to this godforsaken island?"

"You don't like it here?" Robbie asked.

Kerry's shoulders slumped. "What's to like? It's too cold, it's too windy, it rains too much, and it's nothing at all like Texas. Texas is the best place on earth."

"I think I'd like Texas," Birdie said. "They have all those cowboys there, don't they? Men who ride horseback and lasso little doggies?"

Kerry tried not to laugh. "They're dogies. Wayward calves. Not dogs."

Neither girl spoke for a few seconds, then the pretty one said, "We hear you have a couple of brothers. Are they savages too?"

Robbie gasped. "By the holy, Birdie, stop using that word!"

Kerry swung herself down off the mount and led her to a patch of grass under a tree before tethering her. "Yes, I have two brothers, and no, they both aren't savage, as you call them. One has hair nearly as bright as wheat."

Robbie was the first to offer Kerry an invitation to join them. "Come, sit with us. We ha'e much to ask you about your life. And I really like your boots. What are they made of?"

Kerry glanced at her shoes. They're made from cowhide," she offered.

Birdie scooted close. "First you have to tell us about your brothers. How old are they? Do they like girls? Do you think they'd like me?"

Robbie uttered an exasperated sigh, but didn't interrupt.

Kerry sighed inwardly and studied the girl. She was green-eyed and dimpled and had skin so fair Kerry could almost see her veins. But her cheeks had high color, and her nose was just a little button of a thing. "My brothers don't like girls who throw themselves at them."

"Well," Birdie answered, preening in front of her, "I think they'd like me. All the boys like me, don't they, Robbie?"

Kerry saw Robbie glance at the ground and kick at a clump of dirt. Unlike her sister, she was not pretty. Her hair was brown and her eyes were a clear shade of blue, almost like the sky. She had clear skin too, but the sun had given it a bit of color, even some freckles across her nose. Kerry thought she looked the healthier of the two and she was much more likeable. But she still wasn't sure she wanted to make friends, even though she longed for someone her own age.

"Yes, Birdie, dear, all the boys like you."

Kerry picked up a fallen hoop and played with it, sending it on a short spin. She had many questions, but the one that kept eating at her was about the children on the island. "Tell me," she began, "are there really children here who have to steal for their food? Do they really have parents who beat them if they don't?"

The girls glanced at one another and something flicked between them. Finally, Robbie asked, "Where did you hear such a thing?"

Kerry toyed with the end of the long, thick braid that hung over her shoulder. "I've been helping out at the clinic with the lady who treats patients. She told me."

"You mean Mrs. Begley?" Robbie asked.

"Aye," remarked Birdie, "the lady who wears trousers. Is that where you got the idea?" she asked, pointing to the ones Kerry was wearing. "I think they're kind of silly for a girl to wear. But," she added with a shrug, "you're not from around here. I suppose it's natural for lassies to wear pants in Texas."

Kerry shook her head. "Not really; I just like the way they feel."

Birdie made an unpleasant sound in her throat. "Not me. I like to look like a lassie because otherwise the laddies don't pay any attention to you."

Kerry smiled at her in spite of herself. "Well, I really don't care about your laddies."

"So you work for the nurse?" Robbie asked.

Kerry nodded. "She seems to do everything a doctor would."

"What kind of patients have you seen?" Robbie asked.

Kerry shrugged. "A boy whose father had broken his arm. Mrs. Begley told me it was because he hadn't stolen enough that day, so his pa broke his arm." She brushed the braid back over her shoulder and studied the girls. "Why do things like that happen here?"

Birdie snorted. "You think they only happen here? What about where you come from? Is everything so perfect there?"

Kerry felt a wave of homesickness so strong she almost felt physically ill. "It was perfect for me. I didn't want to leave; the only thing that made me come here was my brother, Fletcher."

Birdie giggled. "Oh, the new duke." She snickered again. "I hear they call him the Savage."

Robbie gasped again, the sound more exasperated than shocked. "Birdie, that's enough!"

Kerry was beginning to think she'd had enough of both of them. "He's no more savage than you are." She bid them goodbye; she had more to explore than just this small patch of land and some seemingly witless young people.

She rode her pony into the village center and saw for herself more of the kind of children she had seen the day before, at the clinic. She even recognized one Mrs. Begley had been treating for an earache. He was playing with a scruffy dog outside a ratty-looking saloon.

Kerry dismounted. "Hello. I saw you yesterday. Do you remember me?" She also remembered that his mother had her arm in a sling.

The boy continued to stare at her, but gave her a slight nod.

"My name is Kerry; what's yours?" She spoke slowly in case he couldn't understand her English.

He stuck his finger in his nose and then into his mouth. "Do you have a name, then?"

He nodded. "Clyde."

"Clyde. Well, Clyde, why does your ma have her arm in a sling?"

Without preamble, he answered, "Me da tossed her down the steps."

Kerry's hand went to her mouth. "Why would he do that?"

"'Tis his right."

Kerry frowned. "It's his right to throw your ma down the stairs? She isn't his property, Clyde."

"She is," he asserted.

Just then a huge man with a red face and big nose pushed the door of the saloon open and stepped outside. His hands were the size of hams. He gave Kerry a disgusted glance and then bellowed, "Clyde! Git yer arse in here. There's garbage to toss."

The boy hurried inside, and before following him the man

pointed a sausage-like finger at Kerry and threatened, "And you, missie, you come to spy on me? That witch of a nurse send ya? I knows all about you. Being rich and havin' a title don't mean the lord of that manor is someone he ain't. He ain't nothing more than a savage, I say. And stay away from me kids."

Speechless, her heart in her throat, Kerry mounted Mariah again, prodding the pony with her heels as they trotted away. She wasn't used to being threatened. Not by anyone.

She didn't like it here. Actually, she hated it, and nothing anyone could say or do would ever change her mind. The only thing that kept her from trying to find a way home was that she would disappoint Fletcher. And she couldn't do that.

She and Mariah headed out of the village. The crofts became sparser as she went north, and soon she was alone, gazing as the waves lifted and dipped over the sea. She studied her surroundings as Mariah picked her way over the rough tufts of grass and rocks. When Mariah tensed beneath her, she looked into the distance and saw the wild horses she had heard about from Duncan and Gavin. "Mariah, what a magnificent sight," she murmured to her mount.

A bit further on, an outcropping of rocks caught her eye. As she got close she realized there was a cave hidden behind the rocks, a shelter from the sea. Leaving Mariah near the entrance, she cautiously stepped inside. As she turned, she realized that the cave faced the water. She sat and rested her back against a rock and took in the sights and sounds, foreign to her, yet peaceful. No one would know where she was and she could sit and watch the ocean for hours. She had found her place. She opened one of the books she'd borrowed from the library, settled in, and began to read.

* * *

One late August evening, after the children had been with them for almost three months, Fletcher drew Rosalyn from the solarium and led her upstairs.

"What's this?"

"Do you know that we haven't shared a bed in over a month?" Fletcher had his arm around her.

"More like almost three," she corrected him.

"So you've been counting, have you?"

She shrugged, pretending nonchalance. "I thought it was perhaps because you found me too unwieldy to take to bed."

He stopped and brought her in front of him. "You're not serious, are you?"

She gazed up at him, wondering for the millionth time how he could belong to her. "Not entirely," she admitted. "But you must agree that since the arrival of the children, we've had little time together."

He turned away, clearly upset.

Rosalyn put her hand on his arm. "Please, don't beat yourself up over it. I understand it, believe me, I do. There's much for you to grasp and learn here, and now with the children…"

She had noticed the differences between the children since they arrived. Duncan was wilder, taking off on his mount with a loud whoop whenever he got the chance. No one knew for sure what he was up to, but rumor had it that he was already checking out the island lassies. Gavin remained quiet, most often lost in some great tome from the library, although he could also be seen reading outside on the small terrace by the roses, a hound or two asleep at his feet. One day she noticed him sketching something and when she peeked over his shoulder, she saw that he had drawn the stables and a couple of outbuildings. When she'd remarked on how good it was, he had told her that he really preferred drawing maps and measuring distances. "I would like to be a navigator one day," he had said.

Early on, she recalled, he had asked, rather shyly, to move the two globes from the dining room into the library, where he could study them.

Kerry still helped out at the clinic every morning; what she did with the rest of her day was often a question, but presumably she went exploring. And she seemed more comfortable in her surroundings, often even sitting with Rosalyn in the solarium while Rosalyn sewed. Rosalyn encouraged her to talk about Texas, for she was truly curious to know what it was like.

Fletcher led Rosalyn to her chambers and shut the door behind them. "I hadn't realized I'd been ignoring you, Rosalyn. I wish you would have said something."

Rosalyn smiled. "Like what? Please, I'm sorry I mentioned it. It doesn't bother me, truly it doesn't. I want the children to be happy, too. That's the most important thing."

He frowned and touched her face. "You look tired. Perhaps you should lie down and rest for a while."

She put her hand over his, loving the rough texture against her skin. She hated to admit it, but she was drained. She didn't recall her first pregnancy taking so much of a toll on her body. Feeling a tweak of spirit, she said, "Won't you join me?"

His smile was warm. "Don't tempt me, Rosalyn. If I were to join you in the bed, it isn't rest you'd be doing, I can assure you of that."

"And maybe I don't want to rest; what's your answer to that?"

He drew her to the bed. "If anything were to happen to that child because I thought I needed to exercise my bag of tricks, I'd never forgive myself."

Disappointed, she tilted her head up at him. "It will not harm the bairn."

He bent and kissed her forehead. "I don't want to take any chances, Rosalyn. Now crawl into bed and take a nap like a good girl."

She frowned as she watched him walk to the door and leave. He treated her like he'd treat a sister or an elderly aunt. A ragged thought snagged her. Of course he was concerned about the bairn, his heir. Of course. She had known all along that the babe was his first priority, after his family.

But she loved him already—how could she not? He put everyone's needs ahead of his own. Now that he'd insisted the crofters had paid enough for their paltry land, they treated him like he'd handed them the sun. All the farmers who raised sheep were eager for him to join them at sheep-shearing time, for he had informed them that he had done his share of shearing in Texas. She had heard there were bets being placed as to how good he actually was. No doubt a bit of coin was involved. The castle help adored him. Even the dogs followed him around like he was the Pied Piper.

She turned on her side and took a deep breath, willing herself to relax, trying to get her swelling belly comfortable. Aye, she needed a bit of a nap, no matter who told her to take it. And as long as everything was going well and there were no outbursts or upheavals, she could live with what she had. After all, no one had ever told her that life was always happy or fair.

Chapter Twenty-Five

After months of taking the same route, Kerry took a different path to her hideaway, curious to see more of the island. Far north of the other farms she noticed a lone ramshackle cottage slouched beneath a thicket of pines. At first she thought it was vacant, but then she realized there was smoke coming out of the chimney. Curious, she nudged Mariah closer, dismounted, and sneaked to the window. Cupping her hands around her eyes, she tried to look in but discovered the window was painted.

How strange, she thought. She walked around to the front and knocked. She received no answer. Against her better judgment, she tried the door. And it opened. She squinted into the room, the only light coming from the doorway. There was nothing particularly interesting for her to see. There were empty sawhorses and tables, and a big bag of something against the wall. She peered at it. The letters S-A-L-T were stamped on the front of the bag. With nothing of interest to get her attention, she backed out and closed the door behind her.

Odd little place, she thought. It didn't look like anyone actually lived there. But then she remembered the wisp of smoke that had drawn her there in the first place.

Shrugging, she mounted Mariah and left for her special place by the sea.

As she rode on, an uncomfortable feeling crawled up the back of her neck, a feeling as though someone were watching her. She twisted in the saddle and scanned the area, but saw nothing.

"Must be my imagination, Mariah. After all, I shouldn't have been trespassing." But the feeling continued even after the cottage was hidden by the trees.

The following day, as she was going through the books she had brought with her to the cave over the past weeks, she noticed one of them was missing. Or was it? She had found a volume on horses in the library and she was sure she'd brought it with her. She checked through the books again. It wasn't there. She sat back on her heels and frowned. She must have been mistaken.

* * *

Fletcher and Duncan were returning from a bit of hunting, both using bows and arrows. They had seen a beautiful red doe and a buck, high in the hills, but neither had any interest in killing them. They did, however, bring down a couple of healthy rabbits and decided to have the kitchen crew cook up some rabbit stew like they used to eat it in Texas.

"Kerry must have the recipe in her head," Duncan said. "It was Grandfather's favorite."

At the mention of his grandfather, Fletcher felt a deep sense of loss. "I haven't even asked you how he died."

Duncan stroked his mount's neck. "He had been failing for a while. I think he just wanted to leave. It was hard to lose him, but he went to sleep one night and didn't wake up."

At least he didn't suffer, Fletcher thought, relieved.

As they approached the stream going south toward the sea, Fletcher noticed smoke billowing up through the trees.

"That's a lot of smoke to come from a chimney," Duncan remarked. They rode closer. "Oh, God, it's Fergie the Burn's cottage."

They rode into the clearing and saw that one corner of the thatched roof was ablaze. Fergie's wife, Birgit, and her children were outside; two of the boys attempted to get water from the stream with buckets.

Fletcher and Duncan dismounted and helped the young boys with water to stifle the flames. Amazingly, after their added attempts to put out the flames, a good share of the roof was burnt but not gone. And the cottage itself still stood.

Fletcher returned to Birgit. "I'm sorry. It could have been worse—thatch burns like kindling."

She held Clive in her arms, her eyes filled with tears. "I know, but Fergie will be so upset."

"Have you any idea how it happened?"

She shook her head, unable to speak.

Fletcher looked inside the cottage. Smoke covered much of the room where the roof had caught fire. "You can't stay here. It's not safe." He turned to her. "Have you relatives you could stay with for a spell?"

Birgit, still tearful, nodded. "Me sis lives up the hill."

"Why don't you let Duncan take one of the boys with him and go tell her what's happened."

She called to her son, Archie, a lad of perhaps ten and slathered in soot. She told him the plan. The boy's eyes lit up when he learned he would ride with Duncan on his horse.

Fletcher stayed with her until Fergie arrived and then, when he was sure all would be taken care of until repairs could be done, he left.

As he rode into the yard, Gavin waved to him from his sunny spot in the garden. After Fletcher stabled Ahote, he told Gavin of the fire.

"Will they have to use thatching again?" he asked.

Fletcher shrugged. "I don't know what else they'd use."

Gavin stood. "That building over there, sort of hidden in the brush. Have you ever looked in there?"

Truthfully, Fletcher had not; it hadn't seemed an important part of the estate.

"I looked in there early on out of curiosity. There are stacks of some kind of material. I think it's slate."

"Slate," Fletcher repeated. "Slate is used for roofing." He glanced at Gavin. "Why would the old laird have stockpiled slate?"

Gavin shrugged. "Who knows? I've heard some mighty odd stories about the old man. Maybe he was saving it for something."

"Let's take a look."

And there it was. Stacks and stacks of slate, dusty from neglect. "Now all we need is someone who knows how to build a roof out of it."

As it turned out, a close neighbor, Ferris the Peat, had put a slate roof on his cottage a number of years ago.

In the weeks that followed, Fletcher, Duncan, Gavin, Ferris the Peat, and numerous villagers put Fergie the Burn's cottage back together better than it ever was before. There was a party, with dancing and food and fine whisky from the distillery.

Texans and Scots were no different, Fletcher realized. They worked hard and partied hard.

At the end of the evening, Fergie approached Fletcher. "I canna tell ye how much I appreciate what ye've done for us, Yer Grace. Sorry to say, the old laird would'na been so generous."

Fletcher didn't ask him to elaborate, but the comment stayed with him.

• • •

One day, while all the men in the village were rebuilding Fergie's roof, Kerry skipped her duties with the nurse and rode to her hideaway. She stepped into the cave and a frisson of fear raced through her. Had she stacked the books over there? No. They were on the opposite wall, of that she was certain. She slid to the ground and hugged her knees to her chest. She wasn't afraid, but she was confused. If she didn't know better, she'd think someone was trying to frighten her. That was nonsense, of course. No one even knew she had this special place except Duncan and Evan, and they didn't know the exact location.

She shook away the dark thoughts and settled down to read the book she'd brought with her. Poetry of Robert Burns. She lifted a wry eyebrow. Apparently Rosalyn's favorite. Kerry would have to see what all the fuss was about.

• • •

A few days later, Rosalyn leaned against the doorjamb and watched her husband change into Duncan's buckskins; though years apart in age, they were much the same size. She now felt some guilt about burning his, not realizing that they could have been cleaned. "So, this is the day, is it?"

He turned to her, his expression eager. "I hear there will be quite a crowd there to listen to our stories."

"You look very fierce, my dear. Very fierce indeed." He actually looked delicious.

"Like the first day we met?"

"Aye, like that day. Hopefully you'll frighten no one today, though."

"Are you coming with me?"

"I wouldn't miss it for the world." She might be big and clumsy and not particularly attractive, especially to herself, but she wanted to see everyone's reactions.

"Is Kerry ready?"

"She's waiting in the stable with Evan."

The whole idea had been Kerry's brainstorm to begin with. She had come to Fletcher and suggested that somehow the people on the island should get to know the lot of them, get to know where they came from. A few still looked at them with suspicion.

Later, as they arrived at the tiny town hall attached to the church, they found the place packed with islanders.

Rosalyn touched her husband's sleeve. "Your people await."

After Fletcher helped her down from the gig, Rosalyn watched as Kerry walked proudly to the building in her festive Comanche wear. Fletcher took Rosalyn's arm and they followed behind.

As they had when they'd first laid eyes upon their new laird, they stopped talking and stared, waiting to see what Fletcher was going to do.

Fletcher looked out over the small sea of faces. "I hope I don't need an introduction, but I want to introduce my sister, Kerry MacNeil."

Kerry, who looked like an Indian princess, smiled at the crowd. Rosalyn decided she could be very endearing when it suited her.

"First," Fletcher began, "we want you to ask us any questions you have. I imagine you might have a few."

Questions came mostly from the children; the adults perhaps too reticent to expose their ignorance.

One young lad spoke up. "Have ye ever scalped anyone?" His mam smacked his arm and frowned at him while others murmured, wary of the question and the answer.

Fletcher was relaxed, at ease in the clothing he grew up with. "You might not know this, young man, but we didn't invent scalping."

"Then who did?" he asked, ignoring his mam's continued frown.

"To be quite honest, the Europeans brought it to America. Maybe even the Scots. How do you feel about that?"

The boy perked up. "Scots? Nay, couldna be."

"Tell you what," Fletcher began. "What's your name, son?"

The boy stood. "Mike. Mike MacDougal. Me Pa is Douglas the Lum."

Fletcher nodded. "I know your father. Are you in school, Mike?"

"Aye, I can read, if that's what yer askin'."

"I have a book you might be interested in. Why don't I bring it by your cottage tomorrow?"

The boy deferred to his mother, who nodded proudly.

Another hand was raised. When Fletcher nodded at him, the boy asked, "What's your clothes made of?"

"Mostly deer hide. Sometimes we use buffalo skins."

The boy's eyes went wide. "You see a lot of buffalo? I ain't never seen one except in a book."

Fletcher told them of the herds they had in Texas, and the boy was rapt with wonder. When the questions stopped, Fletcher said, "Let me tell you the story of how the Comanche believed the world began.

"One day the Great Spirit collected swirls of dust from the four directions. From this dust he created the Comanche people. These people had the strength of mighty storms. But a shapeshifting demon was also created and began to torment the people. Great Spirit cast the demon into a bottomless pit. To seek revenge, the demon took refuge in the fangs and stingers of poisonous creatures and continues to harm people to this day."

Archie, Fergie the Burn's boy, shyly raised his arm.

"Yes, Archie."

The boy's chest puffed up; the laird knew his name. "What is a shapeshifting demon?"

"I'll answer that," Kerry said. "It's a being with the ability to change its appearance whenever it wants to. So it might appear to be something pleasant, but underneath, it's very evil and causes people to make bad choices."

The boy nodded. "Sort of like Satan, then? In the Garden of Eden?"

"Very good," Fletcher praised him.

"Would you like to hear about the Comanche Trickster?" Kerry asked. Nods and smiles encouraged her. "Do you know what a coyote is?"

People looked at one another, frowning and shaking their heads.

"It's an animal," Danny McKay, the distillery manager, spoke up. "I've read of them. They are sort of like a wolf, am I right?"

"That's right," Kerry answered. "And I understand that the wolf has not been seen in Scotland for many hundreds of years. Can anyone tell me why?"

Evan, who had been standing in the back, raised his hand.

Pleasantly, Kerry asked, "Evan?"

He cleared his throat. "They were a threat to the livestock. Besides that, they used to dig up the dead."

"How gruesome," Kerry answered.

"What of the coyote?" a boy asked, reminding her of her question.

"Yes, the coyote, who looks much like a wolf, is a trickster. He's very clever. During times when the white people were taking over much of the Indian land, the coyote trickster helped our people cope with the many problems they faced. That's why we call the coyote Brother to the Comanche. But to the white man, he can be greedy, reckless, and dishonest. He takes great pleasure in tricking them into believing something they want very badly is one thing, when it's actually something that will do them no good, perhaps even do them harm."

At the end, people were reluctant to leave and milled about Fletcher and Kerry, admiring the buckskins and the beads, asking about the porcupine quills. Kerry's was the only outfit that had painted figures on it, and there were many questions about their meanings.

Rosalyn closed her eyes and sucked in a sigh as a twinge bit into her back. She would be grateful to get home. When she opened her eyes, Nessa MacNab was watching her.

"Ye got a great bairn in there."

Rosalyn almost laughed. "Indeed I do."

Nessa's face was a study in earnestness. "Ye nay ha'e burning, do ye?" She motioned to her neck and throat.

"Heartburn? Sometimes. The bairn gets wiggly in there and sometimes it's hard to eat."

"Ye know that if ye ha'e the burning, the bairn will be a hairy one, don't ye?"

Rosalyn stopped herself from rolling her eyes. She had heard many myths and sayings about pregnancy; fortunately, she didn't believe in any of them.

"Thank you for your concern, Nessa. How are you doing?"

Nessa lifted one shoulder. "I can live wi' me life." With that she walked away, but Rosalyn noticed that she limped.

Fen ambled up next to her. "She's limping."

"Aye. Poor thing, what a life she must have."

"And you, dear one, you need to be checked. It's been two weeks, and I need to see how things are progressing. I want to see you first thing in the morning."

By the time Rosalyn got home and went to bed, she realized she had not told Kerry what a wonderful job she had done. She had meant to say something right away, but Nessa MacNab's and Fen's appearances had shaken the thought right out of her head. It was no wonder the girl didn't warm to her; she probably felt purposely ignored.

* * *

Although Kerry was becoming more comfortable with her new life, she still loved to be by herself. The afternoon with Fletcher and the villagers had been quite fun, and since then, on her way to her private lair, she had seen some of the children who had attended the function. They waved and smiled, and she did the same.

Taking the same path she'd taken before, when she'd seen the rundown cottage, she rode by it slowly, noting that today there was no smoke coming from the chimney.

As she approached her hiding place she tethered Mariah among the clover behind the cave and went inside. She couldn't see the ocean today—the fog hadn't lifted. She crossed to the spot where she'd last put the Robert Burns collection. It wasn't there. In its place was her volume on horses that had gone missing weeks ago!

Fear climbed her throat. She had hoped she'd imagined all of it, but someone was being the trickster, and she didn't appreciate it one tiny bit. She certainly didn't feel like reading now; she couldn't concentrate.

She lit the torch she had brought in weeks before and carefully stepped back into the farther reaches of the cave. It was cool and damp. She loved the musty smell. She always expected to find dried animal bones or maybe even something more sinister, but as usual found nothing. Disappointed, she started back toward the cave opening, then stopped.

Someone was outside. Her heart racing, she extinguished the torch and flattened herself against the rocky wall. What would she do if that person looked inside? Could it be Evan, playing a trick on her? Or Duncan? It must be one of them. Who else knew she'd discovered this place? If that was who it was, she would give him a piece of her mind. She bravely stepped out into the light but no one was there. It was time to head home. Things were getting too eerie for her. When she went to get Mariah, she was gone. Thinking maybe she'd pulled loose from her tether, Kerry looked around, toward the woods, toward the sea, down the beach. She wasn't anywhere. Mariah wouldn't have left her, she knew she wouldn't!

Whoever had been outside the cave had stolen her pony!

• • •

Fen stopped her gig outside of town, pensive as she thought about Kerry and how she hadn't spent more than a few hours each morning at the clinic since she first arrived.

She studied the land in front of her, noting that the heather had been cleared so the grass could grow for the sheep. Every few years some of the crofters burned it, and in a few years it returned, sending the sheep elsewhere until the heather was burned again. A cycle, it was.

A rabbit sprinted across the path, startling the horse, which whickered and pawed at the ground. Fen knew the rabbits had been on the island for centuries. The sheep were new. Interlopers, like the people.

She drew in a sigh and continued on to the castle. She hadn't seen Rosalyn in so long she felt they almost needed an introduction. At this stage of Rosalyn's pregnancy, she should be checked every week, not monthly.

Rosalyn ushered Fen into the solarium and poured her a cup of tea. "I'm so happy to see you! It's been weeks, hasn't it?"

Fen sat on a tufted settee and accepted her wee cuppa. Bonnie, who had been asleep by the window, rose and joined her. Fen stroked her fuzzy head. Rosalyn carefully lowered herself into a chair across from Fen, trying not to sound like the enormous cow she felt she was. Sima stood and went to Rosalyn, nudging her legs, as if to tell her she understood her predicament, having been in it not so long before.

Fen seemed to notice Rosalyn's discomfort. "You're pale, dear. I have been ignoring you, haven't I?"

"Nonsense. No one can do anything for me now, not until this behemoth of a bairn decides to leave his cushy spot."

"I'd like to check you again."

"You're the boss." Rosalyn settled on the length of the settee, a small pillow under her head.

"Are you getting enough rest?"

"I never seem to get enough rest, but that's my problem. No one is holding a gun to my head."

"Well, since Kerry spends only the mornings with me each day, I thought maybe the two of you had finally bonded." Fen continued to probe, momentarily frowning.

"What's the matter?" Rosalyn felt a quiver of fear.

Fen immediately calmed her. "It's nothing. You just seem so big. If I didn't know your story, I'd think you got pregnant sooner."

Rosalyn tried to get comfortable. "I feel like I'm carrying around a baby elephant. And as for Kerry, we haven't bonded, I'm afraid. 'Twas my thought as well that we might grow close, but she's rarely here until tea time, or even dinner."

Fen finished prodding. "What do you suppose she does all afternoon?"

"What can one do on this island? She says she explores; I guess that's possible. I can't imagine anything else."

"Well, at least we know she can't go far, not without leaving the island."

Rosalyn brought her hands to her cheeks. "Now that I think about it, if she hadn't come home every afternoon, I wouldn't be surprised if she hadn't tried to do that, too."

They left the solarium and just as they stepped outside, a

horse-drawn wagon driven by a neighbor stopped near the entrance and Kerry jumped from the seat, her expression pained. Startled, Rosalyn hurried to her. "Kerry? What's wrong? What happened?"

Much to Rosalyn's surprise, Kerry threw herself into her arms and sobbed.

Rosalyn enveloped the girl in her embrace and glanced up at the man on the wagon seat. "Ferris?"

Ferris the Peat doffed his cap. "I dunno, ma'am. She was walking along the path near the spot where I dig me peat. She won't talk to me, but she's very upset, as ye can see."

Rosalyn gently pulled herself away from Kerry and looked into her tear-stained face.

"Kerry?"

The girl's chin quivered and tears continued to stream down her cheeks. "Someone stole Mariah." She broke into fresh sobs.

Evan came running from the stables. "Where's the pony?"

Rosalyn continued to hold Kerry, gently rubbing her back. "If Mariah is the pony, then someone stole her."

Evan's expression was nearly as pained as Kerry's. "Stolen, ye say?"

Kerry stared straight at Evan. "I thought maybe you did it to scare me."

Evan's face crumbled. "Nay, I'd never do that to ye."

"Then maybe it was Duncan. You two are the only ones who know of my secret hiding place. Books have been missing and then returned, and it's almost as if some trickster is trying to frighten me. It would be just like him to do this."

"Tell us exactly what happened," Rosalyn urged.

She did, and when she'd finished, she said, "Oh, I wish I'd looked out to see who it was, but I was scared and now Mariah is gone."

"Fletcher will know what to do," Rosalyn promised. "And he wouldn't have wanted you to put yourself in harm's way, so you were wise to stay hidden."

Kerry brightened some. "I'm sure it was Duncan. I'm sure of it. He's probably got Mariah hidden somewhere. Where is he?"

Evan still looked upset. "Lassie, he and Gavin went fishing with Donnie the Digger."

Kerry bit her lip." He still could have done it."

"Let Fletcher figure it out, all right?" Rosalyn said.

"He'll be mad."

"How can he be mad? It wasn't your fault, Kerry. You can't blame yourself." She drew the child with her toward the castle. "How about something nice and hot to drink? And maybe a fresh scone?"

Kerry shook her head. "I'm too upset, thank you just the same."

Rosalyn thanked Ferris the Peat and the women returned to the castle.

• • •

They had barely settled into the morning room when Fletcher rushed inside, visibly concerned. "I saw Ferris the Peat on the road." He settled down beside Kerry on the small settee. "Tell me exactly what happened, sweetheart."

Kerry pressed her lips together. "Someone stole Mariah. Are you mad? I think maybe it was Duncan, just to scare me."

Fletcher put his arm around her. "Of course I'm not mad. Just tell me what happened."

She explained that shortly after they arrived on Hedabarr she had ridden to the far north end of the island on Mariah, and she had found a cave. "I can look out over the ocean. It's very peaceful, Fletcher, and I love watching the waves. We have nothing like it in Texas, do we?"

"No, we don't. So, was anything different about today?"

She frowned, thinking. "Not really. I usually see the wild horses, but today I didn't because I took a different path. I had taken it before. I go into the hills a little—you know, where there's one of those big stone markers."

"The cairn monument?" When she nodded, he asked, "What made you change your course?"

Shrugging, she said, "No reason. Sometimes I just go down the coast. It just depends on how I feel."

"Could someone have followed you?"

"No," she answered a bit too quickly. "No one followed me. I would have known. There's too much open space up there." She paused. "But Duncan is an excellent tracker. He could have done it, couldn't he?"

Fletcher stroked her hair. "Why would Duncan want to scare you like this?"

"Who else could it be? No, I'm sure it was Duncan."

"Could someone have taken your pony for one of the wild ones?" Fen asked.

"No. She was saddled and bridled." She gasped and her hand flew to her mouth.

"What?" Fletcher asked.

Kerry looked teary again. "The books. I took some books from the library and put them in the saddlebags. Now they're gone. And I had some stacked up in the cave, too."

Fletcher felt a wave of relief. "If that's all that's worrying you, don't."

"But I wanted to read them," she explained. "Can I go back and get the ones in the cave? Please?"

Fletcher took Kerry's hands in his own. "One thing at a time, Kerry. The first thing is to find that pony. We'll get the books too, I promise." And the son of a bitch who stole Mariah and scared his sister, he vowed.

• • •

Later, Rosalyn changed into her nightclothes and waited for Fletcher to check the doors and windows. He smiled ruefully at her as he closed the door behind him and began to undress. "Everyone's accounted for except Duncan."

She went to him and wrapped her arms around his waist. "So this is what it's like. You stop worrying about one of them and turn around and begin worrying about another."

"Not exactly what you signed up for, is it?"

"It's exactly what I signed up for, my husband. Your worries are mine." She looked up at him. "Do you really think Duncan did this?"

Fletcher frowned. "It wouldn't be beyond him to play a trick on someone, but I can't imagine him scaring Kerry. No, not his little sister."

"Then who and why?" When he shook his head, she asked, "How will you start looking for the mare? She could be anywhere by now. Even halfway to the mainland aboard the ferry."

"I'll check that out in the morning. Whoever took her won't leave her out to be noticed, that's for sure."

She looked at him and gave him a triumphant smile.

"What's that look for?" he asked, amused.

"Maybe it was because of the trauma, but the first thing Kerry did when she got here was throw herself into my arms and sob. You can imagine my surprise."

His smile was warm. "I'm sorry a horse thief is what it took to change her mind about you, but I'm happy. And we'll find the pony."

They climbed into bed and Fletcher tucked her against his chest and rested his arm on her stomach. When her breathing became regular, he began thinking about the mare. And who might have taken her. And why. He had no positive answers, but before he fell asleep, one thought began to percolate in his brain.

* * *

The next morning, when Fen rode up to the clinic, Geddes was waiting for her. It brought her such simple joy she almost felt like shouting. He helped her down and followed her inside. "I'm happy to see you this morning,"

She grinned. "I'm always happy to see you."

While Geddes pumped water into the tea kettle, she told him what had happened to Kerry and her pony the day before.

Geddes frowned. "Hadn't you and Rosalyn been concerned because the girl disappeared every day?"

"Of course, but I certainly didn't think she would be in any danger. For God's sake, Geddes, Hedabarr is probably one of the safest places in the world."

Geddes prepared their tea. "There's always a couple of rotten apples in the barrel no matter where you are."

"So, if that's the case, who are they?" Fen questioned.

"If I could answer that question, I'd be in a different line of work."

They drank their tea in comfortable silence. When Geddes had finished his, he crossed to her, pulled her up, and put his arms around her.

She gave him a happy smile and nestled close. Amazing how good it was to have someone to lean on after so many years. How she'd missed this kind of intimacy. She let out a sharp laugh.

"What's humorous, dear girl?"

She stayed where she was, reveling in his strength, his warmth. "I was just thinking how much I'd missed this closeness, when, in truth, I don't believe I've ever had it before."

"Not in your marriage?" He rubbed his hands over her shoulders and waist, resting them there.

"It was a strange union, but it wasn't a marriage in so many ways. I thought it was just fine at the time; he and I were always working, rarely saw one another, and when we did we were so exhausted we fell into bed without so much as a 'good night.'" She turned in Geddes's arms and gazed up at him. "Not until now did I realize that we may have had a partnership, but we certainly had no marriage." She cocked her head. "And I don't want to scare you off, Mr. Gordon, but I think I want a marriage. A real marriage in my old age."

Geddes raised an eyebrow. "If I marry you, you must promise me a few things."

"Oh, really? What, pray tell?"

"You must promise to always tell me what's on your mind. You must never assume I don't want to listen to what you have to say. If you feel the need to touch me, you are ordered to do so, until penalty of a paddling."

She gave him a wicked smile. "You would actually paddle me?"

He reached down and ran his hand over her behind. "Indeed. And I would insist that you remove all clothing before I did so."

Warmth spread through her like thick molasses. "You would paddle my bare behind?"

"I would put you across my lap and fondle your breasts with my free hand and paddle you pink with the other."

Fen thought about that, her temperature rising. "I'd never have thought you were the sort of man who would take pleasure in such folly."

"Folly, is it? Nay, woman, 'tis something I've thought of since the day I discovered you nose to nose with that sot MacNab."

"Well, you're just full of surprises, aren't you, you devil?"

"I have many more," he promised, pulling her so close she could feel him hard against her belly.

Her knees went weak. "Geddes Gordon, what I want right now is your naked body. I want to feel you drive into me so deep I'll feel it in my throat."

He growled into her ear, dragged her to the cavernous linen closet, and began unbuttoning her trousers.

In her haste to make herself available to him, she completely forgot where they were, what time it was, or who could stop in and discover them any moment.

Chapter Twenty-Six

Her husband was already up and gone when Rosalyn awoke. She dressed quickly and went down the hallway to Kerry's room and knocked. At Kerry's faint "Come in," Rosalyn opened the door and stepped into the room. Kerry was sitting cross-legged on her bed, reading, her glossy curls in sweet disarray over her shoulders and down her back. She looked up. "Is Fletcher gone?"

Rosalyn sat on the bed. "He was gone before I woke up. I'm sure he's out trying to discover who took your pony right now."

Kerry stared at the window. "Duncan came by earlier. He didn't take Mariah." She placed a bookmark in her book and put it on the bed.

Rosalyn read the title. "*The History of Scotland*?"

"It's really interesting. Did you know there was once a black king in Scotland who came here from Africa?"

"I had no idea," Rosalyn answered, surprised that a twelve-year-old would find such a dusty tome readable.

Kerry couldn't quite look at Rosalyn. "I've been such a terrible brat."

Something in Rosalyn's chest melted. She touched one of Kerry's curls and watched it wind itself around her finger. "You've been through a lot. Your whole life has been turned upside down, and just when you become even a little comfortable with your new environment, someone steals your pony." She gave Kerry a sympathetic smile. "No one blames you."

"But you should. I've been mean and cross."

"Who else could you be mean and cross to? Not to your brothers, certainly." She gently stroked Kerry's bare arm. "I knew that under all that frustration was the sweet girl her brother told me about." A sudden twinge gripped her lower back, and she sucked in a harsh breath.

Kerry sat up straight. "Are you all right?"

Nodding, Rosalyn said, "It's just this bairn; he can't seem to settle down when I want to. 'Tis nothing to worry about."

Kerry continued to watch her, her expression fearful. "Will it hurt—you know, when it comes out?"

Rosalyn tried to get comfortable, finally opting to leave the bed and sit in the small settee beside it. "I won't deny it. I've been through this once before."

"You had another baby? What happened?"

"She died."

Kerry's eyes welled with tears. "Oh, Rosalyn, I'm so sorry. I didn't know. I'm so, so sorry."

"'Tis in the past. And you know," she added, trying to lighten the mood, "it wasn't your fault." She motioned to Kerry. "Come here and sit with me."

Kerry scooted off the bed and nestled herself snugly beside Rosalyn. "I don't hate you, Rosalyn."

Smiling, Rosalyn pulled her close. "I know you don't, sweetheart."

"But I've been so awful."

"Let's think about something we could do together. I know, why don't you and I take a rig and go find your cave and retrieve those books you left there? Then I can see what you found so interesting every day."

Kerry's face lit up. "Can we do it now?"

"Let's at least wait until we've had some breakfast, all right?" She wasn't at all sure she should be leaving the castle in her condition, but at the moment, Kerry's priorities were first and foremost in Rosalyn's mind.

• • •

Astride Ahote, Fletcher rode north, hoping to find the path Kerry had taken the day before. At the cairn monument, he took the fork that went a short way into the hillside. As he rode further, the crofts became fewer and fewer, especially now that he wasn't as close to the ocean. Out of the corner of his eye he saw movement in the trees. A wisp of smoke coming from a rundown cottage. The thatched roof was in dire need of repair and the place didn't look habitable.

He left Ahote behind a line of beech hedges whose fire-bronze leaves blazed in the September morning. The place appeared vacant but for the smoke. He noticed a path had been worn over the coarse marram grass, one that went directly to the cottage. He found the door to the cottage padlocked, and the small window in the door was painted over. He circled the building, noting that all the windows were painted from the inside. He suddenly remembered seeing windows exactly like that somewhere else. It was when he made the decision about the goat. Douglas the Lum's shed. Curious.

As he returned to the front of the cottage, something winked at him from the grass. He picked it up and turned it over, his gaze lingering over the object. He knew what it was. But what was it doing here?

* * *

Wrapped in warm clothing and lap robes, Rosalyn and Kerry settled into small carriage. Marvella had put extra blankets in the back. She had insisted on packing them a small lunch. By the looks of the box, they could be gone for a couple of days and still have food left over.

Rosalyn briefly took her eyes off the mare, glanced over, and saw Kerry chewing at her nails. Kerry noticed and put her hands in her lap. "I know I shouldn't do it."

"We all have habits we'd like to stop."

"Grandfather always told me it wasn't good, and I knew that too, but I just kept on doing it. When Grandfather died I dipped my fingers in vinegar so I wouldn't bite them during his burial ritual."

"What kind of ritual was it?"

"We wrapped Grandfather in his favorite blanket. Then Duncan took his body to a cave in the mountains where he was buried. Then we burned all of his belongings." She gave Rosalyn a shy glance. "I suppose it sounds barbaric, but that's what Grandfather wanted, and we would never have buried him any other way."

"Why did you burn his things?"

"So he would have peace in the afterlife. Comanche custom is that if his clothing remains, some of what ailed him is left behind and someone else may suffer because of it." She shrugged and gave Rosalyn a slight smile. "It's quite different from a Christian burial, isn't it?"

"The end result is the same for all of us," Rosalyn assured her.

"As for my nail biting, Dorcas tried to get me to quit, too. She also tried to tell me you weren't a bad person, but I didn't want to hear that. Once I even put my hands over my ears so I couldn't hear her. I'm so ashamed of myself."

Unwilling to say anything against the woman, Rosalyn said, "She cared very much for you."

"I know, but once she was gone, I realized I had depended on her for everything. I did whatever she told me to do, except be nice to you. I'm usually not like that. I have a mind of my own. Just ask my brothers."

Rosalyn gave Kerry a gentle nudge. "I think I knew that from the beginning."

"Well, I promise I won't ever be a problem for you and Fletcher. Not ever again."

Rosalyn had to laugh. "Oh, sweetheart, don't start making promises like that."

The wind came up, bringing with it an icy bite, and there were whitecaps on the water, slapping at the shore.

They had seen the wild horses, and just behind that, Kerry pointed to an outcropping of rocks and shrubbery. "It's there."

Rosalyn brought the rig over the rough ground and pulled the mare to a stop. She held her breath as a cramp twisted in her back.

She'd had a few since before breakfast, but she wasn't due yet, so she wasn't concerned. She didn't want to frighten Kerry.

The girl brought everything into the cave. There was an old chair leaning against the wall, and Kerry covered it with blankets.

Rosalyn was impressed. As she waddled to it and lowered herself onto it, she asked, "You brought a chair in here?"

"It was easier to stay and read. Sitting on the rocks got hard on my bottom." She started going through her books. Rosalyn thought she must have dozens stacked against the wall.

"Is everything here?"

Kerry sorted through them. "Odd—everything is here, even the one I thought was missing." She looked at Rosalyn. "I've been reading Robert Burns."

Pleased, Rosalyn asked, "How do you like him?"

"He's all right, I guess. I'll get a better picture of it when I understand his language better."

Rosalyn looked out onto the roiling ocean, imagining what it must look like on a sunny, calm day. Even now, as weather threatened, she could understand Kerry's feelings for such a view. "It is peaceful here," she said, feeling the damp breeze on her face. "All this fresh air makes me hungry."

Kerry unpacked the lunch, and the two of them ate heartily.

Rosalyn was reluctant to leave, but she was also experiencing more frequent cramping in her back and sides. She almost told Kerry they should go, but the girl was so deeply engrossed in one of her books that Rosalyn didn't have the heart.

• • •

After checking with the station master and learning that no horse had been ferried off the island lately, Fletcher rode to the new distillery. So far Fletcher had been impressed with what they were doing. Some of their Scotch whisky was available at the wedding, and he had enjoyed the taste and texture. Danny McKay met him at the door and ushered him into his office.

"Yer Grace. To what do I owe the pleasure of this visit?"

Fletcher laid the item he had found at the cottage on the desk.

McKay picked it up and studied it. "Aye, for sure 'tis an old ale faucet. Where did ye find it?"

Fletcher told him how he'd come by it.

"'Tis the kind MacNab uses in his pub," McKay informed him.

Fletcher nodded. "MacNab."

"Ye know," McKay began, "I've offered that man plenty for his business but he refuses to sell." He shook his head. "How he stays open is a mystery to me."

"Explain," Fletcher said.

"Ye been in there?" At Fletcher's nod, McKay continued. "Ye look like a drinkin' man, Yer Grace. Would ye call the place yer home away from home, so to speak?"

Fletcher recalled the dirty windows and filthy floor, the near-dilapidated condition of the furnishings, and the unpleasant smell. "No, I wouldn't."

"He has very few steady customers. That's why I can't understand how he stays in business. The only friend he has is his wife's brother, Douglas the Lum."

Fletcher stopped halfway to the door.

"The same fellow who shot Bill's goat?"

"Aye, the very same."

Fletcher thanked him, and just as he left, McKay said, "Yer Grace, we have a new whisky we've been aging, sort of a labor of love. Might I send a flask over when it's ready?"

"I'd appreciate that, McKay. You are doing fine work here."

He had to find a way to get into that cottage. And what, if anything, did it have to do with Angus MacNab? What about Douglas the Lum?

On his return to the castle, he met the tall, rangy Fergie the Burn on the road. The man waved at him. Fletcher met him at his cart and saw that his boy, Clive, was with him.

"Good to see you, Fergie," Fletcher greeted him. "Getting

settled back into the cottage?" Fletcher reached out and tousled Clive's hair.

Fergie took off his cap. "Aye, things are coming together. And Birgit can't stop singin' yer praises, Yer Grace. First ye save little Clive here, then ye come along when the house is afire."

"I'm glad we were at the right place at the right time."

Fergie lifted Clive onto his lap. "See here, Yer Grace?" He wiggled the lad's foot and Fletcher saw that little bells had been tied to the laces of his shoes.

Fletcher broke into a smile. "Bells on his toes. I hope it helps you keep track of the little guy, Fergie."

"Aye, and besides that, I got me a fine litter of collies."

"Ah, yes, from…Donnie the Digger's Sarge, that right?"

With his other hand, Fergie reached down and brought up a squirmy pup. "Fer you, sir."

Fletcher accepted the pup as it licked his face.

"It's a beauty, Fergie."

"He be a male, sir."

Fletcher gave Fergie a wide smile. "Thank you. Thank you, Fergie. Maybe I'll call him Little Sarge."

Fergie the Burn guffawed. "'Twould make Donnie proud, Yer Grace."

Fletcher waved goodbye and rode toward the castle, the pup tucked inside his greatcoat.

Evan met him at the stable door and Fletcher handed him the pup.

Evan took the little collie and looked him over. "He's a fine-looking pup, Your Grace."

"Can you make sure he's got a place here, in the stable?"

Evan shook his head. "When Miss Kerry sees him, she'll demand he be raised in the castle."

"Yes, but a good herding dog shouldn't be coddled, should he?"

"It'll be hard to convince her, Your Grace."

Fletcher frowned. "Speaking of Kerry, have you seen her today?"

"She and the mistress left in a rig after breakfast," Evan answered.

Fletcher sighed. So much for ordering his wife to stay close to home in her condition. "You don't know where they were going?"

He shook his head. "They were just anxious to be on their way. If I were to guess, though, I'd say they probably went north."

Of course, Fletcher thought. Probably to Kerry's special hideaway.

Fletcher glanced at the sky. "Weather coming in."

Evan put the pup inside his shirt, where it wiggled a little, then settled against Evan's chest. "The old laird could tell a change in the weather by the ache in his bones."

Curious, Fletcher asked, "Did he treat you well?" Seldom did anyone even mention his grandfather.

Evan glanced away. "Aye, he were good to me."

Fletcher frowned. "Something bothers you?"

Evan chose his words carefully. "He were good to some folks he shouldna been—nay, I gabble too much, I do."

"Evan, whatever you're thinking, I want you to tell me. I need to know as much as I can about these people. I depend on you to keep me informed, all right?"

Evan kicked at a clump of dirt with his toe. "He were friendly with that pub owner, MacNab."

Fletcher recalled the remark MacNab had made during his visit. And the wink, as if they had something in common. "I see."

"Ye upset, Your Grace?"

"Not with you, by any means. Evan, I will always appreciate any information you might have for me."

He strode to the castle, hoping to find some answers as to his wife's whereabouts. Annie came out of the kitchen. "Have you seen your mistress?"

Annie curtseyed and kept her eyes down. "No, Yer Grace, but seein' as how she's been so tired, she's prob'ly in her room resting."

Fletcher frowned. "I've checked; she isn't there."

"I have been worried about her, Yer Grace, ever since—" She popped her hand over her mouth.

"Ever since what?"

Annie shook her head. "She made me promise not to mention it."

He took Annie's shoulders gently and said, "You must tell me."

Still Annie couldn't look at him. "If I hadna been with her the other day to catch her, she would ha'e fainted and fallen flat to the floor, she would ha'e."

Fletcher cursed and rushed outside. Nothing to do now but try to find Kerry's hideaway and hope that he wouldn't discover havoc.

* * *

Rosalyn had drifted off but a strong cramp brought her awake. She glanced at the cave entrance and gasped. "What are you doing here?"

A nasty smile crawled across Angus MacNab's face as he took in the scene. "Well, well. What do we ha'e here, then?"

Kerry rushed to protect Rosalyn. "She's going to have a baby; you can't hurt her."

MacNab snorted. "What makes ye think I want ta hurt anyone?"

"What are you doing here, then?" Kerry grilled him.

"Jes' wanted to make sure ye noticed that all yer books are back in place."

She glared at him. "It was you. You stole my books."

"Nay, how can I steal something I returned?"

Kerry's eyes narrowed. "You tried to scare me."

"Young lassies shouldna be roamin' around the island alone," he retorted.

"You probably stole my pony, too." She was on the verge of angry tears.

Rosalyn took Kerry's arm and brought her close to her, partly to keep her from physically lashing out at MacNab.

"Do you get pleasure out of scaring women and children, Mr. MacNab?"

He looked at Rosalyn, one furry eyebrow raised as he took in her mammoth stomach. "So yer goin' to have the spawn of the savage, are ye?"

She refused to egg him on. "What do you really want?"

"I tol' ye," he said quite innocently. "Jes makin' sure the lassie is fine."

"What about her pony?"

"What makes ye think I took it?"

"You are a bully, Angus MacNab. Just a big bully. You enjoy picking on those who aren't strong enough to fight back."

His smile was sly. "Ye be careful there—ye don't want nothin' happenin' to that bairn, now do ye?"

"That's just the thing a bully would say," she answered.

"You leave her alone!" Kerry had broken away from Rosalyn and was in MacNab's face.

Rosalyn felt another strong twinge in her back and suddenly everything was wet. Her water had broken. She kept silent. They were in dire straits here, and she had to think clearly.

"Kerry? There's another blanket in the two-seater. Would you get it for me?"

"But I don't want to leave you, Rosalyn."

Rosalyn gave MacNab a saccharine smile. "Nothing will happen to me, dear. Deep down in Mr. MacNab's bones there must be a gentleman of some sort, am I right?"

"I don't hurt nobody," he snarled.

Only your wife, she thought, but was wise enough not to say. But by the holy, she didn't want him around when the baby came.

* * *

As Fletcher rode north along the coast, he saw the cairn monument in the distance.

Slowly he and Ahote moved through the grassy brush, hoping no one was watching him. The cottage appeared empty, but he couldn't be sure. When he reached the shack, he dismounted and crossed to the door. Surprisingly, it was open.

When his eyes adjusted to the dim light, Fletcher noticed two sawhorses that made a makeshift table. He touched the items thrown over them. Hides. As his fingers felt the texture of the skins, he knew what they were and he simmered. "Horse hides," he whispered. He glanced around and saw large sacks of salt resting against the wall. Was it MacNab who was killing off the herd? If so, how was his brother-in-law involved?

He recalled McKay saying that he wondered how MacNab could stay in business. Was this his way of keeping his head above water, or had it actually made him a wealthy man?

Fletcher's stomach clenched. If what he was thinking were true, had Kerry's pony met the same end?

As he left the shack, he was surprised to find Douglas the Lum driving an empty cart across the grass. Douglas expressed shock and horror when he came face to face with Fletcher.

• • •

Rosalyn hadn't had a cramp for a while and hoped to God her labor had stopped for the moment. "What do you want? You say you don't want to hurt anyone, but if you were any kind of human being at all you would ride to the village and get us some help."

Kerry sat with Rosalyn and each time Rosalyn had a cramp she squeezed Kerry's hand.

MacNab faked an innocent yawn. "To help deliver the spawn of the savage? It don't matter none to me. 'Tis not man's business, birthin' bairns."

Suddenly Kerry stood, an unlit torch in her hand, and lunged at the man.

He guffawed and did a little boxer's dance. "Ye gonna strike me, lassie?"

"If she doesn't, I will."

All eyes went to the cave entrance, and both Rosalyn and Kerry yelped with relief.

Fletcher gave his wife a questioning look.

"I'm fine, now that you're here," she answered.

MacNab recovered from his surprise. "Now, ain't this a picture. What do we got here, two savages and a whale?" He guffawed.

Fletcher ignored his remarks. "I came across a little shack in the woods. Interesting little place, filled with bags of salt and treated horse hides. Looks to me like someone has gone into business for himself."

MacNab stopped laughing and gave him a surly shrug. "Don't know what ye be talkin' about."

Fletcher pulled the ale faucet from his pocket and showed it to him. "Is this yours?"

MacNab frowned, his caterpillar eyebrows forced down over his eyes, but he didn't answer.

"I found it in a strange place. Behind that tacky little shack with all the hides and salt in it."

"Don't mean it's mine," MacNab answered.

"Dan McKay seems to think it's the kind you use."

MacNab snorted. "That little ass. Tryin' to run me outa business, he is."

"He wonders how you stay in business, MacNab. From what I hear, you don't have too many steady customers. It's usually customers who keep a business open." Fletcher let that sink in, then added, "What keeps your business open, MacNab? Are you a horse thief?"

"Ye can't prove nothin'."

"I saw the proof with my own eyes. In your little shack in the woods."

"Me and the old laird had a deal. I gave him a cut of the profits, I did. I could cut ye in, too."

"What you've done is against the law. And it's theft, MacNab. The island belongs to me, therefore so do the horses."

MacNab pulled out a small firearm. "What ye gonna do about

it, savage?" He trained the weapon on the three of them and backed away, toward the entrance. Once outside, he grabbed Ahote's reins and pulled himself into the saddle.

But with a strange rider on his back, Ahote bucked and reared, throwing MacNab to the ground. The last thing the man saw coming was Ahote's hoofs as they were about to crush his skull.

Rosalyn and Kerry shuddered, closed their eyes, and looked away.

"Nasty way to go." Fletcher pulled the body to the side of the cave, out of sight.

Back inside, he knelt by Rosalyn. "Have we time to get you to Fen?"

Another cramp, more severe than any she'd had, gripped her. She took Fletcher's hand and gave it a squeeze. "I don't think so. I'm sorry."

He glanced at Kerry. "I guess we've got a job to do, little sister."

• • •

Later, when everyone was back at the castle, Kerry was still teary-eyed. "I can't believe it. I helped deliver two babies. I have to tell Evan!" She sprang to the bedroom door and was gone. Fletcher couldn't believe it either. Two boys. Here they were, small and wrinkled, with thick black hair that stood on end and little noses pushed against their faces. And they wailed. And they were beautiful.

Fen had checked out the twins and Rosalyn, and after everyone had had a peek at them, she ushered them out of the room. "Tomorrow is soon enough to ask your questions," she ordered. And then she was gone as well.

Fletcher stared down at Rosalyn. "My love. You have scared the living shit out of me. Pardon my crudeness, but there's no other way to describe it."

One of the twins began to squeak. Rosalyn unfastened her bodice and Fletcher brought the wrinkled little thing to her breast.

He watched her nurse. "I wish I could do that."

"What? Deliver twins?" Her eyes twinkled.

He grinned. "You know exactly what I mean." He was quiet a moment, then said, "Until you came into my life, I didn't know what this kind of love was. I love you, Rosalyn."

"And I love you, my husband. I'm afraid from nearly the moment I saw you I thought of you in very unladylike ways."

"It was probably my bag of tricks you couldn't resist."

Rosalyn's laugh became a little snort. "That trick bag. I'm forever grateful for it."

They lay quietly together, watching as one bairn nursed and then the other.

"Fen will insist she find you a wet nurse," Fletcher mused.

"Well, I'd like to think I could do it all by myself, but I know I can't. I trust she'll find someone wonderful."

Fletcher put his arms behind his head. "I think I'm going to like this fatherhood thing."

Chapter Twenty-Seven

The next morning, everyone was abuzz with curiosity. Fletcher had gone out to tie up some loose ends, and when he returned, they were all gathered in the morning room.

"Apparently MacNab had been up to no good for a few years. He was killing the horses, removing the hides, and preparing them for sale to someone on the mainland."

"No wonder the herd was so low," Rosalyn mused.

"Was he doing this alone, or did he have help?" Duncan wanted to know.

"His brother-in-law, Douglas the Lum, kept the fifty-pound bags of salt in his shed to be used for curing the hides to keep them from rotting."

"How did you discover that?" Gavin asked.

"When I went to see about the goat he'd shot, I noticed that his shed windows had been painted over. The same was true of the old cottage I'd come across in the forest. And then, I ran into Douglas himself at the shack."

"How will you handle Douglas, since he was implicated?" Rosalyn tucked a twin close to her chest while Kerry cuddled the other.

"He was under MacNab's thumb and Nessa is his sister. And MacNab threatened to hurt Nessa even more than he already had if Douglas didn't become his accomplice. In any case, I have a feeling everyone connected with that family will have a better life from now on."

"Will Nessa MacNab run the pub?" Rosalyn asked.

"Dan McKay, who runs the distillery, had shown interest in

buying it a couple of times but MacNab wouldn't sell. Maybe now she can get rid of it and finally concentrate on her children."

There was a rather feeble knock on the door and Barnaby poked his head in. "There's a gentleman here to see Miss Kerry, Your Grace."

Kerry sat up straight. "Me? Who can that be?"

Fletcher took the baby from her. "You'd better go out and see."

She threw them all a skeptical glance and disappeared. In a very short moment, they heard her shout. "Mariah!"

Rosalyn looked at Fletcher, who explained, "Douglas the Lum had been ordered to get rid of the mare but he couldn't do it. That's another reason I think he's paid his dues."

* * *

Two weeks had passed, and everyone in the castle, from the family to the help, was immersed in the care of the twins. They still had not been named; there was some disagreement among the parties involved. Duncan and Kerry both agreed they should be Abe and Gabe, after Abraham Lincoln and Gabriel, the angel they'd heard about in their father's Bible. At least the names rhymed, they said. Gavin thought they should be Hamish and Shamus. Ham and Sham. No one liked that idea, either. Barnaby suggested Albert and Victoria, but he had to be reminded that they were both laddies.

Rosalyn and Fletcher were in the sunroom, the boys asleep nearby, Sima as close as she could get without tipping the cradle over, when Fen and Geddes peeked in.

They exchanged shy glances, something that wasn't lost on Rosalyn.

"What? What is it, you two? Is something wrong?"

Fen bent down and brushed Rosalyn's cheek with her lips. "Not a thing. At least it now seems that everything is grand. We just came by to see the boys."

Rosalyn gave them a skeptical look. "Really? That's all?"

"Well, of course. You have named them, haven't you?" Geddes put his hand on Fen's hip and Fen didn't push it off.

"If you two don't tell me what's going on, I'll never tell you what we've named the twins."

"Well, you may as well know. Geddes and I are getting married."

Rosalyn's mouth hung open. "You're what?"

"Getting married. You know, like the two of you." Fen rested her hand on Geddes's chest.

Rosalyn bit down on her lip. "But I thought you didn't like each other."

"We discovered we like each other very much, dear sister. Now, are you going to be up and about for the ceremony?"

"We wouldn't miss it," Rosalyn and Fletcher both answered.

"And you've named the twins?"

Fletcher lifted the double-wide cradle and set it in front of them. "This is Rory," he said proudly, touching the bairn's head with gentle fingers, "and this is Robert. They will be Rory and Rabbie."

"After Rosalyn's Rabbie Burns, no doubt," Geddes said, his voice warm.

Rosalyn continued to study the babes. "Indeed."

"How do you tell them apart?" Geddes peered into the cradle, his expression bemused.

"'Tis easy, really. Rabbie has a tiny mole on his left thigh."

"So that means every time I want to know which boy I'm holding, I have to undress him." Fletcher returned to sit beside his wife.

Everyone laughed, and Rosalyn snuggled against her husband. "Yes, my husband is quite a handy man to have around the bairns."

Geddes handed Fletcher a letter. "I received this the other day. It's a response to the letter I sent Fergus MacBean, explaining that you had been found, and that there was an heir on the way. And that he need not come by to claim the inheritance."

Fletcher opened it and read it, shaking his head. "Not a very pleasant chap, is he?"

"I shudder to think what might have happened if I hadn't found you," Geddes admitted.

Fletcher clamped a hand on his shoulder. "But you did, old man, and since you've been my brother-in-law for many months now, and you're marrying my wife's best friend, you're going to have to stop Your Gracing me and call me Fletcher. Agreed?"

Geddes grinned. "I believe I can do that now, Fletcher."

• • •

Later, when they were in bed together, the twins between them, Fletcher told Rosalyn of his grandfather's part in MacNab's mission to slaughter the herd.

She sighed. "'Tis a shame, to be sure. We all knew he had been a wily old Scot, but somehow, this is different."

"Yes. And after speaking with Douglas, I learned that MacNab sold the horse meat to someone on the mainland, and also used it himself to feed his customers." He shuddered, wondering if that was what he had smelled that day in the pub.

All things settled, Fletcher tugged his wife closer and murmured, "My heart is full."

"As is mine." Rosalyn didn't try to stop the tears of happiness that sprang into her eyes.

"Our life has a new beginning," he reminded her.

Yes, she thought, touching the dark hair on Rabbie's head. And nothing could be more perfect. They had procured a tutor for the children and Gavin absorbed everything the tutor said. Duncan, on the other hand, had become sullen. Kerry willingly did her lessons and helped with the bairns as often as possible. Evan had joined the children in their lessons and was doing well. And Rosalyn had the love and respect of a wonderful man. There was nothing more she could want.

More from Jane Bonander

Winter Heart

Desperate to escape a dark past, Dinah Odell will do anything, even risk her freedom by posing as a nurse and accepting a job to care for Tristan Fletcher's mentally fragile sister. She thinks she's prepared for anything, except the sensitive, generous, and mysterious man behind the facade that Tristan Fletcher presents to the world.

With a dark past of his own, Tristan survived the barbs of childhood by closing his heart off from the rest of the world. He sees something similar in Dinah, a desire to flee, and it sparks his desire to protect her. To marry her, even. But to love her? When Dinah's secret past is revealed, it threatens to ruin everything she and Tristan have worked so hard to create. Will it tear them apart, or strengthen their bond even more?

A Taste of Honey

Seeking one last night of passion before entering into a loveless marriage, Honey DeHaviland finds that and more in the arms of Nick Stamos—the very man tasked with delivering Honey to her betrothed. Although it is in Nick's embrace that Honey finds the love she longs for, she knows that marrying a penniless man would mean her father's financial ruin.

But when Honey discovers that Nick is indeed wealthy beyond comprehension, she knows that she cannot give in to her yearning to stay with him without appearing shallow and mercenary.

When he learns the reason for Honey's arranged marriage, he vows to have her for himself. Will he convince her that he's all she needs before he loses her forever?

The Dragon Tamer

Widowed, alone, and penniless, Eleanor Rayburn is devastated when she learns that her late husband sold his shares of the ship before he died. Desperate to take back what she believes is rightfully hers, she sets out to fight back against the handsome but arrogant owner of the whaler.

Marine naturalist Dante Templeton survived a hard life, and has found success as an activist against the killing of whales or any marine animal for profit. But it's his own personal grudge against an enemy from his past that fuels his disdain for Eleanor, and his determination to keep her from reclaiming her share of stocks in the whaler.

As the feud heats up between Dante and Eleanor, so does the blaze of passion. But is Dante's love for Eleanor enough to smother his fiery hatred for her husband?

Dancing on Snowflakes

Susannah Walker has fled to Angel's Valley with her three-year-old son, seeking safety and a place to anonymously restart her life. What she didn't count on was bounty hunter Nathan Wolfe being hired to find her and take her home to stand trial for her crimes. Carrying his own wounded past in his heart, Nathan is committed to fulfilling the job, until he gets to know Susannah and begins to wonder if she's truly the criminal he's been told she is. But in order to get to the bottom of the mystery he'll have to gain her trust, and trust is one thing Susannah does not give easily.

Fires of Innocence

An act of kindness may lead to her greatest loss, or the greatest love she's ever known.

The wilderness of Yosemite Valley is no place to be caught alone. When Scotty MacDowell rescues a wounded stranger from a fierce blizzard, she is thinking only of saving a lost traveler. She never expects to find a passionate lover in Alex Golovin through nursing him back to health.

Seven months later, Alex returns to Scotty's tiny cabin in the wilderness, but not to take her back into his arms. Instead of the man she loved, Alex returns as an angry lawyer, determined to run Scotty off of her beloved land. Caught between passion and responsibility, Scotty and Alex endure a daily struggle to stay true to their hearts, no matter the cost.

CPSIA information can be obtained at www.ICGtesting.com
Printed in the USA
BVOW01s1445070816

458237BV00005B/137/P